VICTORY
DAY

RACHEL CHURCHER

Victory Day (Battle Ground #5)

First published by Taller Books, 2020
Reprinted by Taller Books, 2022

ISBN 9781916386846

Cover design by Rachel Churcher and Medina Karic:
www.fiverr.com/milandra

WWW.TALLERBOOKS.COM

From the Author

Thank you for your interest in the Battle Ground series! If you're new here, welcome.

Here's the part where I do something crazy, for an author. Here's the part where I tell you not to read this book.

Victory Day is Book Five in the Battle Ground series. If you've read the earlier books, ignore me. Keep reading. You know the story, and you're waiting to find out what happens next. But if you haven't read the earlier books, go back and do that now, before you start Book Five.

Jumping into the series with *Victory Day* is like opening a book near the end, and hoping you'll figure out what's going on. The Battle Ground series is one long story, from Book One through to Book Five, and you'll need to know what happened to the characters before you meet Bex, just over the page.

It might sound bossy, me telling you how to read my books, but here's why it's important. I rely on reviews to promote my books. I rely on readers leaving honest and thoughtful reviews on Amazon and Goodreads and Library Thing. That's what encourages other people to pick up my books and read my stories.

If you read *Victory Day* without knowing what happened to my characters before the start of the book, the chances are that you're going to leave me a bad review. This book references events that took place in Books One, Two, Three, and Four, and without knowing what those events were, and how the characters felt about them, they won't mean anything – and neither will the story.

Bad reviews are bad for me, and bad for my writing. Good reviews help me to reach new readers, and that allows me to write more books.

The good news is that it's easy to find *Battle Ground* (Book One). You can buy a paperback copy, or download a Kindle edition, from Amazon – and it's free on Kindle Unlimited. Just search 'Rachel Churcher Battle Ground' on your local Amazon site, and you'll be reading the start of the story in no time.

And when you've read *Battle Ground*, *False Flag*, *Darkest Hour*, and *Fighting Back*, please pick this book up again and dive right in. Thank you for your patience. Bex and Ketty will be waiting for you.

Notes

Margie's name is pronounced with a hard 'g', like the 'g' in Margaret: Marg-ie, not Marj-ie.

Leominster is a town in Herefordshire, UK. It is pronounced 'Lem-ster'.

MARCH

BEX

Prologue

We're out of time.

I need to see paper targets, not people. I need to take my training and use it to save my friends. I can't let my feelings stop me.

I close my eyes, and focus.

Save Margie. Save Dan. Rescue Mum.

The rifle is heavy in my hands.

I lift it, take aim, and pull the trigger.

PART 1

MARCH

(TWO WEEKS EARLIER)

Waiting

Bex

The metal stairs creak as I climb the fire escape to the roof. The last of the light is fading from the sky, and I wrap my winter coat around me, pulling the sleeve down to protect my hand from the cold banister rail.

Dan is waiting at the top, and Amy follows behind me. We sit on the roof-level landing, our backs against the cold brick parapet, and look out at the rooftops around us. Amy pulls a slab of chocolate from her pocket, breaks off a square and hands the rest to me. I take some, and pass it to Dan. We sit for a while, eating chocolate and passing the bar between us. The sky glows orange and pink, then gold, and the buildings look like black shapes pasted onto a mural. There are church spires and square blocks of flats, and in the distance we can see skyscrapers, clustered together.

I can't help smiling.

We're in London.

The landing shakes and creaks as someone else climbs the stairs.

"Bex?" It's an urgent whisper, one floor down in the dark.

"Charlie! Up here!" I keep my voice as quiet as I can.

The landing shakes again, and Charlie leans against the railings, looking up at us.

"Fiona's looking for you. She's got a briefing to give, and she's waiting for you lot." She looks around, at the dark roof of the empty hotel. "And keep your heads down. You know she doesn't like you coming up here."

"Thanks, Charlie. Tell her we're on our way."

She smiles, and gives me a mock salute. "Yes, Miss Committee Member!" The landing shudders as she heads back down the stairs.

Amy pushes the remains of the chocolate bar into her pocket, and takes a last look out at the sunset.

"We're here, Bex. We're really here." She takes my hand, and squeezes it.

I give her a smile. "We're really here."

Dan stares at the skyline, the golden sky reflected in his eyes. His voice is barely a whisper.

"I wish I knew where she is."

"Margie?" He nods. "Close, Dan. She's close. Margie, and Mum, and Dr Richards."

He nods again, and pulls himself up on the handrail, bent double to keep his head below the level of the parapet.

"Coming?"

"Wouldn't want to keep Chairman Fiona waiting."

We walk together down the rattling stairs in the dark.

*****

The safe house is an old hotel. The windows are boarded up, but the electricity works, and there's running water. We're hidden, as long as we stay out of sight, stay quiet, and keep the lights off as much as we can. There's a service yard between the reception building and most of the rooms, and the OIE smuggled us in through the service entrances, out of sight of the road.

We're working with local resistance cells, who brought us here in private cars and delivery vans. Most of us crossed to the UK from northern France, hidden in fishing boats and dropped off at lonely points along the coast in the middle of the night. Dan and I came in from

Ireland, the boat leaving us on a tiny, cliff-backed beach in Wales. We climbed the cliff path by torchlight, and the resistance met us on the road at the top.

We stopped twice on our journey to London. Once, in a farmhouse near Bridgend, and again near Farnham. We changed vehicles, and slept on sofas and spare beds while we waited for the next drivers to arrive. We travelled at night. People were kind, and thanked us for fighting back. More than once, I saw my photo on an OIE poster, encouraging people to resist, flashing past in the dark as we drove. More than once, I saw the same photo on my Wanted poster. I pulled my hood up, and slumped down in my seat.

It's strange, being back in the UK. Having to hide my face, in case the government catches me. Exchanging the safety of Scotland for the danger of London.

If we get this wrong, if the government finds us, we'll be executed. The country will watch, live on TV, as the Home Forces put bullets in us all. As they wipe out the Face of the Resistance and the Opposition In Exile. As they wipe out hope. We're all targets, and we're all here to lead the invasion.

The Home Forces are afraid of us, and they should be. We've got twenty armies behind us – a coalition of governments, heading for the ports and airports. If we're lucky, no one knows they're coming. If we're lucky, no one knows we're here.

I'm the Face of the Resistance, and I'm here to inspire an uprising.

I open the door to the hotel ballroom, and my friends follow me inside.

*****

Fiona holds up her hands for quiet, and the room falls silent.

"Congratulations," she says, smiling. "Stage one of the liberation is complete. Everyone we're expecting is here. You've all arrived safely, and we've had no surprises on our way in. A special welcome to our local resistance supporters – thank you for joining us. We couldn't do this without you." There are some quiet cheers, and a few people clap. Fiona holds her hands up again.

"New arrivals – you've all found your rooms?" She looks around at the people in front of her. "Any problems?" No one speaks up.

"You know the rules. No going outside. Make sure you're not visible from the street. No excess noise. Keep the lights off unless you really need them. Use table lamps and torches if you can. Charlie and Maz," she waves a hand in our direction, "have set up the kitchen, and they'll be providing us with meals. No more ration bars – I'm sure we're all looking forward to some real food. They're operating under challenging conditions, so no complaining, please!" There's some quiet laughter, and someone pats Maz on the back. "There will be an OIE committee member on duty in the dining room at all times – go to them with any problems. We will do our best to keep things safe and working.

"Please remember – one mistake is all it would take for the government to find us and arrest us. Under this roof," she points up at the ceiling, "are all their most wanted resistance fighters. That's you, and me. We are all responsible for the safety of everyone here. Stay quiet, and stay out of sight. And be ready. When the signal comes to make our move, we might have minutes to act. Keep your armour ready, and your guns loaded. Be organised, and be prepared to move out at any time.

"For now, get some sleep. We don't know how long we'll be here, so make the most of the quiet while you can. We'll have a full briefing after breakfast in the morning."

*****

The hotel rooms are empty – stripped back to bare floorboards and peeling walls. The bathrooms still work, and someone's put camp beds and sleeping bags out for us to use. Amy's sharing with me, and Dan's next door. Charlie and Maz are on the other side. I'm glad I'm not in a room by myself – the floorboards creak, the boarded-up windows cut off any escape, and navigating the pitch-black room by torchlight throws up creepy shadows against the walls. With two of us, it's easier to laugh at the shapes in the corners of the room.

Our crates of armour sit just inside the door, and we've pushed our guns under our beds. I didn't think the Scottish government would let us take them when we left, but they've told Fiona that they're backing the invasion, and they've sent guns and armour for all of us. We'll need them when the invasion begins. I know we won't stand a chance if the government raids the hotel, but it's comforting to know that we could do some damage. I feel better, knowing the rifle is within reach.

"It's going to be OK, isn't it, Bex?" Amy sounds sleepy, curled up on her camp bed. "We got here, and we're safe, and we're going to rescue your Mum."

I smile in the darkness. We're still in danger. The government could find us, and take us all to the cells. Fiona's plan could fall apart.

But this feels better than lying in my safe, comfortable bed in Scotland.

I'm here, and I'm doing something. We're standing up to the Home Forces, and we're bringing the coalition together.

"We're going to make it OK, Amy. You, me, and the resistance. We're ready."

Silent

Ketty

"Miss Watson. Ready for your big day?"

Brigadier Lee lounges in the interrogation room chair, and I can hear the smirk in his voice. Margaret looks ahead, at the one-way mirror. She sits up straight, as usual, and there's a defiant look in her eyes. As usual, she's refusing to speak.

Lee has two weeks to get a soundbite we can use at the trial. Like all terrorist suspects, Margaret Watson is guaranteed a guilty verdict and a public firing squad. Hers is scheduled for two weeks from today. The Public Information Network has been running trailers for the event for weeks – we need her friends to be watching. We need the country to be watching. She was caught at Makepeace Farm, and she's a friend of the Face of the Resistance. Executing her sends a message to Bex Ellman, and the Opposition In Exile. It shows them what we can do, and it shows them what to expect, when we bring them back to London.

Conrad is busy with final arrangements for the trial, so I'm running the cameras and the recording equipment today. The bruises I gave Margaret last time we met have mostly healed, and Lee doesn't trust me to question her again, so I'm behind the one-way mirror, waiting for her to speak.

"It must be hard, knowing your life will be over before you're eighteen. Any regrets, Miss Watson? Any unfulfilled ambitions you'd like to share with our audience?" Lee tilts his head, and I know he's still smirking.

Margaret closes her eyes for a moment, then lifts her chin and fixes her gaze on the mirror.

Tough kid. That's what Conrad called her. And he's right.

"You have parents, don't you?" Margaret blinks, but keeps her eyes on the mirror. "And a little sister, if I'm not mistaken." Her gaze shifts, and she's looking at the ceiling, her eyes filling with tears.

Getting to you, is he?

"Nothing you want to say to them?"

She shakes her head, slowly. Her hands are shaking, and she pushes them flat against the table, her handcuffs digging into her wrists.

"And what about Bex Ellman? Anything to say to her?"

She glances at Lee, almost too quickly to notice, and then stares straight ahead, tears spilling onto her face.

Come on, Margaret. Give us something to use on PIN.

Lee leans forward in his chair. "And Dan Pearce. I'm sure he's watching. I think he'd want to hear from you. What would you like to say to him?"

I think of the look on Margaret's face when she saw the photo of Dan. The brief smile she couldn't hide when she realised he was free – that we hadn't found him.

She closes her eyes, tears spilling down her cheeks, and her shoulders shake. She sobs, twice, then takes a deep breath and shakes her head again, eyes closed.

When she opens her eyes, she's looking at me through the mirror.

She's looking through me.

And I think of Camp Bishop, after Jackson threw his punches. The Enhanced Interrogation room, throwing punches of my own. Margaret Watson looking through me, as if nothing, and no one, could touch her.

*****

16

Lee slams open the door to the observation room as the prison guards arrive to take Margaret back to her cell.

"Show me," he says, sitting down next to me in the cramped space.

I play back the interview, and he shakes his head.

"Too sympathetic. We can't risk public opinion shifting in her favour." He looks through the mirror at the empty room. "Do you have anything else?"

"Nothing where she speaks. We've already used that."

"PIN needs footage for tonight, Corporal. What else have you got?"

"There's an interview from last month, with Bracken."

"Does she have anything to say?"

"No ..."

He cuts me off, standing up from his chair. "Find something, Corporal."

I nod. " ... but everyone will see the bruises."

He gives me a long stare, then sits down. "Show me what you've got."

I find the drive from a month ago, and load the footage. Margaret and Colonel Bracken, facing each other in the interrogation room. Like Lee, Bracken sits to one side, asking his questions – and this time the camera picks up colourful week-old bruises all over Margaret's exposed skin. On her face and neck, on her hands, on her arms as she shifts in her handcuffs. Her orange prison jumpsuit hides the rest of the bruising, but I know it's there. The bruises came from my orders, and my fists.

Lee nods. "And we haven't shown this yet?"

I shrug. "PIN's been too busy with Craig Dewar and Elizabeth Ellman. And I wasn't sure whether you'd approve it, Sir."

He looks at me again, holding his gaze for a moment too long.

"I'll approve it, Corporal. Things have changed. Get this to PIN."

"Yes, Sir."

*****

The car is supposed to drop me at Dover House, but the driver is happy to leave me on Westminster Bridge. It saves him dealing with the security checks on Whitehall, and keeps me away from Bracken for a few minutes longer.

I walk to the edge of the bridge and look down at the river. It's a cold, grey day, and the scar from the South Bank Bombing looks like the aftermath of an earthquake. Cranes and diggers shift the remains of the buildings, and there's scaffolding along the edge of the water. Metal barriers keep the river from washing more of the broken bank away, and there are barges under what's left of the London Eye, cutting crews crawling over the metal frame as it lies across the river.

The Home Forces building is hidden behind scaffolding and plastic sheets. They're replacing the windows, and fixing the bomb damage, and it's going to take at least another month. Another month, working in a tiny office with Bracken. Collecting the whisky bottles every evening, and pretending I don't see when he drinks his way through every day. Fetching coffee, and ignoring the bottles under his desk.

You can do this, Ketty. Keep your head down and keep Bracken standing.

The guard on duty at the end of Whitehall tells me off for walking in. We're at high alert, and we're supposed to be escorted during working hours. No one knows what else the resistance is planning – what else they can use to send us a message. There could be another bomb, or a personal attack, at any time.

But I've seen how Londoners reacted to the South Bank attack. To devastation in the heart of their city – to the worst attack here since the Crossrail bombing. I've seen how they refused to show their fear. They went out. They carried on. They made sure their lives weren't affected.

I touch my gun in its holster, and smile at the guard.

No point living in fear. If you change your behaviour, the terrorists have already won.

*****

The clouds have thinned by the time I climb the stairs to my flat. There's an orange-pink glow coming through my windows, and I stand and watch the colours change before I go out for a run.

There's a moment when the sky looks as if it's on fire, and I have to close my eyes. All I can see are the flames on the riverbank. People, injured and bleeding. For an instant I'm back on Hungerford Bridge, carrying stretchers and helping medics treat the wounded.

I shake my head.

It's over, Ketty. You're safe.

But my hands are shaking as I close the curtains.

This time, the bombers missed me by hours. If I'd been out running, I would have been in the middle of the attack. We didn't see them coming, and they punched a hole in the city. Next time …

I force myself not to think about it.

Get out there. Run. Show them you're not afraid.

Worry

Bex

There's a quiet knock on the door as I'm lying awake. I reach for my torch and check my watch, and it's half past two. I pull the sleeping bag over my head, but whoever's outside the door knocks again. I crawl out of bed, push my feet into my trainers, and open the door a crack.

"Dan!"

"Bex. I'm sorry. Were you …?"

"No. It's OK." I step out in to the corridor, pulling the door closed behind me. The beam of my torch picks out peeling wallpaper and splintered floorboards.

"Did you mean it? Can I talk to you any time?"

I nod. "I meant it. What's up?"

"I don't know." His voice catches in his throat.

"Can't sleep?" He shakes his head. "Me neither. I just want to make our move. I want to start fighting."

He sits down on the corridor floor, and when he speaks, his voice is choked.

"I'm scared, Bex."

I shrug, sitting down next to him. "We're walking into something dangerous. We don't have all the facts. We're hoping this will work."

He shakes his head. "That's not it." He looks at me, and there are tears on his face. "I know all that."

"So what …?"

"This is our last chance." He takes a ragged breath. "We don't get another opportunity to save them."

I shake my head. "We can't think like that. This is our best chance. This is how we make a difference."

"What if we're not ready?" He puts his head in his hands. "What if we're too late? What if I can't save her?

The trial's in two weeks, Bex. What if we don't move before then?"

I put my arm round his shoulders, and he leans against me, sobbing quietly.

I know what he's feeling. And I know what's keeping me awake. We could sit here, waiting for a signal to start the attack, and we could be too late. We could be sitting here while they show Margie's trial on TV. While they show Mum, bruised and injured, on PIN every night.

We might be ready, but if the coalition isn't ready to move we could still lose this fight. We could still lose our friend.

"You can't think like that. You're doing the best you can."

He nods. "But what if it's not enough?"

I move away, dropping my arm from his shoulders. He leans back against the wall, watching me.

"We're doing the right thing, Dan."

"How do you know that?"

"Because staying in Scotland wasn't helping."

He nods, looking down. "I just …"

"I know, Dan. I get it. I don't want to lose Margie, and I don't want to lose Mum. As soon as we can, we'll lead this invasion. We'll go and rescue them."

He nods. "You're right." He rubs his hands over his face. "You're right. So why am I so afraid?"

I reach out again, and put my hand on his arm. "Because you're right, too. This might not work. The government might find us, and stop us. The coalition might wait too long to start the invasion. We might lose Margie, and Mum, and Dr Richards."

He puts one hand over his face, and his shoulders shake.

"But it won't be because we didn't try. We're making the best choice here. We're doing the right thing. We're doing the brave thing."

"Yeah. I just … I hate feeling this useless. I want to go in and rescue her now. Today. I want to take her out of their horrible cells and their horrible interrogation rooms, and I want to set her free." He glances at me. "I don't even care if she walks away from me. From us. I just want to be useful. I want to save her."

"I know." I give his arm a squeeze. "And she knows that, too."

He nods. "But that doesn't change anything."

"This is our chance, Dan."

He pushes the tears from his cheeks with his hands.

"You're right. I know you're right. I just …"

"I know, Dan. I know. I'm scared too."

He reaches out his hand, and I take it in mine. We sit for a while, without speaking.

And somehow the fear seems easier to face when we're facing it together. We've both got so much invested in what happens next. We both need to do something – for Margie and for Mum. We might fail. We might not get to them in time. But whatever happens, we both have somewhere to turn.

*****

There's a crowd of people in the corner of the dining room when we come down for breakfast. Someone's rigged up a TV, and people are gathering to watch PIN. I glance at Dan, and he looks back, the fear from last night showing on his face. We walk over and join the audience.

The morning news is recapping headlines from last night. There's a clip of Mum and Ketty – no sound, but Mum's arm is still in plaster. There's a clip of Craig

Dewar, addressing the camera. And there's a clip of Margie, covered in fading bruises. PIN hasn't run footage of Margie in weeks – just the endless trailers for her trial – and we haven't seen bruises like this before.

Dan staggers beside me, and I pull a chair over from the nearest table. He waves me away, and steps towards the TV.

The bruises are everywhere. All over her face and neck, and on her hands and arms. They're old – they're not black and blue, but ugly shades of yellow and green and brown.

"What have they done, Bex?"

I shake my head. I know how this feels. When Ketty did this to Mum, I nearly punched my Liaison Officer when she claimed there was nothing we could do.

"We're here, Dan. We're going to save her."

"Two weeks, Bex. Two weeks until they ..."

"I know." Two weeks until the rigged trial, and the firing squad.

He clenches his fists and closes his eyes. "We have to move soon, Bex. We have to."

*****

Fiona's briefing is short. No word from the coalition, so for now we stay where we are and hope the government doesn't find us.

Dan walks out, fists clenched, and Amy goes after him. I stay, waiting for a chance to talk to Fiona.

Charlie pulls up a chair and puts her hand on my shoulder.

"Everything OK?"

I shake my head. "I can't sit here forever. We need to fight. We need to act."

"We will. Just as soon as the coalition is ready."

"But that could take weeks. Months." She nods. "But we don't have weeks. Margie doesn't have weeks."

"I know, Bex. But marching in without the coalition? That's suicide. You know that."

"I know." My voice is a whisper, and I'm looking down at the table when Fiona sits down next to me. Charlie gives my shoulder a squeeze and pushes her chair back.

"I'll leave you to it. OK, Bex?" I give her a smile, but I'm blinking back tears as she stands up and walks away. I turn to Fiona, and force myself to stay calm.

"Dan's not happy with us?" She glances at the door, and back at me.

I shake my head. "He's worried about Margie."

She nods. "We're doing the best we can, Bex. We're in place – we're where we need to be, but we have to wait for the coalition before we can make our move."

"And if that's not enough?"

She looks down at the table. "You know the answer to that. We'll do everything we can to rescue Margie, and the other prisoners, but taking down the government has to be our first priority."

"That's not good enough." She looks up at me, surprise on her face. "We need to move before they execute my friend."

"Bex, I can't tell the coalition what to do!"

"You can make sure they know about the trial, though. You can make sure they know that this is PIN's biggest event of the year. You can remind them that stopping the trial would embarrass the government. And that it would save my friend. It would keep me and my friends in a helpful mood, too."

She looks at the expression on my face. "Are you threatening me, Committee Member Ellman?" She's whispering, but there's nothing soft about her words.

I fight the urge to shake my head and back down.

"I'm reminding you what's at stake. I'm reminding you that we're here to rescue our friends and our families, as well as to lead your invasion. And I'm asking you to pass that on to the coalition, Madam Chairman."

She looks at me for a few moments longer, then pushes her chair back from the table.

"I'll bear your comments in mind, Miss Ellman. I hope you'll take note of mine."

Rumours

Ketty

"Have you heard?"

I shake my head and carry on making notes. "I don't need to hear anything from you, Corporal."

Conrad rolls his eyes, and pulls a chair over to my desk.

"You want to hear this."

Bracken is at a meeting with Lee, so I have the tiny room to myself. I give Conrad a cold look – he's come to leave some papers on Bracken's desk, and I'm expecting him to leave. I have nothing to say to the person who killed my best friend.

"Troop movements, across the North Sea," he says, ignoring the look on my face.

I shrug. "So?"

"So we think they're going to try to invade."

I put my pen down and fold my arms. "Who?"

He smiles. "We think it's the OIE. And we think they're working with the Netherlands." He waits for me to react. My missing recruit is in the Netherlands, rescued from deportation to London by a deal with the Scottish government.

I don't want to talk to Conrad, but he's right. I need to hear this. "OK. I'm listening."

He shrugs. "That's all we know. Troop movements. Some sort of training camp. And a lot of warships at the Den Helder military base."

"They don't stand a chance. We've got the Army, the Navy, the Air Force, and the Home Forces. What do they think they can do?"

"No one knows. But something's happening. And your recruit is in the middle of it."

*****

Bracken's face is pale when he comes back from his meeting. He reaches for the whisky bottle as soon as he's sitting down, and I focus my attention on the papers in front of me while he drinks two glasses and slumps back in his chair.

"Coffee, Sir?"

He nods. I leave him with his bottle, and walk down the corridor to the kitchen. The coffee is instant, and terrible – there's no space for the coffee machine here – but it's better then nothing. I shake two painkillers from the bottle in my pocket, and carry the coffee back to the office.

"Thank you, Ketty."

I leave one mug of coffee and the painkillers in front of him, and he swallows the tablets before putting the whisky bottle back under his desk.

"Bad day, Sir?"

He looks at me, trying to decide what to say.

"Bad news, I think."

"The invasion?"

He raises his eyebrows, and he's about to say something.

"Conrad was here," I say, quickly. "He told me."

"I thought you two weren't speaking."

Not when I have a choice.

I shrug. "This concerns Jake, and the other recruits. I let him talk."

There's a ghost of a smile on his face. "Very commendable, Ketty."

I can't help smiling back. "Thank you, Sir."

He wraps his hands round the coffee mug, and stares at his desk.

27

"So are the Netherlands invading? Is this the end of the UK?" I keep my voice steady, but I can see that Bracken is worried.

He shakes his head. "We don't know."

"But they can't have enough people …"

"We don't know, Ketty. We don't know what they've got." He looks up at me. "The government of the Netherlands worked with the Scottish government to make sure Jake wasn't sent back here." I nod. One of the list of failures that Lee is holding against us. "Who knows what else they're cooperating on?"

"Are they working with the OIE?"

"We think that's likely."

"So the other recruits could be heading for the Netherlands."

"I think that's a fair assumption."

Which means we've lost our leverage with their hosts. We've lost *them*.

"So Craig Dewar …"

"Threatening the life of a Scottish citizen might have had exactly the effect we were hoping for, Ketty."

"Persuading Scotland to expel the OIE, and the recruits?" He nods. "But that doesn't help us, if they've found another safe place to stay."

"It doesn't."

I stare at my coffee mug.

"Did we screw this one up, Sir? Putting Craig Dewar on PIN?"

Did my suggestion prompt an invasion?

"Who knows, Ketty? Maybe this was happening anyway. Maybe this is to do with the bombing." He shakes his head. "Maybe the OIE has been planning this from the start."

"Is Lee blaming us?"

Bracken gives a harsh laugh. "He's blaming everyone. But yes, we're on his list."

Just what we need. Giving the brigadier something else to use against us.

I think about what Conrad told me. Warships and troops. Cooperation with the OIE. If they're planning an invasion, they must be confident that they can win.

"Can they do it, Sir? Can they defeat us?"

He shrugs. "They must think so." He takes a sip of his coffee. "But we're sending troops to the ports. The Air Force is on high alert. The Navy is positioning its ships to defend us. Major General Franks is working with the head of the Army. We're doing everything we can."

"Can we persuade them not to invade? Can we show them that fighting would be a mistake?"

"We need to wait and see how they respond to our defences."

So this could be war. This could be fighting in the streets.

"What are we telling people? Is PIN covering the troop movements?"

He looks at me, and smiles. "Absolutely not. PIN is stepping up its coverage of local news. Raids on safe houses. Interrogations. Terrorist trials."

"Margaret Watson?"

"Margaret Watson. She's the big distraction. Keep everyone looking at her, and we'll keep them from noticing what's going on beyond our borders."

*****

My run takes me round St James's Park, past Buckingham Palace, and the lines of Home Forces soldiers protecting the King, and back along the Mall. I can't run along the South Bank any more, and the roads around the bomb site are all closed. I miss running along the river, but running under the trees on Birdcage Walk I can forget about the bombing. Forget about how close I came to being one of the casualties. I can forget the flames, and the smoke. The London Eye, falling.

And I can forget about standing with Conrad next to the water at midnight. About the touch of his fingers on my skin. About all the mistakes I've made.

Come on, Ketty. Focus on running.

But my thoughts circle in my head, and I keep coming back to the invasion.

Is this the OIE, putting pressure on us? Are they sending a signal to the resistance cells in the UK? Is this the start of more bombings?

Bracken said things would get worse before they get better. What if he's right? What if the resistance thinks it can get away with more attacks like the South Bank bomb?

A line of soldiers in black uniforms blocks the pavement in front of me, and I turn to run through the park.

There are more guards on duty today. Is the threat of invasion making the Home Forces concerned for the safety of the King? Or are we worried that he's working with the resistance?

Are the guards keeping bombers out, or are they keeping the King locked in?

Where are the good guys in all this?

Focus, Ketty. This isn't about good and bad. This is about survival.

So how do I survive? How do I protect myself from whatever's coming?

Stick with the Home Forces? Put my trust in Franks, and the Army?

Or find a way out?

There are more soldiers lined up in front of the Victoria Memorial as I turn to run the length of The Mall. They're armed with power-assisted rifles, cradled in combat-ready positions. The weapons we used at Camp Bishop. The weapons my recruits stole from the coach. I feel a jolt of pain as I think about the coach raid – Dan firing his rifle, sending the bullet through my knee. I see Saunders' look of surprise when I sent a bullet into his chest at the bunker. I know how much damage those guns can do, and I can feel them behind me as I run.

Is this how it feels to be a target?

If the Dutch army invades, will we be targets? How far will they get? I can't imagine a foreign army marching into London. I think about defending the capital – lining up in my armour with the Army and the RTS to keep the invaders out. It feels absurd.

And I wonder how it would feel if they win. How it would feel to be on the losing side.

Visions of prison jumpsuits and handcuffs distract me from the rhythm of my run, and I stop for a moment, bent double to catch my breath.

Prison jumpsuits, and the inside of a cell.

I shake my head.

Come on, Ketty. You're overreacting. Just keep running.

Keep Bracken working. Keep your job. Keep yourself safe.

But it's a relief when I reach Whitehall, and the guns are out of sight.

Despair

Bex

"Dan?" I knock on his door again, but he doesn't answer. I shout as loudly as I dare. "Dan!"

There's a shuffling sound from inside the room. He unlocks the door, and walks back to his camp bed, crawling under his sleeping bag and switching off his torch before I can stop him. I take my torch from my pocket and use it to find my way across the room.

I kneel down on the floor next to his bed and put my hand gently on his shoulder.

"Dan." He shrugs. "Talk to me."

"What's the point?" He lies, curled up, with his back to me. His voice is rough, and I realise he's been crying.

"Because we promised. Any time this gets too much, you're supposed to talk to me."

"Like that's going to help." His words are muffled by the sleeping bag.

I rest my head on the edge of his bed.

"It's not going to make it worse."

There's a long pause. "No. I don't think it can get any worse."

I squeeze his shoulder, and move to a more comfortable position on the floor.

"I'm here, Dan. I'm not going away."

For a while, he says nothing, and then he nods.

"Thanks, Bex." His voice is quiet, and he doesn't move. I put my hand back on his shoulder.

*****

Dan didn't come to breakfast this morning, and he's been ignoring everyone who knocks on his door. I'm lucky he let me in.

It's been nearly two weeks since I reminded Fiona that our friend's life is in danger. That we're here to save her, and that we need the coalition's help to do that.

And Margie's trial is tomorrow.

We've heard nothing. The invasion was always going to take time, but no one thought we'd be waiting this long. Fiona gives us updates every day, but so far there's been nothing to report. Stand by. Hold position. Even when the OIE committee meets, she doesn't have anything else to tell us.

And now the worst is happening. Now we have to watch the government execute our friend, and there's nothing we can do to help her.

So I sit with Dan. I'm missing a committee meeting, but Fiona doesn't need me there to discuss the running of the hotel, again. Dan needs me this morning. He's said everything he can say, and he's told Fiona what we need to do, and nothing's happened. He's at the end of his road, and all he can think about is Margie.

I don't know what to do. Fiona can't help. There's nothing we can do until the coalition is ready. Charlie's right – anything else would be suicide.

I know Dan doesn't care. I know he wants to go to Horse Guard's Parade tomorrow. To see for himself that there's nothing he could do to save her. But that's suicide, just as much as if he stormed the stage with his rifle. Our faces are on posters all over London, and there's no way he'd get near the trial without being caught. I just have to make sure he doesn't try.

*****

"I can't do this, Bex. I can't wait like this." He turns to look at me, his face grey in the torchlight. "If I knew where she was …"

"If you knew where she was, you'd be doing something brave and stupid, and it would take everyone here to wrestle you into a chair and stop you."

"I'd like to see them try."

"Anyway. Brave and stupid is my job. You're supposed to stop me, not the other way round."

"I didn't stop you from visiting your Dad."

He throws his words like a punch, and I feel as if he's winded me.

"Dan …"

"You went to the nursing home, and you had the chance to say goodbye. I didn't stop you."

He's right. I had the chance to give my Dad a hug. To make sure he knew I was there, before he died.

But I screwed up. I let Ketty take Mum away. Dad died alone, because of me. And Mum's in the government's cells, and on PIN every night, because of me.

"Maybe you should have stopped me." He turns away from me, and stares at the dark ceiling. "All the damage I caused by going to the nursing home? Maybe it would have been better if I'd stayed in Newcastle."

"So because you messed up, I have to let them execute Margie."

"Come on, Dan. It's not like that. People are in prison because of what I did. People are in exile. We betrayed a safe house network, and Neesh lost her business, because of me."

"So …"

"And I nearly got killed. Ketty nearly took me away, as well as Mum. I honestly thought she'd found me …"

My pulse races as I think about hiding under Mum's bed. Ketty, searching the room for me. The box, pulling away from my knees as she checked my hiding place. The darkness, keeping me hidden.

"You screwed up, so you won't even let me try?"

"I learnt a lesson, Dan. I stayed hidden, and Ketty took my mother away. I hurt so many people that day, and I nearly lost everything." I can feel my hands shaking. Tears stinging my eyes. "I'm not going to let you make the same mistake."

"Why should you get to ..."

There's another knock at the door, and we both stop talking.

"Dan? Bex?"

"Amy?"

"You need to get out here. You need to come downstairs."

"I don't think Dan wants to ..."

"It's the signal, Bex. Fiona's had the signal. We're moving."

*****

Dan's out of bed and pulling on a pair of jeans before I've made it to the door. We follow Amy down the stairs, our torch beams bouncing on the walls as we run. There's a tiny slice of light between two of the wooden panels on the windows, and I have to check my watch to convince myself that it's still morning outside.

The ballroom is full when we walk in, and the atmosphere is electric. People are talking and whispering as they find places to sit in the rows of seats. Charlie waves us over to the places she's saved for us at the front.

"You two OK?" She raises her eyebrows at Dan, and I notice that his hair is matted and tangled. He's wearing the old white T-shirt that he usually wears to bed, and socks, but no shoes. There's stubble on his cheeks, and he hasn't switched off the torch in his hand, even though the lights in the ballroom are on.

I've never seen him like this.

I look back at Charlie. "I think that depends on what Fiona has to say."

*****

"Listen up!" Fiona steps up to the front of the room, a grey folder in her hands. The room falls silent. "It's been decided. Everything is in place, and we make our move tomorrow."

I feel Dan tense up next to me, and I reach out and take his hand. He grips my fingers tightly, holding his breath.

"As you all know, Margaret Watson's trial is scheduled for two in the afternoon, at Horse Guard's Parade. After the South Bank bomb, Home Forces staff were evacuated from their building, and accommodated in offices along Whitehall – buildings that back on to Horse Guard's.

"We're going to use this, and the distraction of the trial, to take out the chain of command."

There's a murmuring from behind us, which dies away as Fiona carries on.

"We've had some useful intelligence from our resistance partners. There are several key meetings happening while the trial gets started. The heads of the armed forces – Army and Home Forces, Navy, and Air Force – are meeting in a room overlooking Whitehall. The regular meeting of senior Civil Servants is taking place close by. And there's a meeting of the Terrorism Committee, overlooking Horse Guard's Parade.

"Our role will be to enter these meetings, keep the senior commanders in their seats, and cut off their communications. When we've done that, the coalition

36

will make its move, and the forces on the ground will be cut off from their chain of command.

"We are going to decapitate the military government."

There's a muted cheer from the seats behind us, and Fiona raises her hands.

"This won't be easy. We won't have much support. We need to take, and hold, positions in the heart of London." She looks around the room. "There will be troops behind us – British fighters, from the Netherlands camp – but they can only move when we've taken away the command structure." She looks down, and opens the folder. "We have limited supplies of armour, uniforms, and weapons. If you haven't been issued any yet, come and see me at the end of the briefing. If you have, make sure everything is in working order before tomorrow morning."

She pauses, and people start to whisper all over the room. Charlie takes my free hand and holds it in hers.

"In addition to taking the commanders hostage, we also need to change the mood of the public. PIN is expecting a huge crowd for the execution tomorrow." Dan grips my fingers more tightly, never taking his eyes off Fiona. "We can't be sure what mood they'll be in when we start our operation. So we're going to make a broadcast. We're going to patch into the PIN feed, and the feed to the screens on the stage, and we're going to send them a message."

There's a twisted feeling in my stomach. I know what Fiona wants me to do.

"We're going to show them the Face of the Resistance, and we're going to ask for their support."

I slump down in my seat, my head on Dan's shoulder. She's not going to let me save Margie. She's going to put me on TV in my armour, looking like my photo, and she's going to expect me to inspire people.

She wants me to appeal to the people who've come to watch the murder of my friend, and she's not going to let me fight.

"Front-line doll." I don't mean to speak, but I can't stop myself, and there's frustration in my voice. Charlie glances at me, and squeezes my hand.

"Bex," Fiona points at me. "We'll escort you to the meeting room, when the Terrorism Committee is under guard. We can patch into their feed from there. You'll give your speech, and we'll follow yours with other broadcasts to keep the crowd in line."

I lift my head. "And Margie? What about Margie?"

"When we've done what we can to the commanders, then we'll see about saving your friend." She turns to the room. "We've divided you into teams …"

I pull my hands back from Charlie and Dan, and stand up.

"No."

Fiona looks at me, her face carefully calm.

"No, what, Miss Ellman?"

"No. I'm not doing it."

"Bex. You're a critical part of this plan."

"And so is my friend."

Dan looks up at me, eyebrows raised. I give him a nervous smile.

"Can we talk about this later?"

I shake my head. I can feel the blood rushing to my cheeks, but I don't care.

"No. I want this agreed now."

She closes the folder carefully, and holds it against her chest like a shield.

"Go on then. What's your objection?"

I take a deep breath. I need to ask for the right thing. I need to make her understand.

"I'll make your broadcast. But my friends? They get to save Margie." Dan sits up straight in his chair, and

Amy nods. Fiona shakes her head and opens her mouth, but I cut her off. "While I'm addressing the crowd – while I'm *distracting* the crowd – my team gets to break the prisoner out. And when I'm done speaking, I'm going to help them."

Fiona glares at me, her eyes flashing with anger.

"Bex – our resistance contacts have spent weeks on this plan. We can't …"

"Then neither can I." I sit down, returning Fiona's glare.

She hangs her head for a moment, one hand massaging her forehead.

"Are you serious, Bex? Are you putting this whole plan in jeopardy, just to free one prisoner?"

I'm about to answer, when Dan stands up next to me.

"Yes. Yes she is. Because that prisoner is our friend, and we're here to rescue her." Fiona opens her mouth, but he doesn't stop. "And when we've done that, we're rescuing Bex's mother, and our teacher, and all the people who are locked up because of us. All of them." Fiona's shoulders are sagging, and she's shaking her head. "That's our price, Madam Chairman. We'll agree to your plan, if you agree to ours." And he sits down.

Fiona sighs.

"How many of you are in on this?"

I look at Dan and Amy, and Charlie and Maz. They're all looking at me. I reach out, and hold hands with Dan and Charlie again. Charlie reaches out to Maz, and Dan takes Amy's hand, and we stand up, holding our joined hands up between us.

Fiona nods.

"Right. We'll talk about this after the meeting."

"Is that a yes?" Maz calls out.

Fiona bows her head. "That's a yes. Can we move on with the meeting now?"

She doesn't get an answer. I'm too busy being hugged by my friends, and pushing tears from my eyes with my sleeves.

Deception

Ketty

"Corporal Smith." Lee walks into the office, checking his watch. "As of now, you no longer have clearance to be in this room."

I stand up behind my desk. "Sir?"

"Bracken and I have matters to discuss. I need you to be elsewhere."

Don't mind me, Sir. I'll get out of your way.

"Yes, Sir." I start to gather the papers I'm working on.

"Now, Corporal. Not next week."

"Yes, Sir." I push a pen into my pocket, and shuffle the papers into a folder, stepping round the desk.

"And bring some coffee. I think the Colonel could use some refreshment."

Bracken is sitting at his desk, watching Lee throw me out of the room. He doesn't react.

I think he could, too, Sir.

"Yes, Sir."

*****

"You've been evicted?"

Conrad smirks as he pushes past me into the tiny kitchen. He shakes his head as I ignore him, and concentrate on spooning instant coffee into two mugs. He pulls another mug from the cupboard and lines it up next to mine. I ignore that, too.

"Enjoy that," he says. "There's a chance we'll run out soon."

More cryptic comments, David?

I turn to face him. "I've had enough of your secrets, Corporal. Tell me what you're talking about, or shut up."

"Coffee." He grins, watching my reaction.

The kettle boils, and I give him a recruit-scaring glare before turning away and pouring water into my mugs.

"The blockade? At the ports?" He sounds as if he's trying to jog my memory. He thinks he's telling me something I already know. I shake my head, reaching for the milk in the fridge.

"I thought we had that under control. I thought the Navy was handling it."

"Bracken really hasn't told you?"

I slam the milk carton down on the work surface.

"Told me what, David?"

He takes half a step back, holding his hands up in front of him. The smirk is back on his face.

"How bad it is."

I roll my eyes, pour the milk and put the carton back in the fridge. I don't want to play his game, but I need to know the truth.

I make myself keep talking.

"How bad is it?"

"We're under siege, Ketty. Nothing's getting out, and nothing's getting in."

I shake my head, trying to clear my thoughts.

"The Dutch Navy isn't big enough to block everything."

"It's not just the Dutch." Conrad reaches past me to the coffee, and puts a spoonful in his own cup.

It's not just the Dutch?

I don't want to talk to Conrad. I don't want to have friendly conversations with him in the kitchen. I don't want to be distracted by his beautiful eyes and his gorgeous smile.

But I need to know what he knows.

"OK, David. Who is it? Whose Navy is big enough to blockade all our ports?"

He shrugs. "It's everyone."

I put my hand on the work surface to steady myself.

"What do you mean?" I ask, slowly.

"It's Scotland, It's France, It's Germany, It's Norway …"

I hold up one hand. "Working together?"

He nods. "Working together."

They could win. They could starve us out, they could invade, and they could win.

"How long do we have?"

He waves a hand. "Oh, ages. We'll run out of some things soon, but we can hold out for a long time. Plenty of tinned food in the stockpiles." We waves his hand. "We'll come to an agreement with them before they're ready to attack." He grins.

"Won't people notice?" I glance at the mugs. "What happens when the coffee runs out?"

"Franks is talking about rationing …"

"Rationing?" I can't help shouting.

He waves his hand again. "Don't be so dramatic. It won't be everything. Just the things we have to import."

"So what's your plan, Corporal? Keep talking to the invading hordes, and hope that people don't notice?"

He grins again.

"Distraction. Keeping them entertained."

The trial. Margaret's trial.

"And after tomorrow?" I can't help smirking. "What will you do when you've executed your main distraction?"

"Plenty more prisoners in the cells, Ketty."

He leans past me again to flick the kettle switch and pour the water into his mug.

He's right. There are. Elizabeth Ellman, Craig Dewar, William Richards. The other terrorists from Makepeace Farm.

I lean back against the work surface and fold my arms.

"So they'll all get show trials?"

He nods. "Keep the public watching what we want them to watch, and they won't notice what's going on."

"And tomorrow? How many people will be in London tomorrow for your show trial?"

The trial I was supposed to be running. The trial I'm going to miss, while I'm sitting outside a Terrorism Committee meeting.

He shrugs. "A hundred thousand? Two?" He reaches for his mug. "We've got screens in St James's Park, and more in Trafalgar Square and Hyde Park. There are coaches coming in from all over the country."

I can't help looking impressed.

"And who's making sure they all behave themselves?"

"You mean apart from the bars and the streetfood and the other distractions?" I nod. "Home Forces, mostly. RTS. The Army's busy at the ports, so we're the ones in charge."

"Is your team up to that, David? After what happened on the South Bank …"

"My team has everything under control." His voice is frosty.

Don't want to be reminded that it was you who gave the weapons to the South Bank Bombers, David?

And I realise. Part of me wants him to fail again. This was my event. This was my trial, until Lee took it away from me.

Part of me wants David to make another mistake.

Part of me wants trouble at the trial.

I turn away and pick up the mugs of coffee. Bracken and Lee will be wondering where I am.

"There is one thing …"

I turn back to Conrad.

"What?" My impatience is obvious.

"Lee hasn't managed to get Margaret to talk."

"Of course he hasn't." I can't help smiling. I hope I sound smug.

Conrad looks at his coffee cup, cradled in his hands.

"I wondered if you had any more footage. Anything else we could use."

Are you asking me for help?

I stare at him for a moment.

"What do you want, Corporal? My secret footage of Margaret confessing to everything? Confiding in me about all the attacks she's masterminded?"

He shrugs.

"Anything, Ketty. Anything you can think of."

I lean towards him, raising my voice.

"There's nothing, Corporal. She hasn't spoken, and she won't speak. You've got everything she's ever said to the camera. She's a tough kid, and she's going to beat you on this." I'm frustrated with the progress we've made with Margaret, but I can't help laughing at Conrad. I couldn't break her, but neither can he.

And it's his job to make the trial a success.

His job. Not mine.

And I don't need to help.

Unless …

I put the mugs down on the work surface.

"Do you have the footage I recorded with Lee? Where he asks about her family?" He nods, watching me carefully.

This is your chance. This is your ticket to the trial.

"Get me a backstage pass, and I'll give you the footage you need."

He gapes at me. "How?"

"Backstage pass, David."

He stares at me, and then nods. "Fine, fine."

"Now."

"OK."

I follow him out of the kitchen, leaving my mugs of coffee on the side.

*****

"So what's your plan?"

I look at the backstage pass in my hands. My name, my details. Signed by Conrad.

I can take myself down, during the meeting. One of the guards can cover for me. With the backstage pass I can get from the conference room, into the crowd, and back again before they'll miss me.

It's risky, but I get to watch. I get to see what happens to the person who nearly cost me my job. What happens to the tough kid who dodged the RTS. Who ran away with her teacher, and joined the terrorists rather than joining us.

Lee doesn't get to take this from me.

I nod towards the screen. "Play the footage."

Lee, off to one side in his chair. Margaret, facing the camera.

"Ready for your big day?"

No reaction from the prisoner.

"Can you find the part where she's reacting? Where she's shaking her head?"

Conrad glances at me, then skips the footage forward.

"There. Now go back and play the question."

He moves the footage back.

"Nothing you want to say to them?"

Margaret shakes her head.

He pauses the footage. "I don't see …"

"Whats she shaking her head too, David?"

"Lee's question?" He sounds confused.

"Right. So what if we dubbed in a new question?"

He stares at the screen, a smile spreading across his face.

"Oh, that's good, Ketty. That's genius."

"So, let's get Lee to ask whether she regrets joining the terrorists. Whether she regrets wiping out Leominster. She reacts again, a bit later."

He plays the next section. She glances quickly at Lee, and tears run down her face.

"That's the Leominster question."

He nods, watching her sob, and regain control.

"And something about how many people she's killed, there at the end."

He pauses the image: Margaret staring, expressionless, into the camera.

I didn't need to break you. I just needed to out-think you.

We've got our clip for the trial.

*****

I hurry back to the kitchen. The coffee is cold, so I pour it away and make two fresh mugs, then carry them back to the office, my pass in my pocket and my folder tucked under my arm.

Lee opens the door when I knock, and waves me inside.

"Have your desk back, Corporal," he says, taking one of the mugs.

I put the other mug on Bracken's desk, and sit down at my own.

Lee whispers a few words to Bracken as I take the papers from my folder.

47

I glance up at the screen on the wall. They've been watching something. There's no sound, but the images look like a news broadcast. There's no badge or channel logo visible, but the screen shows a helicopter view of a port. There's a Union Jack flying over the harbour, but out to sea there are ships.

Warships. Thirty or forty of them.

And they're not ours.

My breath catches in my throat, as I count five – no, six – different flags.

Conrad was right. It's not just the Dutch Navy.

It's everyone.

They could invade, and they could win.

My small victory over Margaret, over Conrad, fades. It doesn't matter what I do here. Who I help, who I support.

If those governments decide to move against us, I'm wearing the wrong uniform.

I can feel my pulse racing. I press my hands against the desk to stop them shaking.

Find a way out, Ketty. You don't want to be on the losing side.

Departure

Bex

"You slept?"

Dan sounds incredulous. He shakes his head, and takes another mug of coffee from Charlie. He looks pale, and the bags under his eyes look like bruises.

"She was snoring all night." Amy nudges my elbow, and picks up another piece of her armour.

It's true. I slept better than I have since we arrived in London.

For the first time, I know what's expected of me. For the first time, I have a chance to save Margie, and Mum. I have a chance to put right the mistakes I've made. And there are people standing with me, making all this possible.

For the first time, I'm hopeful. I'm allowing myself to believe that we can do this.

I'm allowing myself to believe that we can win.

Dan picks up the last of his armour, and I help him clip the panels to his arm.

"You didn't sleep?"

He shakes his head again.

I put my hand on his shoulder, and wait for him to meet my eyes.

"This is it, Dan. This is our chance." He looks away, but I don't let him move. I lower my voice to a whisper. "Margie needs you, Dan. She needs you awake and thinking straight." He closes his eyes, and nods. "Drink your coffee. Eat something." He shakes his head. "I'll check your gun."

He sits down on one of the ballroom chairs, coffee mug in his hands. I pick up his rifle, and run the pre-combat checks we learnt at Camp Bishop. I check the battery, and all the connections; the sights, the clips and the grips. I check that it's loaded.

"Are these AP bullets?" He nods. "And you've got spare APs?" I point to the magazines clipped to his belt.

"They're all Armour Piercing, Bex." He sounds tired, and he sounds afraid.

"Good." I hold out the rifle. "Everything's working. You're ready, Dan." He takes the gun, and rests it on his knees, but he doesn't respond.

I hate seeing him like this. Dan is the person who has my back. In all the time we've been running from the RTS, he's stood with me. He's believed in me. He's been brave with me, and he's killed people to keep me safe.

I can't lose him now. Not when Margie's life depends on us.

He's right to be afraid. There are so many things that could go wrong today. Any one of us could be killed, or captured. The Home Forces could stop us before we can reach Margie. They could stop us before we reach any of our targets.

We could fail.

And our friend will die.

But we can't walk into battle thinking about what we might lose. We need to be brave, and we need to believe in ourselves. We need to believe in each other.

I kneel down in front of him, the plastic panels of my armour clicking on the wooden floor.

"Dan." He looks at me, and all I can see is the pain in his eyes. His fear that we might not save her.

He needs me. He needs me, and Amy, and Charlie, and Maz. He needs to know that we're standing with him.

"You're ready, Dan. You can do this. *We* can do this." I take the empty mug from his hands and put it on the floor. I reach out and take his gloved hands in mine.

"This isn't all on you. It's not your responsibility to save her. This is on all of us, and we're all here."

He looks around at the ballroom. At tables, covered in crates of armour, sent with us by the Scottish government. At OIE staff, trained to fight during our last weeks in Edinburgh, dressing themselves in the black panels and helmets. At Amy and Charlie and Maz, checking their guns and clipping ammunition to their belts.

And he nods.

"I know. I just …"

"You're thinking about everything that could go wrong." He nods. "Then don't. Think about what happens if everything goes right."

The ghost of a smile appears on his face, but he shakes his head. "I don't dare, Bex. It's too hard."

I stand up from the floor and wrap my arms round his shoulders. "I need you to be brave. Margie needs you to be brave. Think about what happens if we win."

He sits still for a moment, then reaches up and hugs me back. When I pull back, there's a new look in his eyes. He's almost smiling, and I can see determination on his face.

"We're going to make this work," he says, and there's surprise in his voice.

I smile back. "We're going to make this work."

*****

There's a fleet of cars waiting in the service yard when Fiona sends us out of the hotel. All the local resistance fighters, driving up in their family cars and people carriers, ready to take us to Whitehall.

It's a crazy plan, but it's simple. All these mismatched cars, everyday vehicles that might belong to anyone, will take us to the roads around Whitehall. We'll group together and we'll walk in, posing as routine patrols. We'll use our armour to get past the guards, and the trial as our distraction. By the time the Home Forces see what's happening, the backup forces will be behind us.

Neesh and her rebel fighters are already in place, waiting for us to make our move. All we have to do is follow the plan.

Fiona sends us to a 7-seater van parked near the road. We climb in – Dan, Amy, Charlie, Maz, and me. The driver turns and gives us a smile.

"The Face of the Resistance, in my car." He shakes his head. "This is a big responsibility. I'll be careful – I promise!"

"Thanks, mate," says Maz, covering my angry silence. "We appreciate it."

We balance our guns and helmets on our knees, and shuffle in our seats so that we're not elbowing each other with our armour panels. There are cuddly toys in the seat-back pockets, and brightly coloured child-friendly sun screens attached to the windows. This vehicle wasn't designed for a troop of soldiers, and it suddenly seems absurd to be sitting here, waiting for the driver to take us to war in his family car.

Charlie slides the door closed, and I feel as if she's trapped us inside. It feels dark and cramped and dangerous in here, and I can feel my panic rising.

I close my eyes tight, and take a long, deep breath. And another. I need to be calm, and I need to be ready.

Dan reaches across from his seat and takes my hand. When I turn to smile at him, I can see that he's fighting the same feelings. We're trapped, and we're under someone else's control.

But this isn't like the helicopter, carrying us to Scotland. This isn't like the cars that picked us up after the raid on the bunker.

We're not being driven to safety. We're being driven into danger, and Dan's right – this is our only chance.

The driver starts the engine, and the doors lock. I grip Dan's fingers, and he squeezes mine back. As we pull away from the hotel, I wonder whether any of us will be coming back.

I start to feel alive as the car turns a corner and leaves the safe house behind. I feel as if I've lit a fire inside my chest. I feel as if I've crawled out of a cocoon – as if I'm a new creature, brave, and ready to fight. As if all the training we've done and all the preparations we've made are part of another life, falling away behind me.

As if all that counts is today. As if this is everything I've been living for.

No one speaks as we drive towards Whitehall, and Margie.

PIN

Ketty

I send Bracken into the Terrorism Committee meeting, and sit down outside the room. Since the last meeting, someone's set up a desk for me in the corridor, and there's a TV on the wall opposite. I guess I'm not the only runner who has to sit here while the conference room is in use.

I put my document bag down on the desk, and switch the TV on, flicking through the channels until I find PIN. Everyone in the conference room is enjoying a view of the backstage area in Horse Guard's Parade, but PIN is showing the front of the stage, and the crowds. The platform is huge – like the stage for a music festival, draped in black cloth and lit with bright spotlights. Conrad was right – there are thousands and thousands of people here, waiting to see Margaret Watson confess to her crimes.

I touch the corner of the backstage pass in my pocket. There are no guards with me in the corridor, but there are guards on the doors at the bottom of the stairs. If I'm lucky, I can get one of them to cover for me while I sneak out to watch the trial.

I sit down behind the desk and pull out the paperwork for this morning, splitting my attention between the reports in my folder and the images on PIN.

*****

The build-up to the trial is slow. PIN is running promotion after promotion, reminding everyone about this afternoon's show. The coverage alternates between the audience and the soldiers guarding them; and the preparations on the stage. I watch the crowds gathering, the stage taking shape.

They're building the elements of the trial in front of the audience and the cameras, keeping everyone's attention focused. I watch as a group of workmen constructs the bullet-proof backdrop at one side of the platform, ready for the firing squad. They're all dressed in black, with matching T-shirts. They could be roadies at a concert, or staff at a bar. I watch as they clear the space behind the backdrop, and fire a rifle into the reinforced boards. The bullet lodges in one of the panels, raising an explosion of dust, and a cheer from the crowd.

They know what they're doing. They know how to manipulate the audience.

Conrad appears on camera, pointing at the backdrop, and the workmen bring out a roll of black cloth, pulling one end out and stapling it to the top of the panels. They pull out the rest of the fabric, and staple the other end to the stage. Now the prisoner will stand in front of a black curtain, bold and unmissable in her orange jumpsuit.

Very dramatic, David.

I check my watch. Not long until I need to attract the attention of one of the guards, and get myself in front of the stage.

Real

Bex

The car pulls up in a narrow street near Charing Cross Station.

"Good luck," the driver says as he turns to face us. "Good luck, and thank you."

I look around the car. This is it. This is the moment when everything gets real.

We need to get out. We need to let the driver get away.

But I can't move.

There's a lump in my throat as I look across at Dan, and his face is grey as he looks back at me, the circles under his eyes dark in the shadows of the car.

I don't want to lose him. I don't want to lose anyone.

I reach out, and touch his cheek with my glove. He takes my hand, and holds it there.

I can't breathe. Everything we've done together seems concentrated into this moment. I remember the day we met, at school. How his friendship made a strange place more bearable. I remember Camp Bishop, and Makepeace Farm. I remember the bunker. I remember waiting for him to come back to the gatehouse, and the fear that he might not return. I remember Newcastle, and driving lessons, and Dan, keeping me going. I think about Edinburgh, and finding him in the common room. Finding out about his relationship with Margie. How happy I felt that they'd forgiven each other.

And now we have to go and save Margie.

And we might not come back.

"Bex?" Amy's hand is on my shoulder. "Bex. We have to go."

I nod, and pull my hand away. I try to speak. I want to say something encouraging. I want to inspire my friends, as I inspired the South Bank bombers, but I can't. My throat is tight, and I can't find the words.

I make myself think about today. About what happens next.

"Helmets," says Charlie, watching my face. "Helmets and guns."

I pick up the helmet from my knees and pull it over my head, clipping it onto my armour, watching as my friends do the same.

Silence. The helmet shuts out the sound of the engine, and the noises from outside the car. I'm cut off from my friends and I can feel the panic rising again. I sit still, and force myself to breathe as Charlie slides the door open.

I watch as Charlie steps out onto the pavement. Maz follows, then Amy.

This all feels like a dream. It's everything I've been waiting for, but I can't make myself move.

Dan tips the seat in front of me forward, and waits for me to climb out. I pick up my gun, and look out of the door.

I can feel the silence filling my head. This isn't real. This can't be real.

Dan reaches over and touches the controls on the back of my glove.

And there are voices in my helmet. My friends, calling me out of the car.

The radio breaks the spell. The silence is gone, and I'm moving. Crawling out of my seat. Standing on the pavement. Helping Dan out of the car.

The driver waves, and closes the door. I watch as he drives away, leaving us alone in the middle of London.

I look around.

We're alone, but we're armed. We've got our armour, we're trained, and we're together.

I'm surprised to find myself smiling.

"Come on!" Maz's voice is loud in my helmet. "We've got people to save. Better start looking as if we're supposed to be here."

I shift my gun into a combat hold, and make myself stand up straight.

"Brave and stupid," I say, a smile on my face. There's no going back now. This is what we've been training for. This is what we've asked for and fought for and argued for. The fire is back, and I'm ready to fight.

Charlie laughs as she turns to follow Maz. "Brave and stupid."

I follow her along the pavement, towards Whitehall.

Soldiers

Ketty

It's almost time.

Lee puts his head round the conference room door and sends me to make coffee. The rest of this corridor, like the ones below, is taken up with offices. Clerks and support staff, mostly, doubling up in their rooms to free up space for the rest of us, while the bomb damage to the Home Forces building is fixed. Most of the offices are empty, and I'm guessing that everyone's out on Horse Guard's Parade, watching the stage.

The kitchen is empty, too, and it doesn't take long to fill the coffee jugs and take them back to the committee.

The coverage on PIN is gathering pace when I come back to the desk. They're running the footage from the interrogation room, Lee's new questions dubbed in over the original soundtrack. They flash Margaret's face on the screen, alongside Lee's images from Makepeace Farm: the tables of bomb-making equipment, the rocket launcher, the maps. All planted by Lee to incriminate the members of William Richard's cell, but the audience doesn't know that. PIN will have the crowds shouting for Margaret's firing squad before they've even started the trial.

On the stage, the workmen have installed a podium and a lectern for the judge, and a chair for the prisoner. I watch as they anchor the chair, screwing each leg to the stage. Someone attaches straps to the arms to make sure the prisoner can't interrupt the trial by trying to escape.

The crowd responds with cheering and chanting. This is the standard setup for every trial, but the audience has never seen the preparations happening live before. They've never witnessed this build-up, this level of hype from PIN. Huge screens above the stage are showing the PIN coverage, beaming images of themselves back at the crowd.

And it's working. I can feel the excitement building.

Lee is right. This is Margaret's big day. We've made her the star of an unmissable show – Conrad, Lee, Me – and we're going to send our message to Bex and her friends.

I wonder whether there's a TV set up at Belmarsh. William Richards should see this. It would remind him what we can do to his daughter, if he doesn't help the Terrorism Committee.

Elizabeth Ellman should see this. She should see what will happen to Bex, when we find her.

I hope all the prisoners are watching. It will make it easier to convince them to help us.

I rest my elbows on the desk, watching the screen.

The view cuts away from the stage, and onto the crowds. There are kids in grey RTS armour, patrolling the edges of the public enclosures, and there are Home Forces soldiers in black armour, guarding the gates and the stage. In Hyde Park and Trafalgar Square there are lines of soldiers under the giant screens, keeping people back from the equipment and the speaker stacks. The chain of guards around Buckingham Palace is an unbroken circle of armour and guns, protecting the King.

There's a PIN presenter – she must be on the roof of this building – talking through the arrival of the prisoner. The camera swings down, pointing along Whitehall, as a prison van makes its way past a line of guards and drives at walking pace towards us.

Time to use the backstage pass.

I'm standing up, pulling the pass from my pocket, when I notice the soldiers. They're walking down Whitehall towards the camera. Twenty or thirty of them, in single file. Helmets on, guns ready.

I've seen the plans for security. I helped write most of them. And this wasn't on the plan.

As I watch, another group walks out of Whitehall Place, behind the prison van. They join the first group, doubling up and walking two by two, following the van along the road.

Are these our soldiers? Extra security for the prisoner?

Or is this something else?

Is this a rescue attempt?

You're paranoid, Ketty. This is Conrad's trial. This is a change to the plans.

I sit down again, perching on the edge of my chair.

I could warn the Committee. I could warn the guards. I could hurry out to the stage and warn Conrad.

But what if this is nothing? What if this is part of the plan?

This isn't your trial any more, Ketty. This isn't your job.

And part of me wants Conrad to fail.

I sit back in my chair, and watch.

Whitehall

Bex

We're on Whitehall. We marched up to the guards on a side street, and our armour was enough to convince them to let us through.

We're following the prison van as it drives slowly towards Horse Guard's Parade.

There are more of us now – we've joined up with others from the hotel, and we're heading for the meeting rooms Fiona's been told about. Another line of OIE soldiers joins us from a side street, and another. We're three abreast, now, marching towards the leaders of all the UK's armed forces. Marching towards the government that wants to put us in front of their firing squads.

Marching behind Margie in her prison van.

Dan's walking in front of me, and I switch my radio to our private channel.

"You OK?"

He touches the back of his glove. "Absolutely not. You?"

I can't help laughing.

"Nowhere near."

"She's in there, isn't she?" He says, quietly.

"And you're right behind her, Dan." I can't let him do anything stupid. Not when we're this close. "Dan?"

He sighs, and his breath is loud in my ears. "Yes, Bex."

"Stick to the plan. OK?"

There's a pause before he answers, and I know how he's feeling. I want to run ahead. I want to open the doors, and pull Margie out. I want to save her before she gets near the trial.

But it wouldn't work. It wouldn't help her. We'd all end up dead – here, or with her on the platform.

"OK, Bex. I'm not an idiot."

But he sounds exhausted. He sounds as if he's got nothing left to lose.

"I know. Just … be safe. No heroics. OK?"

"OK." He switches his radio back to the general channel, and I do the same.

The van pulls up ahead of us. We have time to walk past it before the guards open the doors. We march together, turning to walk through the gates and into the courtyard that marks the start of the trial cordon.

There's a door, ahead of me and to the left. I'm heading that way, with a group of OIE fighters. Dan's heading straight ahead, into Horse Guard's Parade, with Amy and Charlie and Maz.

I want to stay with them. I want to fight this together. But that's not the deal we made with Fiona.

I want to say something. I want to give Dan a hug. I want Charlie to tell me we're OK.

But I can't stop.

I take a deep breath, and turn away from my friends, heading for the Terrorism Committee.

Suspicion

Ketty

There are more of them now. More soldiers in armour, marching out of the side streets and joining the procession behind the prison van.

This feels wrong.

If the soldiers are part of the plan, why are they appearing bit by bit? Why weren't they all waiting in Trafalgar Square? They could have formed up in advance, and followed the van past the guards.

But not if the guards wouldn't let them through.

The van pulls up outside the building. PIN is still running the feed from the roof. Everything I'm watching is happening meters away, on the street outside.

The van stops, but the soldiers don't. They file past the prison vehicle, and through the gates. No one stops them, and they march out of shot.

I can't see them any more.

They're at the bottom of the stairs, outside this building, and I can't see what they're doing.

If this is an invasion, if these are terrorists, then you're in the line of fire.

I stand up, reaching for my gun.

There's a noise from the stairwell at the end of the corridor. Shouting.

I glance along the corridor in the other direction, but it's empty.

There are footsteps on the stairs, and someone fires a shot. The shouting stops.

On the screen, the prison van opens, and two guards step out. I pick up the remote, and mute the sound.

I should warn the committee. I should warn Bracken. I should run.

You're better off with Lee and the Committee behind you. If you run, you're on your own.

I feel sick. I'm taking quick, shallow breaths, and I can hear my pulse, thumping in my ears. My hands are shaking.

Make a decision, Ketty.

More footsteps. Someone's running up the stairs.

Run, or warn the committee.

And I'm back in the worst place in the world, fear kicking into me like a bullet.

Out of time, Ketty.

On the screen, the image switches to a camera in the street. The prisoner steps down from the van, her hands cuffed, chains linking her hands and feet.

You're on your own.

The footsteps grow louder.

I step back to the conference room door. I draw my gun, point it at the stairs, and wait.

Sprint

Bex

I sprint up the stairs. They're taking Margie out of the van, and I don't have time to wait. Dan needs my help, and I need to make the broadcast for Fiona.

I run, and I leave the others to catch up with me.

At the first landing, I pause, lifting my visor. I can hear the rest of my team, gathering in the hall below, and I can hear voices on the floor above. I listen for a moment, and I realise it's the sound from a TV, somewhere near the top of the stairs. As I wait, listening to my team, the sound from the TV switches off.

There's no sound from the floor above. Before I can think, I'm running again, up towards the silence, pulling my visor down as I throw myself up the stairs.

Threat

Ketty

A soldier in black armour steps into the corridor, and I see myself reflected in their visor. My bullets won't stop them, but if I'm lucky, they'll hurt. I stand as if I'm in the firing range, gun ready.

Whose side are you on?

My hands grip my gun, aiming at the soldier's helmet.

There's no sound from the conference room. I'm on my own out here.

And I'm wearing fatigues. I have no armour to protect me from the soldier's bullets.

Stand your ground, Ketty.

My pulse is loud in my ears. The soldier raises a hand.

Gun

Bex

I step into the corridor, and I'm looking down the barrel of a gun. Someone in fatigues is pointing a handgun at me, standing between me and the meeting room. I'm wearing armour. I'm safe. I keep my breathing steady. I'm about to raise my gun, when I recognise the guard.

I recognise Ketty.

She's standing here, between me and my target. Between me and Margie. Between the OIE and the government.

I should shoot. I could take her out, with one bullet.

I think of the firing range, and the paper targets.

But I can't. I'm back under Mum's bed in the care home, waiting for Ketty to find me. Waiting for my chance to shoot.

I'm distracted. I need to concentrate. I need to get into the meeting room.

And Ketty can help.

I raise one hand, pointing the gun downwards with the other, and slowly reach for my visor.

Calm

Ketty

I almost laugh. The soldier raises her visor, and it's Bex.

Bex Ellman, walking right into my line of fire. Lifting her visor. Showing me her face.

Nowhere to hide this time, Mummy Ellman.

I adjust my aim, sighting between her eyes. My finger tightens on the trigger.

And she brings her gun up.

I freeze.

I'm dead if she fires. Her bullets will tear through me, and I won't have time to shout.

This is about survival, Ketty. Buy yourself another minute. Another two.

I open one hand and hold it out, letting the gun dangle from the fingers of the other hand. Slowly, I bring the gun down, and push it back into the holster on my hip, then raise both hands in front of me.

I'm amazed at how calm I'm feeling. My hands are steady. Her gun is pointing at me, but her arms are relaxed. She's not ready to shoot.

She swings the gun, pointing it at the door behind me.

"Get out of my way," she says, and there's no kindness in her voice.

I shrug. If this is it, if this is the invasion, I need to find a way out.

And if Bex is on the winning side, maybe this is how I get out of here alive.

Door

Bex

Ketty shrugs, and steps away from the door.

"Fine." She says, standing back, waiting for me to move.

I point my gun at her, lining it up with the centre of her torso. Willing myself to see the silhouette from the firing range, not the Senior Recruit. Not the person who held me down while Jackson punched me over and over. Not my mother's torturer.

I can hear my team, climbing the stairs behind me.

"You first. Get me inside."

She shrugs again, and turns to the door.

William

Ketty

I'm walking into the Terrorism Committee. I'm walking into the conference room, into a meeting so classified that I've never been told who sits behind this door.

I'm about to face Brigadier Lee and Colonel Bracken, with a gun to my back.

I push the door open.

The murmur of voices stops instantly, and as I walk into the room, everyone is watching me. Bracken, Lee, Holden. But their eyes shift to the figure behind me. The person holding the gun.

We're walking into the middle of the room. There's a U-shaped arrangement of tables, lined with committee members, and a clear space in the centre for presentations.

For us.

I keep my hands up, where everyone can see them. I keep Bex behind me, so it's clear I'm being threatened.

"Corporal Smith!" Lee sounds furious, and his face is turning a deep shade of red.

"Sir," I say, quietly, risking a glance behind me.

But Bex isn't pointing the gun at me any more. She's staring, open-mouthed, at the far end of the room.

"Will!"

I look round, following her gaze.

William Richards is sitting at the head of the table.

He's wearing a smart shirt and a tie. No prison jumpsuit or handcuffs, here.

And he's smiling.

Betrayal

Bex

"Will!"

I can't help shouting. It's Will, the leader of the Makepeace Farm rebels, sitting at the table with all these people in uniform.

"You're alive!" I look around, taking in the rest of the committee. The rank insignia on their uniforms. Will, looking out of place in a white shirt and a tie.

He should be locked up. He's one of the rebels these people are hunting.

"What are you doing here?"

Will shrugs. "You escaped from the farm, then, Ellman?"

I can't help nodding. I can't understand what's happening. Why Will is here.

"Good for you," he says, quietly.

He's not in uniform. But he's not in a prison jumpsuit, either. He's not handcuffed. He's here – part of the Terrorism Committee – and he's a free man.

And I realise.

He's the link to the resistance groups. He's the one who's been giving their details to the government.

There's a sick, sinking feeling in my stomach. This is our traitor. This is the person who's been giving targets and weapons to the resistance cells. He's responsible for their bombings, and he's responsible for their trials. Every resistance member caught after an attack, every rebel sent to a firing squad – they're on Will's conscience.

"How could you? How could you help these people?"

He shakes his head, and his smile fades.

"You wouldn't understand," he says.

I roll my eyes. Will has no idea what I would understand.

"What did you do?" He looks down at the table. *"What did you do?"*

He looks up at me, and there's fear in his eyes. "They've got my daughter, Bex. They've got Sheena. If I don't help …"

I think of Mum. Of everything that Ketty's put her through, because she's trying to get to me. I think of Dr Richards, sitting in a cell.

And I think of all the bombs the resistance has planted. All the people they've killed, doing the government's work for them. All their victims, caught up in the attacks. All the resistance prisoners, sent to firing squads while Will sits here, protected, and hands over their names.

"Coward!" I spit the word at him, and he nods, his head bowed.

I'm raising my gun before I can stop myself.

Sides

Ketty

I stare at William. I thought he was in a cell at Belmarsh, locked up with Sheena and Elizabeth and the other prisoners. Bex is shouting at him, demanding to know what he's doing here.

There's a movement at the corner of my eye. Lee, pulling his gun from his holster. Raising it to point at Bex's head.

Waiting for her to turn round.

I drop my hand slowly to my hip.

Keep talking, Bex. Keep everyone's eyes on you.

"If it isn't Corporal Smith, Bracken's mother-figure, and Recruit Ellman, playing at being a soldier." Lee leans back in his chair, draping one arm over the back, and pointing the gun at Bex with the other.

Really? Mother-figure? That's what you think of me?

Bex turns back, spotting his gun too late to bring her visor down. She stares at the handgun, her eyes fixed on the barrel.

"Is this the invasion, Recruit? You and your friends from the RTS?" He looks round the room, laughing. "I'm sure we're all quaking in our boots."

His eyes widen in mock surprise. "Or perhaps you're here to save your friend out there?" He points at the windows, with their view over the back of the stage. "It would be a shame to come all this way, and fail, wouldn't it?"

Bex is shaking. Her gun clicks against her armour as her hands tremble.

"Or perhaps you'd like to join her. Stand with her while she takes a bullet?" He looks at the gun in his hand. "Maybe I shouldn't kill you now. Maybe I should give you a chance to say goodbye before you both face the firing squad, live on TV." He glances at William, and gives him a cold smile. "And maybe it's time for Sheena to join her friends on the stage?" He nods to someone on the far side of the room. The man pulls a radio from his hip and starts barking orders.

William shakes his head, reaching both hands out to Lee.

"Please, no …"

There are footsteps from the corridor. People running up the last of the stairs.

The door to the room starts to open again. More soldiers?

I wrap my hand around my gun.

Whose side are you on?

Object

Bex

I'm staring down the barrel of a gun, and this time I don't have my visor to protect me.

I'm staring at the gun, and the blood is pounding in my ears, but I can't block out this man's words.

He's threatening me, and he's insulting my friends.

And he's stopping me from getting to Margie.

I'm shaking, with fear and with rage. I've come this far. I need to finish my task.

I need to make my broadcast, and I need to help Dan.

I need to live.

"Shame about Margaret, really. She's a pretty little thing." He smirks. "I can think of things I'd rather do to her than fill her with bullets, but you make your choices, and you take the consequences." He raises his voice. "Right, William?"

If Will responds, I don't hear him. The door opens, and solders in armour file into the room, but I'm too angry to notice whether they're here to help me, or arrest me.

He's talking about Margie. He dares to talk about her as if she's an object, as if she's not important. I'm standing, facing his gun, in the middle of a government meeting. I've trained for this, and I've put myself in danger to help my friend. I left my safety and comfort behind, and I feel completely exposed, standing here, surrounded by people who want me dead.

And he's saying disgusting things about the person I'm here to save.

I tighten my grip on my gun.

Choice

Ketty

The soldiers file into the room. I watch to see where they point their weapons.

Lee is insulting Margaret, and Bex is fighting to control her anger. I can hear her tight, quick breathing as she listens to his comments.

The soldiers raise their guns, and they're pointed at the committee. The man with the radio drops it on the table, holding his hands in the air.

We're outnumbered. We're outgunned.

This is the invasion.

And I'm on the wrong side.

Bex starts to lift her rifle, and I watch Lee's knuckles whiten as he grips his gun.

If this is the end, I need Bex on my side.

And Lee is about to shoot.

I think about Lee's manipulations. Giving me the PowerGel to fix my wounded knee, then refusing to replace it after the fight at the bunker. All the humiliations and insults he's thrown at me in London. The way he used Conrad to get to me. His taunts and smirks, and the way he gloated over my mistakes.

I pull my gun from the holster, as fast as I can, and point it at Lee.

Before he can react to Bex's gun, before he can shoot, I fire.

Hit

Bex

I'm done. I'm not letting this smug man insult me, or my friend.

All the fear, all the worry, all the tension of the last two weeks takes hold of me. I don't think I've ever felt this angry.

Fiona wants us to detain the Terrorism Committee. To stop them leaving, and to stop them contacting anyone outside this room.

I can do better than that.

I lift my gun.

And Ketty raises hers.

Before I can shoot, she fires, sending a bullet into his chest.

And I can see the firing range. I can see the target, waiting for my gun.

There's a look of shock on Ketty's face as she drops her gun to her side.

I line up the target, and I shoot, sending my bullet after hers.

A red stain begins to spread across the front of his uniform.

He chokes, once, bright red blood running from his mouth. His head falls back, resting on the back of the chair.

His chest is still.

He's not breathing.

Protected

Ketty

I push my gun back into the holster, fighting panic, trying not to think about what I've done.

Lee is dead, and I killed him. *We* killed him.

Get out, Ketty. Run.

I reach out and grab Bex by her elbow. She stares at Lee, her gun still pointed at his chest.

"You win, Bex," I say, quietly as I pull her towards me. "These are your soldiers?" I tip my head towards the door.

She nods, looking up at me and lowering her gun.

"I just saved your life." She looks shocked. "He was about to put a bullet in your head. I stopped him." She nods, her eyes wide. "So buy me some time. Let me leave." She nods again.

There are more people filing in through the door. The soldiers fan out, each one pointing a gun at one of the committee members. William stands up, hands held up in front of him. One of the soldiers walks over, smiling, and William points towards the door.

I need to move quickly. I need to talk to Bracken. I need to understand what's happening, and I need to stay safe. I have to get Bracken out of here, and I have to work fast.

There are guards in the corridor, and guards around the tables. Keeping Bex with me, I push my way through to where Bracken is sitting next to the door, his head in his hands.

"Come on, Sir," I whisper. "We need to get out."

He looks up at me, and there is defeat in his eyes.

"What did you do, Ketty? Lee is …" He shakes his head.

I grab his elbow, drag him out of his chair, and pull him towards the door. William pushes his way out in front of me, the soldiers shaking his hand and slapping his back as he walks past. A couple of the guards step out to stop me, but they fall back when they see the look on my face, and Bex walking behind me. I push Bracken ahead of me out into the corridor, and leave Bex standing in the doorway. Another group of people in black armour reaches the top of the stairs, carrying heavy equipment between them, and cutting off our escape. I keep my head down, turn away along the corridor, and keep walking.

Broadcast

Bex

There's confusion in the room as the camera crew pushes past me through the door and tries to clear space in one corner. I pull my helmet off and a woman with a clipboard straightens my hair and hands me a list of names. Someone is talking to me, but I can't make sense of what they're saying.

I've just killed someone.

I lifted my gun, and I fired a bullet into his chest.

I look down at the list in my hand. These are the people Fiona wants me to name in my speech. This is the hit list for the resistance – the people we won't allow to escape.

I look around the room. There are voices, and shouting, but it's just noise. Will's gone. Ketty's gone. The committee members are sitting quietly, guarded by soldiers with guns. There are medics dragging the man we shot out of the door, and more OIE fighters lining the edges of the room. The fighters nod encouragement to me as the portable lights make the meeting room impossibly bright, and the director takes me by the elbow and stands me in front of the camera.

The noise drops away.

"You're up, Bex."

My mind is a white space as I face the camera, and for a moment I think I won't be able to speak.

I've just shot someone. I've just *killed* someone. Me, and Ketty.

And I let Ketty walk away.

I can't think about it. I can't allow myself to react.

This is it. This is what I'm here for. This is what I promised Fiona, and this is how I buy Dan and the others time to rescue Margie. I close my eyes. I need to find the determination that brought me here. The fire in my chest. I need to ride the adrenaline before it fades. I think about Mum, locked up and waiting for me. I think about Ketty, standing with me and saving my life, after everything we've been through. I think about pulling my trigger, and sending my bullet into the man in the chair.

And I know what to say. I open my eyes.

"Action!" The Director points at me, and we're live. All those screens in Trafalgar Square, in Hyde Park, and around the platform on Horse Guards Parade. All those people, watching me. I nearly choke, I nearly run from the camera, but Mum's voice comes back to me.

You're a hero Bex. You always have been.

And the words come.

"You know who I am. You've seen my face, and you've described me as a terrorist, but that's not true. My name is Bex Ellman. I was taken from my life, and signed up to fight by your government. I've been a recruit, a public guardian, and a rebel. But one thing I am not is a terrorist."

I push away thoughts of the South Bank bomb. Of the video I made, encouraging the bombers. I force myself to focus on the camera.

"There is a resistance in this country. I am a member of it. But we are not terrorists. The government has been lying to you.

"It's not the resistance that's been planning the bombs. It's the government. It's the army. It's the people who should be protecting you."

I pause. It is so important that the people watching believe this. I think back to Leominster. To the crashed cars and the pieces of people's lives, lying in the road. Teddy bears, handbags, shoes – pieces of lives that had already ended.

"I was there, in Leominster," I say, and give that a moment to sink in. "I saw the weapons. Government issue, planted by people who hide behind their uniforms and their titles. But they can't hide any more. We will name them, these faceless people."

I glance at the list in my hand.

"Commander Holden and Brigadier Lee, and a whole staff of people who closed their eyes and looked the other way as the people of Leominster died.

"Colonel Bracken, who knew what was going on, and failed to stop it.

"Major General Franks, Leader of the Home Forces, who washed her hands of responsibility.

"The government is so desperate for power, so desperate to keep you controlled, that they are creating false flag attacks every day, every week, just to keep you living in fear.

"Right now, I'm on your screens. I'm patched in over the PIN feed, and there are resistance soldiers marching on London. It seems as if the world is ending, I know. It doesn't feel safe. But that's because *their* world *is* ending. Their world is finished. We are ending it – the fear, the hate, the false flags and the false blame. We are ending it today."

I glance at the director, and he's grinning, gesturing for me to go on. I can do this. I can make people see.

"To the recruits on patrol: work together. Forget your training. Stand with your fellow recruits. Protect the public from the real enemy, and take your country back. Take your world back.

"Turn your guns on the soldiers. Turn your guns on the liars who run this country. Take back your lives. No more front-line dolls. No more kids sent to die for the power of others.

"To all of you, wherever you are. Take your power back. Take your freedom back. Take your country back.

Join our resistance. Don't wait. Don't go home and cower in fear.

"Make this happen *today*.

"Together, *we* are an army. Together, we can …"

The director looks down at his monitor and swears.

"We've lost the feed. They've hacked us back out."

I feel winded. I'm caught between the passion of my speech and the fear of what might happen next. I stumble over to the monitor.

The screens around the platform are showing the trial again. Margie in her orange jumpsuit, sitting handcuffed to her chair. The judge at the podium. Soldiers closing in with guns.

We haven't stopped it. We haven't saved Margie. The trial is going ahead, and the bullet-proof backdrop is waiting for her firing squad.

I feel sick. I feel angry.

I'm running for the door before anyone can stop me, grabbing my helmet and my gun from the table as I push past.

There's a figure in a smart suit in the hallway, surrounded by guards. I'm so consumed by the idea of saving Margie that I don't notice the guards moving to stop me. Someone grips my arm and spins me round.

And I'm facing the King.

If we've won, if we've cut off every meeting room and every committee, then I'm facing the only government this country has.

I manage a tiny bow of my head, and I freeze. I don't trust myself to speak.

The King smiles, and puts his hand on my shoulder.

"That was a good speech, Miss Ellman," he says. "Now go and make it happen."

I nod, struggling to find my voice. "Yes, Sir."

And I'm running again. Down the stairs, past guards in armour, past assistants and staff in and out of uniform.

Whatever happens next, I can't let Dan face it alone.

Fight

Ketty

I keep my hand on Bracken's shoulder and push him ahead of me along the corridor. I don't look back. Every step sends a jolt of pain through my knee, and I realise I've twisted it, dragging Bracken from the room.

No time to stop. Just keep walking.

We head down a tiny staircase, and at the next landing I elbow my way past a group of clerks in civilian office clothes and drag him through into the empty corridor beyond. I pick a door, and pull us both into a deserted office. He sinks into a chair as I close the door behind us, and perch myself on the edge of a desk, facing him. Taking the weight off my knee.

He rests his head on one hand, as if he's shielding his eyes from the light.

Or from me.

"I think its time for the truth. Don't you, Sir?"

He groans. "Ketty ..."

"The truth. Who you're working with. Who's involved. Just how many of these attacks were us, spreading fear and blaming the resistance. Making them into terrorists."

"I was doing my best ..."

"How many?"

He shifts in his chair, and covers his face with his hands. His voice is a whisper.

"All of them."

I know he's telling the truth. I realise I've known this for a while, but I want him to confirm it. I want to hear him confess.

"Leominster? Manchester? *Crossrail*?"

He nods.

"*Every* terrorist bombing was a government false flag?"

He starts to protest. "Not to start with. The first attacks were real. But when we saw …"

"… when you saw how frightened people were, you saw how useful that would be. You decided to keep it going. To keep the fear building."

"You have to understand, Ketty – this wasn't me. I wasn't part of it. I was running Camp Bishop. Leominster was the first time I realised what we were doing."

"And what did you do after that? Did you shout out? Did you tell the truth?" He shakes his head, looking up at me. "No. You helped them. And then you came here and took your promotion and carried on helping them. You even used resistance fighters to plant your bombs. It wasn't their idea to bomb civilians – it was yours. You and Franks and Lee – and you blackmailed William Richards into making it happen. There was blood on your hands, and you used it to get here. You went along with the violence, and you turned it into a step up in your career."

He gives me a cold stare. "So did you."

My head jerks back, as if he's landed a physical blow. He's right. I did. I used Leominster and I used the bunker to get here. I even killed one of our recruits, and I would have killed more of them if I'd had the chance. If they hadn't damaged the PowerGel. If they hadn't left me lying in the woods.

But I didn't know the scale of the lies. I thought we were protecting people. I thought we were fighting terrorists, not killing civilians ourselves. Not after Leominster.

Bracken reaches for his cargo pocket and pulls out his hip flask. His hands shake as he fumbles with the lid, but I'm too angry to let him drown his feelings. I step forward and twist the flask from his hands, throwing it across the room, and we both watch as the liquid inside drains out, his whisky a spreading stain on the worn green carpet. He makes to stand up, and I push him back into his chair, shouting. I can't believe that he'd rather drink this away than face me. That after all I've done to keep him in his job, he won't even tell me the truth.

"No, Sir. You do *not* get to drink your way out of this. This is real, and I need you here, with me. I need you to confront this. I need to hear your side of the story."

He lunges up out of his chair, and his voice is an incoherent roar. He throws himself towards me.

I'm not ready for this. I take a step back, but he's too quick. He hurls his hand up and slams it into my neck, hard. The shock and the blow knock the breath from my lungs, and I stumble backwards, his fingers locking round my throat. I'm gasping for air, trying to pull his hand away, but he's too strong. A sick, dizzy feeling hits me – I've lost control, and I'm running out of time.

Don't panic. Breathe. Fight back.

The desk is behind me, and he's throwing me backwards, his face pushed into mine. The room disappears as the edges of my vision fade to black, and his face is all I can see. My knee buckles, and I stumble, fear pushing me to fight as I struggle to stand. His grip on my neck pulls me up, and I can feel my windpipe closing; my neck, bruising.

Breathe! Fight!

I feel the edge of the desk against my legs, and I'm trapped. He's pushing me, shouting as he throws me backwards, and I'm falling. Pain slams into me like a bullet as I crash onto the desktop, Bracken standing over me, pinning me down, his hand crushing my throat. My head hits the desk and I'm choking, coughing. Clawing at his knuckles.

I can't believe how quickly I'm thrown off my feet. How quickly he has total control of my body. I wasn't ready.

Breathe, Ketty. Keep breathing.

My lungs are on fire. My throat is a fist of pain. I'm not thinking clearly. I need air. I need to breathe.

Concentrate, Ketty. Focus.

I've got one hand on his, my nails tearing at his skin, and with the other I'm searching the desktop for something I can use as a weapon. I can't reach my gun, or his. I try to kick and twist against his grip, but I can't move. He's leaning over the desk, his whole body pinning mine.

Fight!

My throat is closing, I'm falling. I can't feel the desk under me. All I can think about is taking a breath, and trying to cough and breathe and fight at the same time.

One more breath.

His face is red with fury, too close above my own as he leans his weight against my neck. He's gritting his teeth and he's looking at me, but he's not seeing me.

One more ...

He's looking through me, his hand crushing my throat, and I'm suddenly sure he's going to kill me. Everything else drops away. I'm vulnerable, I'm helpless, and I'm afraid. He's pushed me to the worst place in the world, and I know there's nothing I can do to stop him. I start throwing punches at his shoulders and head, but there's no strength in my arms.

There's no air in my lungs.

How did this happen so fast?

You should have been ready, Ketty. You should have expected this.

This is failure. This is fear.

I'm drowning. I'm blacking out. His hand is a bar across my neck, and I know I can't fight this.

I want to scream. I want to kick and punch and shout my way out of this, but there's nothing left.

… Iron fists and steel toe caps.

… I'm falling into the dark.

... *Jackson* ...

But then Bracken's eyes seem to focus. He lets out a sob, and as suddenly as he attacked me, he stops. He loosens his hand and he steps back, away from the desk. I stay where I am for a moment, eyes closed, filling my lungs with air in ragged, ugly gasps.

Breathe. Breathe.

I can feel the desktop, hard and cold under my back.

I can feel fire in my throat. Bruises blooming on my neck.

My hands are shaking as I tug at the neck of my shirt, pulling at the buttons until I can breathe again.

Bracken staggers back and drops into the chair, hands over his face. Slowly, I push myself up from the desktop until I'm leaning on the edge, propping myself up with my arms. There's blood in my mouth, and my neck is a ring of bright bruises. Every breath makes a rasping sound in my throat.

Breathe.

He's sitting, hunched over in the chair. The fight has gone out of him, and he's crying, his shoulders shaking with sobs.

I'm watching him, my hand on my neck as I drag fiery air through my bruised windpipe, and I try to feel something. Anger. Pity. Disgust.

But there's nothing. It's as if he doesn't matter any more.

And I'm back in the kitchen, with Dad, the day I left for Camp Bishop. His drunken fury gone, the knife dropped on the table. His broken voice, begging me to stay.

He doesn't matter any more. He can't protect me.

And I know what to do.

Barriers

Bex

I'm running, as fast as I can push myself in my armour. I've jammed my helmet on, and my visor is up as I burst through the doors at the bottom of the stairs. People are shouting behind me, but I'm not stopping, not now. I sprint through the archway, push past a security checkpoint, and out into Horse Guards Parade.

There's a wide open space in front of me, and it's filled with people. People in PIN jackets with cameras and microphones. People in black T-shirts. Guards. Soldiers. I force myself to walk, cradling my gun. I need to look as if I'm supposed to be here.

Above the heads of the people, there's a wall of metal and black cloth cutting me off from the audience. I'm behind the stage.

And the Judge is talking, his voice booming from the speakers. He's reciting Margie's crimes as if my speech hadn't happened. And I realise that a few moments ago, that was my voice.

And my face.

I pull my visor down and touch the back of my glove to activate my radio, trying not to react to the sudden shouts in my ears.

"Dan!" My voice cuts through the shouting, and everything falls silent. "Where are you?"

"Bex!" He sounds breathless. "We're in front of the stage. Where are you?"

"Backstage."

"Can you get to the platform? Can you get to Margie?"

I push my way forwards, past a group of PIN technicians.

Someone steps aside to let me pass, and there's a barrier in front of me. A chest-high metal fence, and on the other side are soldiers, guarding the back of the stage.

I turn away, pushing out again through the crowd.

"Not unless you want a suicide mission."

Turncoat

Ketty

I stand up, and the room spins around me. I walk round the desk, holding myself up with one hand. There's a TV remote on the desktop, and I use it to bring up the PIN feed. I need to know what's happening outside.

But it's Bex's face on the screen. Bex, talking into a camera. She's telling people about the Terrorism Committee, and she's naming names.

Holden, Lee, Bracken, Franks.

They're looking for Bracken.

I need to get out. I need a way to walk out of here, before they work out who I am.

I start pulling out drawers, throwing them onto the floor until I find what I'm looking for, trying to breathe without choking. I pick up a pair of scissors and test the blades with my fingers, then pull my camouflage shirt over my head and start cutting away the name tag on the front. I'm in a hurry, I'm still dizzy, but I force myself to focus. I keep it neat – I can't have people seeing what's missing. I still need to look like a soldier, out there.

I have to stop to cough – violent, choking coughs that leave me sitting on the floor, leaning over, my head between my knees.

Keep going. Keep protecting yourself.

I cut the stitching around the flags on my sleeves, careful not to damage the fabric underneath. The Corporal stripes are next to go – I try to cut them off neatly, but it's easier to slice the epaulets off completely. Two cuts at the top and bottom of the shoulders and I'm anonymous. I'm just a soldier in the crowd. I make sure the cuts are neat along the seams, and pull the shirt back on. I pull myself up on the desk until I'm standing again. I straighten my shirt, and check my belt for the handgun, still clasped in its holster.

My breathing is getting easier. My throat feels full of flames, but I'm not choking any more. I give myself a few slow, deep, burning breaths, and turn back to Bracken.

He hasn't moved. He's still sobbing, curled over and hiding his face in his hands. He looks small and weak, collapsed into himself in the chair.

On the screen, Bex is urging people to fight. To turn their guns on us.

She tells us that the world is ending.

I touch my neck. I can still feel Bracken's fingers gripping my throat, keeping the air from my lungs. I should say something. I should show him that he hasn't broken me, he hasn't beaten me. But he doesn't matter. There's nothing left to say.

"I'm leaving now, Sir." My voice is a rough croak, but I make myself heard. I watch him for a few seconds more, then I walk to the door. As I step out into the corridor, he starts to speak, but I don't wait to hear what he has to say.

Bex was right. His world is ending. I need to make sure that mine is not.

Checkpoint

Bex

"Get to us, Bex. Get to the front of the stage. We've got a plan."

I look around. The backstage crowd is penned in on each side by more of the metal barriers, and there's a walkway behind them that leads round the platform. I push my way through until I'm standing next to the barrier, and watch as two figures in RTS armour walk past, patrolling the perimeter. I glance up and down, but they're the only people in the empty space.

"I'm on my way."

I walk back to the archway, looking for the end of the barriers. Next to the buildings, where the walkway begins, there's a guard. I stand back and wait for another patrol.

There's shouting behind me, muffled by the helmet. I risk a glance at the checkpoint I've just run through.

There are guards, pushing through the checkpoint. Guards in black uniforms, gathering in the courtyard and clearing a passage through the crowd, towards the stage. And there's a prisoner between them. Someone in an orange jumpsuit.

Dan is shouting in my helmet, but I can't let him distract me. I switch off my radio and watch, holding my breath as the guards walk into the courtyard. They're bringing someone else to the execution.

As they walk past, I see the prisoner's face.

It's Dr Richards.

Dr Richards, in handcuffs.

And I know that this is my fault. I let her go, in the farmyard. I let the soldiers take her. I failed to save her, just like I failed to save Margie.

And now the government is showing me what they can do.

If I move now, we'll both die. There are too many guards and too many people here for me to save her.

And Dan needs my help.

The guards walk past me, Dr Richards held by her elbows between them.

I take a breath. I've lost her again.

Two more RTS kids walk past, through the space cleared by the guards, and up to the barrier in front of me. I step out, and fall in behind them, raising my hand to the guard as he lets us pass. The guard raises his hand back. He must assume I'm an instructor, patrolling with them.

I don't have time to think about it.

Blocked

Ketty

I walk away from Bracken, down the stairs and out of the building. I head towards Whitehall, but my way through is blocked by a prison van, and a crowd of guards. I don't know whose side they're on, and I can't risk finding out. I turn back, hiding my face with one hand, and walk through the archway.

I take the backstage pass from my pocket and wave it at the guard, who lets me through into Horse Guard's Parade.

The voice of the trial Judge fills the space. PIN has taken back control of its live feed.

Are we winning? Is the invasion over?

My hands are shaking as I push the pass back into my pocket. I made a choice, in the conference room. I stepped away from the Home Forces, and I killed Brigadier Lee. If the Army has defeated the resistance, I'll have to answer for that choice. If the resistance is winning, I need to disappear.

This is dangerous, Ketty. Keep your head down.

The backstage courtyard is crowded, and there are guards and soldiers everywhere. The easy route to freedom is behind me, and blocked. In front of me is the trial.

And Bex.

I need to find Bex. I need to fight my way out of this, and I need an ally.

There's shouting behind me, and I turn to see a group of prison guards, pushing their way through the crowd. I move away, slipping between someone in a PIN jacket and one of the stage hands, out of sight of the soldiers.

They push the crowd back, clearing a path to the back of the stage.

Escorting a prisoner.

Margaret is already on the stage, and the Judge is reminding us of the injuries her attacks caused. He's shouting about bombings and civilian casualties. I stand on tiptoes to see past the crowd. To catch a glimpse of the prisoner.

And I realise – it's Sheena Richards. Lee had time to give one final order in the conference room, before the soldiers came in. William told Bex what happened, and he's no longer protecting his daughter. The agreement has been broken. This is Lee's last revenge – his insurance against William's betrayal.

The Home Forces are still in control here.

I need to get out of the courtyard.

Margie

Bex

I walk through the second checkpoint, following the recruits. The guard lets me through, and I step behind him, past the barriers and into the edge of the crowd.

The Judge is shouting now, whipping the crowd into a frenzy of anger and anticipation. I'm fighting nausea as I turn back, catching sight of Margie on the stage.

She's handcuffed to a chair, watching the judge with a calm expression on her face. As I watch, she turns her head, listening to the crowd.

I hate what they're doing. I hate that she has to listen to this.

But the crowd isn't all one supportive roar. There are other shouts as well. People arguing with the Judge. Calling my name.

My name. From the people in the crowd.

My knees buckle, and I reach out to support myself on the barrier next to me. I can't take a breath.

People are chanting my name.

I pull my visor up and lean over, aching to get air into my lungs.

I lean on the barrier, face to the floor, and the world spins around me. A hand grabs my arm and shakes me until I look up, and it's Charlie, her visor up. She's pushed through the crowd to find me, and she's here, holding me up. Keeping me from falling. Maz appears beside her, and offers me his arm. I use it to steady myself as I straighten up and take a breath.

"You OK, Bex?"

I nod.

"What's happening?" I shout, as the crowd noise swallows us.

"We're not sure. We're not sure who's on our side, and who's still fighting for the Home Forces." Charlie looks at me, and a smile crosses her face. "Great speech, by the way. You got everyone shouting out here."

"How much did you get, before they cut me off?"

She smiles again. "Enough, Bex. They've been chanting your name. I think you got through."

I look up at the stage. "And Margie?"

Her face falls. "We can't get to her. Too many guards." I open my mouth to protest, but she holds up her hands. "We're working on it. There's a group of Netherlands fighters in armour on their way. There's a plan."

I nod, my mouth dry. We don't have much time for their plan to work. Any moment now, the Judge is going to announce the execution. Any moment now we could be too late.

As Maz pulls me into the crowd I notice the line of soldiers in front of the stage, safe behind another high barrier. A line of guns, cutting us off. Keeping us from getting to Margie.

Pass

Ketty

I walk up to the guard at the barrier, backstage pass in my hand. He grunts, and points at my shirt. At the missing nametag.

"How do I know who you are?"

I hold up the pass with one hand, and reach into a pocket with the other. The guard lifts his rifle.

Slowly, Ketty. Don't screw up now.

I pull out my ID card, and he matches it with the pass. He shrugs, and lowers his gun, waving me through.

I walk quickly round the edge of the stage, showing the pass and the badge to a second guard at the far side. He stares at me for a moment, taking in my missing nametag, and missing Corporal stripes. He raises his eyebrows, but he waves me through, and I turn past him to walk into the safety of the crowd.

Plan

Bex

Amy is waiting in front of the stage. She lifts her visor and gives me a tight hug.

"You were amazing, Bex." She looks out at the shouting crowd. "Everyone loved your speech."

I nod. I can't speak. It doesn't matter how good my broadcast was, if we can't save Margie.

The shouting gets louder. There are people calling for the firing squad, and there are people chanting my name.

I look around, trying to decide whether this crowd will help us, or haul us up on stage and shoot us themselves.

"Where's Dan?"

Charlie points at the stage, but there are too many people in front of us. I can't see him.

"He's getting to the barrier." She looks at me. "I told you, Bex – there's a plan."

"So what are we waiting for? He can't climb over the barrier. Not with the soldiers guarding it."

She taps the side of her helmet. "He's in contact with the Netherlands force, over the radios. They're on their way."

"How long?"

Charlie shakes her head.

"We don't know. But they're coming, Bex. They're coming."

I look around again, but it's just the crowd, and the soldiers under the stage. We need more time.

But the Judge is calling for quiet.

That's it. Time's up.

We're on our own.

Exposed

Ketty

I'm in the crowd, watching the trial on the platform in front of me, the tiny people magnified on the screens behind them. The Judge is speaking, calling for silence, and there are guards walking towards the prisoner, releasing the handcuffs from the straps on the chair and pulling her up by her elbows. The crowd roars as she's dragged to the edge of the stage and left to stand alone in front of the black backdrop.

I watch Margaret Watson, standing tall and proud as she waits for the firing squad.

I remember the look she gave me in the Enhanced Interrogation room. After the interrogators had beaten her, after I attacked her, she looked right through me, as if I hadn't hurt her. As if I hadn't touched her. And I know there's no fear in her eyes now.

Then there's another figure in an orange jumpsuit, being led onto the stage, next to Margaret. Sheena Richards, back straight, head held high. Sheena pushes against her guards until they let her stand shoulder to shoulder with Margaret. Both women look straight ahead as Sheena takes Margaret's handcuffed hand in hers.

The roar of the crowd grows louder, but there's something wrong with the sound. Something is shifting in the mood in front of the stage. I push forward, to see what's going on.

There's a line of soldiers in armour on the ground in front of the platform. They're looking around, nervous as the crowd shouts and chants. They start to raise their guns.

This isn't safe. I look at the power-assisted rifles, pointing at the people around me, power lights glowing on the barrels.

The guns are live, and they're pointing at me.

This is how it feels to be a target.

My pulse is hammering in my ears, drowning out the noise of the crowd. I look around, searching for cover, but there's nothing here. Only people. Only civilians.

We're completely exposed, and there's nowhere to hide.

Execution

Bex

I can't watch as the Judge announces the execution, and the crowd starts to roar again. They'll be dragging Margie to this end of the stage, to the bullet-proof backdrop. To the firing squad. I take Charlie's hand, and press my face into her shoulder. She turns round, and puts her arms round me. Maz stands next to her, with Amy, both of them staring at the stage.

"Don't watch, Bex," she whispers. "You don't need to see this."

The crowd roars again, louder this time, and I look up at my friend.

I see Margie, standing tall in front of the backdrop, facing four soldiers in armour. Four rifles.

I watch as the guards bring Dr Richards to stand next to her.

There's some jostling, and Dr Richards pushes her guards away with one shoulder, then steps right up to Margie and silently takes her hand.

I can't see. I can't see anything through the tears pouring from my eyes. Charlie tightens her arms around me as my shoulders heave with sobs.

I think about Dr Richards in the farmyard, how I took her from her guard. How she was safe with me for a second or two before she pulled away to help Margie, and I had to leave them both. I had to run, and I had to leave them there.

This is my fault. This is my failure, and they're paying for it with their lives.

I stumble forwards, and my knees hit the floor. Charlie pulls me to my feet and I lean on her, waiting for the silence. The word from the judge. Waiting for the shots.

But they don't come.

There's chanting from behind me. I shake my head, trying to clear my thoughts.

They're chanting my name again.

The crowd parts, and I can see Dan at the front of the stage, his gun clipped to his back and his foot on the barrier.

People are shouting, but I can't make out their words.

Margie stands, facing the guns.

And Dan jumps, throwing his arms over the barrier and climbing.

Diversion

Ketty

There's someone climbing the barrier. Someone in armour.

I glance around, but all I can see are angry people, voices loud, fists pumping the air.

The soldiers turn, and step towards the intruder.

And I let out a breath I didn't know I'd been holding.

The guns are pointing at someone else.

Dan

Bex

I'm running, shouting at the people in front of me to move. Dan drops down behind the barrier, and the soldiers in front of the stage move towards him, rifles ready. I pull Charlie with me, clipping my gun to my back and pulling down my visor as I run. When we reach the barrier I throw my arms up and pull myself to the top.

I need to stop Dan. I need to keep him safe. I can't lose two friends today.

Someone grabs my feet and pushes me higher. I pull my legs over the top and drop down next to him.

He's watching the soldiers, lifting his hands into the air. I activate my radio, then lift mine, and wait.

"They'll have APs, Dan," I whisper, my eyes on the the soldiers as they step towards us. "They'll get through your armour."

"I know." His visor is down, and I can't see his face. I can't tell what he's thinking. He's being brave and stupid, and I'm standing with him, but I have no idea what happens next.

My heart starts to hammer in my chest. "What's your plan?"

"Charlie?" He says, keeping his hands up.

The soldiers look back at the crowd, distracted by something behind us.

Charlie's voice is loud in my ear. "We've got this! Get to the stage – both of you!"

Dan looks round, then runs for the steps at the edge of the platform.

I glance back, and watch as three figures in armour lift their guns on the far side of the barrier.

The soldier next to me points his gun at my head, and as I duck down his chest plate shatters, throwing him backwards. The plastic pieces clatter against my helmet and I throw my arms over my head as the soldiers swing their guns towards the crowd.

"Run, Bex! We've got this!"

There's more firing now – Charlie, Maz, and Amy, keeping the soldiers busy for me.

I don't have time to think. I pull my gun from my back, and follow Dan up the stairs.

Shots

Ketty

The Judge is shouting for quiet, but the crowd is roaring.

Another figure climbs over the barrier, and I hear a shot at the front of the stage.

The soldiers are firing. I think they're shooting at the intruders, but then the people in front of me start to panic, running or ducking down, trying to escape the bullets.

They're firing into the crowd.

The only cover I have is the people around me. I need to get away from the guns.

Time to leave, Ketty.

I turn and start to push my way back through the crowd, elbowing people out of the way as they shout and chant. They haven't seen the bullets. They're too busy watching the show.

Bullets

Bex

We sprint up the steps, into the sights of the firing squad.

And the judge gives the order.

Dan throws himself at Margie, locking his hand above her elbow and twisting her round, pushing her onto the stage. He crouches over her, head down, both arms wrapped round her, his back to the guards. She draws her knees up to her chest and ducks her head as he takes bullet after bullet, his armour denting with the force of the shots.

I'm turning to Dr Richards, reaching out to pull her away, when a tall figure sprints out from the curtains at the back of the stage and slams into her, knocking her head back and taking both of them to the floor. I close my hand on nothing, and she's falling away from me again.

I can see the farmyard. Margie, falling to her knees. Dr Richards, pulling away from me to help. The soldiers, firing.

I watch, holding my breath. Time seems to slow down as she falls, her arms out, her hair framing her face.

As the guards fire over and over.

Everything around me seems to freeze.

I see the rifles, powered up and firing at my friends.

I see stray bullets raising puffs of dust from the black backdrop.

I see Dan and Margie, rocked by the impact of every bullet.

And I see Will, his arms round his daughter, shots erupting from the back of his shirt.

I raise my gun, and turn to the firing squad.

The figure in front of me is a silhouette. A paper target.

I line up my rifle, and I shoot.

Panic

Ketty

There's more shooting, now. The judge gives the order, and instead of a line of clean shots there's a rain of bullets.

This isn't what we planned. This isn't what Conrad was expecting.

Get out, Ketty. Get away.

I keep pushing away from the platform as the panic starts to spread. I duck down and muscle my way through people shouting, people trying to run, people too shocked to move. The crowd is reacting, and I can't tell what they're going to do.

Keep calm. Keep moving.

There's no way to know how this ends.

Blood

Bex

The guard falls. His armour shatters, and my bullet slams into him. His rifle bounces on the stage.

I fire again, and again, as the guards switch their target, firing back at me.

My pulse is loud and fast in my ears, and I'm taking quick, gasping breaths.

They're firing at me.

I wait for pain. I wait for Armour-Piercing bullets to rip into me.

The bullets punch my armour, knocking me backwards, but the panels hold. These rounds are designed for executions, not soldiers. They'll bruise, but they won't reach me.

I keep firing. Sending bullets into the targets in front of me. Smashing their armour and throwing them back onto the stage. I don't stop until all the soldiers are down.

When the shooting stops, I lower my rifle. The firing squad is gone, bodies scattered across the stage. I force myself to see paper silhouettes. Neat bullet wounds. Target practice.

The judge is cowering against the podium, holding his hands in the air, eyes closed. His image is repeated on the screens behind him.

As I watch, the cameras turn to me.

And there are voices in my helmet.

"Drop your weapons! coalition forces!"

A soldier in camouflage climbs the steps at the far end of the stage, rifle trained on us. I hold my gun up in one hand, and slowly lower it to the floor. I lift my hands up in front of me.

Someone grabs my shoulder from behind, pulling me round and lifting my visor.

"It's her!" The soldier shouts, over my shoulder. "It's Ellman!"

Is this the coalition, or are the Home Forces taking back control? Are we safe, or are we prisoners?

I can't stand up.

The soldier tries to pull me back to my feet, but I fall to my knees, pulling my helmet off and crawling to where Will and Dr Richards are lying on the stage.

Will's shirt is shredded, and what's left of his back is red and wet with blood. There's no way he survives this.

I take his shoulder and pull him towards me, dragging his weight off my teacher.

Dr Richards lies still, her eyes closed.

And there's a red stain spreading from her shoulder.

Squad

Ketty

The sound of the bullets grows louder, and the people around me stop shouting. I push between them, and they let me pass, staring at the screens.

It's as if everyone's holding their breath.

I glance back at the stage.

The prisoners are on the ground. Someone's crouched over Margaret, shielding her from the bullets.

There's a flash of orange from Sheena's jumpsuit, but I can't see what's happened to her.

And there's a figure in armour, rifle raised at the firing squad, armour-piercing bullets cutting them down as they stand and shoot.

The last guard falls. The judge is crouched against the podium, arms over his head, his face filling the giant screens.

There's a moment of silence, after the bullets. A moment when no one takes a breath.

And then there are soldiers, climbing onto the platform. Soldiers in fatigues, rifles raised.

You're not safe yet, Ketty.

I turn, and keep pushing back through the crowd.

Pulse

Bex

"Medic!"

I'm screaming as I drag Will away from his daughter, and lift her head into my lap. I tear off my gloves and check her pulse. It's weak, but she's still with me.

"Medic!"

There are soldiers helping Dan and Margie to stand, leading them through the curtains at the back of the stage. There are soldiers crowding round me, filling the platform.

And there's more blood on her jumpsuit. There's a ragged hole in one leg, just below the knee, and another on her arm.

I feel as if I'm watching someone come apart in front of me.

I shout again, feeling the tears on my cheeks.

There's shouting, and there are voices on the radio, but no one's listening to me.

I can't tell whether we've won or lost. I can't see Charlie or Amy or Maz.

All I can think about is losing Dr Richards in the yard at Makepeace Farm. Feeling her slip out of my grip as she ran to help Margie.

I don't want to lose her again.

Trapped

Ketty

I need to find a way out. I don't know who's in control here.

I don't know who's in control of the country.

There are soldiers on the stage. If they're Home Forces, they'll execute me for shooting Lee. If they're the invasion, they'll be hunting the Home Forces.

I need to get out of here without being seen.

King

Bex

Dan and Margie disappear behind the curtains.

I want to follow them. I want to get off the stage. I want to walk away.

I want to get far away and forget that this ever happened.

But Dr Richards needs me.

Someone puts a hand on my shoulder, and they're pointing to the back of the stage. I can't hear them over the noise from the crowd and the hammering sound of my own heartbeat. I don't know whether they're helping, or arresting me.

I shake my head.

There's a noise like a explosion from the speakers, and the soldier looks up in surprise. He crouches next to me and draws his gun, looking around, one hand protectively on my arm.

And then the King's voice booms out over the crowd. The shouting dies away, the crowd falls silent, and the King starts to speak.

And I know we've won.

Speech

Ketty

The speaker stacks let out a deafening squeal, and I turn back.

The image on the screens skips and changes, and it's the King, standing in the conference room. Standing in front of Bex's cameras. Holding up his hands to calm the crowd.

A murmur moves through the people watching, as the King begins to speak.

"People of the United Kingdom," he begins. "Whether you are part of the crowds in London, or whether you're watching from home, please remain calm.

"I'm not the first intruder on your screens today. A few minutes ago, you heard a speech from a brave young woman – a woman who asked you to join with her, and with the resistance, to save your country. She's a tough act to follow," there's scattered laughter from the crowd, "but I'm here to ask you to join her."

Bex has the support of the King?

"She's right. This world is ending. I'm asking you all to join together to build a new world – a new country. A new United Kingdom. To banish fear, and hate. To win back your rights and freedoms."

And then I know it's over. I don't need to hear the rest of the King's speech – the fact that he's quoting Bex is enough. Martial Law. The Home Forces. Franks, Bracken, Lee. The whole structure is toppling. We're not going back to false flags and conscription and child soldiers.

It's my world that's ending, not just Bracken's, and I need to make sure I don't go down with it.

Bad situations don't have to end badly.
Use the confusion, Ketty. Find a way out.

Medics

Bex

The soldier points again to the back of the stage, and leans over to shout in my ear.

"There's an ambulance coming." He looks down at my patient. "Do you want to stay with her?"

I nod.

The soldier stands up, and clears a path for the medics as they push through the curtains onto the stage. Someone pulls me away, and Dr Richards is surrounded by figures in camouflage. I watch, helpless and shaking as they cut away her jumpsuit to expose the wounds.

And I glance over at Will, his eyes closed, his body crumpled on the stage.

Before I know what I'm doing, I'm kneeling next to him.

There's blood, everywhere. He's not moving. He's not breathing.

I think about the conference room. About lifting my gun.

About calling him a coward.

I take his hand.

"I'm sorry." It's all I can think of to say.

He proved me wrong. He's not a coward. He's just done the bravest thing I've ever seen.

He's just sacrificed himself for his daughter.

"Ellman! Are you hurt?" One of the medics is in front of me as I stand up, staring into my eyes as the King's voice echoes around us.

I shake my head, and she nods, eyeing the cracks and scratches on my armour. My hands, red with Will's blood.

There's laughter from the crowd, and the medic raises an eyebrow.

The King is talking about me.

Disguise

Ketty

The speech ends. The crowd cheers, and starts chanting again.

Bex's name, over and over.

And I know what I need to do.

Stay calm. Find Bex. Offer her your support. Get yourself out of here alive.

There's an ambulance in the walkway at the edge of the crowd, moving towards the side of the stage. The people around me are pushing forwards, straining to see what's happening on the platform. It's impossible to move in the crush.

I look up at the soldiers on the stage. At their images on the screens. Medics, kneeling round the prisoners.

The Medics are dressed like me, in camouflage fatigues.

I could blend in. I could get to Bex.

I need to get to the ambulance.

I think about the South Bank bomb. Running stretchers and bandages and medical kits to the people treating the injured.

If I can reach the edge of the crowd, I can jump the barriers. I can follow the medics and make myself useful.

I can find a way out.

Stretcher

Bex

The medics are lifting Dr Richards onto a stretcher. I pick up my rifle and helmet, and follow them as they carry her through the curtains at the back of the stage. I wait while they negotiate the steps, and then follow them down, through the dark backstage area and out into the courtyard.

I'm bracing myself to push with them through the crowd, but when we step out into the daylight the courtyard is empty. The barriers behind the stage have been pushed away. There are soldiers in camouflage guarding the archway and the walkways, but the people who were here earlier have gone.

The ambulance is waiting. A couple of medics run towards us, taking the stretcher and carrying it while the others walk alongside, making sure the bandages are holding.

I walk behind, and as they lift her into the ambulance, I realise there's nothing more I can do.

Ambulance

Ketty

Moving sideways through the crowd is easier than pushing backwards, and I make it to the barrier while the ambulance is still in front of the stage. I pull myself up on my arms, and throw one leg over the top of the fence, letting myself drop carefully on the far side.

My knee protests, but I make myself ignore the pain, and take off running towards the stage.

I reach the ambulance as it drives through the checkpoint, and I walk confidently alongside it, as if I'm supposed to be there. The guard waves me through. The second checkpoint is the same, and I'm in the courtyard again.

And there's no one here.

I look around, staying close to the ambulance. The crowds have gone – evacuated, or arrested. It's going to be hard to stay hidden out here.

Make yourself useful, Ketty. Make yourself invisible.

The ambulance pulls up, and someone opens the back doors. I stand outside, waiting to help.

A group of soldiers walks out from the black curtains, and I make myself stand still. They have no reason to suspect that I shouldn't be here. I glance over, and I notice that they're escorting someone.

Margaret Watson, in her execution jumpsuit, and Dan Pearce in full armour.

I duck behind the open doors, and wait for Bex.

*****

There's a shout from behind the stage. Someone calling for help with a stretcher.

I step away from the ambulance and look around. Dan and Margaret are standing together, with eyes for no one but each other. A medic jumps out of the back doors, and I follow as he jogs to the back of the stage. We take the stretcher and walk with it while the medics check the patient.

It's Sheena Richards, her jumpsuit cut and torn. Bullet wounds padded with bandages.

And behind her is Bex, her armour pitted and cracked. I duck my head and make sure she can't see me.

Keep walking Ketty. Almost there.

Together

Bex

My knees buckle. I'm falling, until someone catches my elbow and hauls me to my feet.

"You OK, Rugrat?"

"Maz!" I drop my gun and my helmet and throw my arms round his neck. "You're OK?"

He grins. "I'm fine." He steps back and looks at my armour. "You're looking a bit dented, though. You're sure you're alright?"

I nod.

There's a shout from the ambulance, and I look up to see Margie, reaching out as the medics close the doors. Dan holds her back, whispering something to her, and she slumps against him. Someone's taken off her handcuffs.

They're sitting on the ground by the time I reach them. Margie sobbing, and Dan with his arms around her.

I sit down beside them as the ambulance pulls away, blue lights flashing.

"I'm sorry, Margie. I'm so sorry."

She looks up at me and nods. "Is she …?"

"She's breathing. She's hurt, but she's alive."

"And Will?"

I shake my head. "I'm sorry."

She nods again, eyes closed.

Dan's face is white, and he doesn't speak as he reaches one arm out to me. I lean my head against his shoulder and close my eyes. I want to forget. I want to leave this all behind, but all I can see is Will, taking the bullets that were meant for his daughter, his white shirt turning red as he sheltered her from the guns.

When I open my eyes, Charlie is sitting next to me, and Amy is standing with Maz, watching us.

Charlie nudges me. "Good job, Bex. I think you took down the firing squad single-handed."

"And the soldiers by the stage?"

She looks up at Amy and Maz. "We took care of them. Group effort." She smiles at me.

"They'll be playing that clip on TV forever." Maz is shaking his head. "You, Dan, the firing squad. You're even more famous than you were before."

Backstage

Ketty

I lift Sheena into the ambulance and step back as one of the medics climbs in, and someone closes the doors.

There's a shout from behind me, and Margaret is standing, touching distance from my shoulder. I step away, covering my face with one hand as I step behind the vehicle.

The other medics are walking back towards the stage, so I follow, keeping my face hidden as the ambulance drives away. We head through the curtains, and as they walk back up the steps to the platform I hang back, losing them in the backstage darkness.

There's no one here. I'm expecting to see the technicians, or someone from PIN, or Conrad.

But they've gone.

The coalition is in control, here. They must have been arrested.

Or shot.

There's an icy feeling in my spine as I look around.

Don't think about it. Get yourself out.

I step back to the gap in the curtains, and watch the gathering outside.

Deal

Bex

Dan tightens his arm around me. "Thanks, Bex. We couldn't have done this without you. Famous together?"

He's smiling, but I'm already pushing him away and standing up, suddenly sick of all of this.

"Bex?" There's a chorus of concerned voices as I turn my back on the group and walk away.

I'm not ready to stop and smile about what we've done. I'm not finished. There's more to do.

Half way to the barrier, there's another voice calling my name. I turn round to shout, to tell them to back off and leave me alone, and I realise it's Ketty. The name tag's gone from her uniform, and there are livid purple bruises on her neck, but she's here, and she's not pointing a gun at me.

"Ellman," she says, in her recruit-intimidating voice, and then her face softens. "Bex. I need your help."

There's something wrong with her voice, as if she's talking through gravel, or sandpaper. I stare at her, trying to make the words make sense. "You need my help?" I repeat, my voice flat. She nods, slowly.

The sound of her gun plays in my head. The committee member, choking as first her bullet, then mine, slammed into his chest.

I don't know why I saved her. I don't know why I didn't shoot her at the top of the stairs.

I should have hurt her, while I had the chance. I should have hurt her, the way she's been hurting Mum. The way she hurt Dad, leaving him to die alone.

She watches me, waiting for me to react.

"I helped you. I got you out of the committee room." My throat is tight, and I have to make myself speak up. I lift a hand to stop her interrupting. "You saved my life, I saved yours. Why are you still here?"

She clenches her fists, and I take a step back, but she pushes her hands down to her sides.

"Bex, listen. I'm Bracken's assistant. Colonel Bracken, who you named and shamed in your speech." She waves a hand at the backs of the screens. "They're going to be looking for me."

I stare harder, and put all the anger I'm feeling behind my voice. "So *what*?" I spit the words at her, and spin on my heel, walking away. Putting space between her and me. Between me and everyone.

"Bex!"

I keep walking. I can hear her footsteps behind me, but I don't stop.

"I know where your mother is."

And I'm turning round and swinging my fist before I can stop myself.

She deflects the blow from her face, but lets it land in front of her shoulder. My knuckles meet her collarbone with a satisfying crack, and she steps backwards in surprise. My fist explodes with pain, but it doesn't stop me raising the other hand and swinging again.

This time she stops me, grabbing my fist out of the air and holding my arm still.

"I can take you to her." I pull my arm out of her grip and square up in front of her. She stands her ground.

"I can take you to your mother, but I want your protection."

So that's it. Get her out of a life sentence or a firing squad for choosing the wrong side, and I get to see Mum.

"You want me to protect you? You want me to dig you out of this hole so you can – what? Take up torturing children again for a living? Lock someone else up and interrogate them for kicks?"

She pulls herself up straight, hands out in front of her, warding me off.

"Fine. I'll do it myself. I'll find my own way out." She shakes her head. "But after today, I'm guessing I'm the only free person who knows where your mother is."

And she starts to walk away.

I kick the floor in frustration, and I'm screaming before I know what I'm doing. She turns back.

"Do we have a deal?"

I look over her shoulder. There are figures in black running towards us.

Dan. Amy. Maz.

She follows my gaze, and slowly lifts her hands in the air. Dan has his gun drawn, and he brings it up to point at her chest.

She looks back at me and smirks.

"You're going to let him kill me? You're going to lose your mother to get revenge on me?" There's a swagger in her step as she turns away from Dan. "Come on, Bex. I'm worth more to you than that. You need me alive."

Bargain

Ketty

Bex shakes her head at Dan and he drops his aim, lowering his gun to his side.

I nod, keeping my hands where he can see them. He steps towards me and pats me down, lifting my shirt to take the gun from its holster on my belt.

"Is that it, Ketty? Is that all you've got?" Bex stands with her hands on her hips, shouting at me.

"That's it."

"She's clean, Bex. There's nothing else." Dan clips my gun to the belt of his armour.

"So? Where is she? Where's Mum?"

I smile. "Can you get a car?"

Bex stands for a moment, then starts running. Amy runs after her and I follow at a walk with Dan.

She stops to speak to Margaret and Charlotte, and pick up her rifle and helmet. There's some shouting and handwaving, and she walks away again as we reach her.

"Bex!" Charlotte calls after her. "We're supposed to wait here. They said the King wants to speak to us!"

But she doesn't stop. "The King can wait," she calls over her shoulder as she marches through the archway and out onto Whitehall. Charlotte helps Margaret to her feet, and they take off after her at a run.

Dan pokes me in the back with his gun, and I realise I've stopped walking. "We've radioed for a car, from the coalition." He smiles. "Well, more like a fleet of cars." He nudges me again until I start walking. "Now it's up to you."

*****

We make the trip to Belmarsh in convoy. Bex and her friends, and some of the soldiers guarding Whitehall. We use the military lanes, and the journey takes half an hour.

Half an hour in a car with Bex and Amy, both of them armed, and both of them angry.

I can think of better ways to spend an afternoon.

"Ketty," Bex begins. "I'm not sure what it is you're expecting me to do. I'm not sure who's in charge yet, and I don't know whether anyone will listen to me."

Amy laughs. "They're all going to listen to you. You were the one on the screens. It was your speech. You told them *their world was ending*. The King quoted your words. Of course they're going to listen to you."

Bex ignores her. "What is it you want me to do? Save your career? Tell them you had nothing to do with all this?"

I hide a smile. It hasn't occurred to her to double-cross me. It hasn't occurred to her to go back on her word. She's really going to help me. After Saunders, after interrogating her mother – after everything Jackson and I did to her, and to her friends, she's still going to help me.

Careful, Ketty. Don't take anything for granted.

I take a deep breath. "I'm a soldier, Bex. I signed up for it, I volunteered for it. I chose to fight for my country. I thought that meant fighting terrorists and training you lot, but today it means bringing you to your mother, and tomorrow it will mean – who knows? Fighting for the King? Defending elections? Guarding politicians?" I shrug. "Whatever it means, that's what I'm signing up for. So that's what I want.

"I'm a good soldier. I'm a fighter. I don't give up." She raises an eyebrow at that.

"So what's this, then?" She waves her hands at me. "Looks like giving up to me."

I let out a sigh. "This is what my country needs today. So this is what I'm doing, today. It might not look like it to you, Bex, but this is fighting."

You have no idea how hard I'm fighting. I intend to stay alive.

"So, what? A good word in the right ear? A recommendation to the King? A letter to the Opposition In Exile?"

I smile. "Something like that, yes."

She fixes me with a stare, and I think of her mother in the nursing home, steel behind her eyes as she sized me up.

She nods, finally. "OK. OK."

"Thank you."

She nods again. "But my Mum had better be OK when we get to her. You had no right to kidnap her. You had no right to take her away from home. From my Dad." There are tears in her eyes as she speaks.

I close my eyes and nod, accepting her accusation. "She's fine, Bex. I promise."

The car pulls up at the prison.

Rescue

Bex

Ketty is right. Mum's OK. She lets us into the prison with her pass, and down into a waiting room. I follow her to the cells, and there's Mum, sitting in her wheelchair, waiting for another interrogation.

"Corporal Smith. No guards today?"

Ketty steps back and waves me into the cell. Mum's jaw drops.

"Bex!" She holds out her arms and I kneel down in front of her chair. She wraps her arms round me and I drop my helmet and hug her back. There are tears in my eyes as I pull back and take in her orange jumpsuit and the fading bruises on her face. The plaster cast is gone, but she's still wearing a support bandage on her arm.

"Mum. Are you …?"

She nods, and smiles, her eyes searching my face, hands gripping the arm panels of my armour.

"What happened? Why are you …?" Her smile fades, and she looks over my shoulder at Ketty. "What is this, Corporal? Is this the reunion you promised me?" She raises her voice. "What are you going to do to my daughter?"

She moves her arm protectively round my shoulders.

"No, Mum – it's OK. We won. We fought, and we won."

"No strings, Mrs Ellman. No more questions. I'm here to let you go. You and your daughter."

Mum looks at me. "I don't understand."

I smile. "We won, Mum. There's a coalition of armies running the country. The Home Forces? They're done. They're all under arrest." My smile widens. "We're getting our country back."

She nods towards the door. "Then what's *she* doing here?"

I shrug, her arm still round my shoulders. "Ketty helped us. She brought us here. She's going to let you go."

Mum raises her eyebrows, and looks at Ketty.

"So you're happy to sit on the bully's side of the table, but you're not willing to take the consequences, Corporal?" She shakes her head, a faint smile on her face. "That doesn't surprise me." She looks at me again, her hands on my shoulders. "She's not threatening you, is she, Bex? She's not hurting you?"

I shake my head, and there are tears on my cheeks.

"No, Mum. This is real. She's here to get you out."

Mum gives Ketty a long stare, then looks around the cell, and shrugs.

"What are we waiting for?"

Alone

Ketty

They're all here. Bex, Dan, Amy, Charlotte. Margaret in her execution jumpsuit, and some faces I don't recognise, all crowded into the Top Secret Belmarsh waiting room. I've opened all the cells, and people are helping themselves to coffee and tea, and everyone's talking at once.

Bex sits with her mother, the two of them deep in conversation. Elizabeth hasn't seen anything that happened this afternoon – there's no TV in the cells – and Bex is bringing her up to date. She's explaining something, waving her hands to help her descriptions, and pointing out people round the room as they show up in her story.

Amy is talking to a man I don't know, waving her hands and gesturing with excitement. The man laughs and grins. Charlotte Mackenzie is talking to Craig Dewar, her hand on his arm. She glances at me, and excuses herself. She sits down in the chair opposite mine, and looks me in the eye.

"Do you know how lucky you are to be here?" She asks, her voice cutting. "Do you know how lucky you are to see this?" She waves her hand. "Oh, I know why you're here. You've bargained yourself a reprieve from the witch hunt that's going on in the Home Forces right now. Bex is desperate enough – and kind enough – to let you in here. She could have left you outside." She thinks for a moment. "She could have left you in the courtyard at Horse Guard's Parade. She could have handed you in to the people in charge. But she didn't." She indicates the room. "So now you get to see what you don't have, Ketty. You get to see friendship. You get to see love, and kindness, and caring." I shake my head. I don't want to hear this from the kitchen supervisor. I wave her away, but she doesn't stop. "Take notes, Ketty. Life isn't all about winning. Sometimes it's about standing still and finding your tribe." She shakes her head at me. "But you don't have a tribe, do you?"

Watch who you're talking about. My tribe is dead, and the child who killed him is on the other side of the room.

I bite down on the temptation to shout at her. To tell her what happened to Jackson. What happened to Bracken, and Lee. What happened to Mum, and Dad. What happens to everyone who cares about me. But I bite my tongue. I have an advantage, here, but it won't last. I need Bex to believe I'm on her side.

Charlotte stands up, and walks away, and it's harder to watch the group mixing around me.

Because she's right.

And then I notice Dan, standing in a corner with Margaret. He's holding her shoulders, and she slides her arms around his waist. I look away as their lips meet, and see Bex watching them as well, a smile spreading across her face. I raise an eyebrow, but she doesn't see me. She's too busy with her tribe.

I sit, alone in the centre of the room, watching the groups divide and join up around me. There's no harsh joking. There's no one pushing each other to react. There's nothing of Jackson here. And there's no manipulation. No Bracken. No Lee. No Conrad. No broken promises.

This isn't my tribe at all.

I sink down further in my chair.

"So you're using my daughter now?" Elizabeth crosses her arms and sits back in her chair. She's pushed herself over to my seat, and we're eye-to-eye in the middle of the room.

Careful, Ketty. You don't have any friends here. Don't forget that.

"I'm working with her," I say, carefully, pulling myself up straight in the chair. "At least – if she'll let me."

She watches me for a moment, a smile twitching the corners of her mouth. "You've decided not to point guns at her any more?"

I make myself smile, too, and look round the room. "I don't think that would get me very far here. Do you?"

She shakes her head. "Or anywhere else." Her gaze is almost as piercing as Lee's, and I feel myself shrinking back from it. "Is it true, what she told me? What you did to her and her friends?"

My mouth is dry, and I have to force the words out. I try to sound unconcerned. "What did she tell you?"

Elizabeth looks at me again, and it's like being back in the interrogation room. Except that this time there are no handcuffs. Nothing to protect me from her. No power on my side. Nothing to be gained from provoking her. She tilts her head to one side, and appraises me. "I think that's a yes."

I look down, my face heating up as she continues to stare.

"What is it you think my daughter can do for you?" She asks, as if she's asking about the weather. As if this means nothing, to either of us. I make myself meet her gaze. "What are you hoping for? A pardon?"

"Something like that."

She watches me, her eyes searching my face.

"How old are you, Corporal? Twenty-one? Twenty-Two?"

I shrug.

Close enough.

"I don't envy you. The rest of your life? Sixty years, give or take? That's a long time to spend behind bars."

She glances at Bex. "I can see why you'd want to make a deal. That's a lot of time to spend answering their questions." She looks down at her jumpsuit. "Plenty of time to get used to wearing one of these."

I look away. I don't want to think about this.

Don't let her get to you.

She leans forward so her face is inches from mine, her anger finally showing. "If you ask me, you deserve a firing squad, *Ketty*." She leans away again, and shrugs. "But if you ask Bex? Maybe she's a better person than me." She glances over to where Bex and Amy are talking. "Maybe she can see something worth saving. She certainly knows what you're capable of."

She touches her neck, then points to the bruises on mine. "Whoever did that – they had the right idea. Send them my regards."

She watches me for a moment more, a hint of amusement on her face, and then she turns her chair and pushes herself away.

I take a deep breath and run my hands over my face.

I'm here. I'm alive. That's what matters for now.

Insight

Bex

Ketty opens the doors and we bring the prisoners to the waiting room. There's tea and coffee, and comfortable chairs. It's all so normal, and so safe, and it seems impossible, so close to the cells.

Everyone's reaction is different. The guard from the gatehouse has tears in his eyes when I step into his cell, and I can't help crying as I walk him to freedom. Neesh's friend throws his arms around me and tells me he can't believe he's being saved by the Face of the Resistance. Ketty and I both roll our eyes at that, but we take him to the waiting room and make sure he's OK.

When the cells are empty, I thank Ketty and leave her sitting alone in a chair, the reunion going on around her. I step over to the interrogation room door, and rest my fingers on the handle.

Mum pushes herself to my side and takes my hand in hers.

"You don't need to go in there, Bex. You don't need to see."

I look at her, blinking back tears. "I've seen it, Mum. Every night on PIN I've watched you, and Ketty, and all the prisoners. I know what's inside."

Mum shakes her head. "It's not the same, Bex. Not when you're on this side of the cameras." She squeezes my hand.

I nod, and open the door.

She's right. This isn't a TV image. This is harsh white lights and a cold metal table. This is a smell of disinfectant and a one-way mirror. Cameras, bright light, and my own eyes, looking back at me.

This is fear.

I walk slowly into the room, leaving Mum in the doorway. I put my hand on the prisoner's chair, then slowly pull it out and sit down, my hands on the table, one on each side of the handcuff loop. I look down at my hands, and then up, at the mirrored wall in front of me. I watch myself, sitting where Mum sat. At the view I've seen so many times on PIN.

And it feels cold. Empty.

Then I stand, and walk to the other side of the table. To the chair where Ketty sat, questioning Mum. I put both hands on the back of the chair and look across the table.

There's a feeling of power on this side of the room. A feeling of safety. No handcuff loop on the table. No one-way mirror, watching me. Slowly, I pull the chair out and look at it, as if I'm expecting an explanation.

Mum watches from the doorway as I sit down, hands in my lap, back straight. I try to imagine someone across from me, fear in their eyes. The questions I would ask. How I would feel.

I shake my head. I feel sick. I close my eyes and lean over, taking deep breaths.

I'm shaking when I stand up and leave the room, pulling the door closed behind me. Mum takes my hand, and turns me to look at her.

She shakes her head. "That's not who you are, Bex. You're better than that, my beautiful girl." I stare at her, trying to shake the feeling of power. She points at one of the chairs in the waiting room. "Come on. Sit with me. Tell me everything that's happened." I nod. "Tell me how you got here."

So I tell her. I tell her about Camp Bishop, about Ketty and Jackson and Bracken. I tell her about Leominster, and how we escaped from camp. I tell her about the bunker. About Joss Saunders and the gatehouse guard. About Newcastle and Edinburgh and

145

the Netherlands. I'm pointing people out as we reach each part of the story – Charlie, Dan, Margie, Amy, Maz. Ketty.

Mum listens. She holds my hand and she listens to everything that's happened. I tell her everything as quickly as I can, and then I tell her about today, and my speech in the meeting room. What happened at the execution.

She puts an arm round my shoulders again, and we sit quietly for a while; Mum looking round at my friends, and me fighting tears as I realise what we've done today.

I look at the room – at my tribe, talking and laughing – and I see Amy with Maz. Charlie, talking with the gatehouse guard. Dan and Margie in the corner of the room, stealing a kiss. I can't help smiling, knowing they've found each other again.

Mum gives my shoulders a squeeze. "So these are your friends."

I nod, my eyes filling with tears. "Yeah."

She nods. "They're good people." She looks at me. "You've kept each other safe, through everything. You should be very proud of that."

I nod, my eyes closed.

"Mrs Ellman?" Mum looks up. "I'm Charlie. It's an honour to meet you."

I brush the tears from my eyes as Mum takes her arm from my shoulders and shakes Charlie's hand.

"It's an honour to meet one of Bex's friends."

I stand up, giving Charlie a smile and putting a hand on Mum's shoulder. I leave them to talk, and make my way around the room. None of this feels real. I need to talk to Dan and Margie. I need to know that my friends are still with me.

"Bex!" Amy jumps up and throws her arms around me. "This is amazing! All these people …"

I nod. "I know. I can't believe we're here."

"We've done it, Bex!" And she hugs me again. She pulls me to a chair, chattering with excitement, and tells me what happened to her earlier. How she helped to rescue Margie and Dr Richards, and how she reported what was happening to the coalition. Jake worked with her, talking with her on the radio as she described the events in the crowd, and on the stage. How she's thrilled to have her friend back.

I look up. Mum is talking to Ketty, and I'm about to get up and interrupt when Mum pushes herself away, and the door behind her opens.

Taken

Ketty

The room falls silent as a group of guards in olive uniforms walks in from the corridor. I turn in my chair, heart pounding, searching for some kind of identification on their uniforms. There's nothing to indicate which side they're on. I watch as they draw their guns.

Someone has tracked us to Belmarsh.

I'm half-expecting to see Conrad, or Franks, and I realise that it's my pass that opened all these cell doors. I'm in trouble if this is the Home Forces, and I'm in trouble if its not.

Time to call in the debt, Ketty. Time for Bex to step up.

I glance across the room at Bex. She's watching the guards with the same expression. We're both trying to guess who they're here for. She stands, pulling herself up tall in her armour, waiting for whatever is coming.

I reach for my gun, but the holster is empty. Dan took the gun, back at Horse Guards Parade. If this is the Home Forces, there's going to be a fight, and I'm unarmed. If this is the King's soldiers, I'm on their wanted list.

I glance around the room, looking for shelter and safety, but there's nowhere to hide. I could run for the cells, but there's no way out. We're trapped down here. If the guards are here for me, there's no one I can count on. Already I can see hostile looks on the faces around me – Charlotte, Elizabeth, Amy. There's no safety here, but I'm amazed at how calm I'm feeling. I feel exposed, I feel vulnerable; but I feel calm, as if the end is inevitable.

I stand, and slowly move towards the interrogation room, putting the chair between me and the guards.

Charlotte is watching me. Bex is watching the guards. Everyone is waiting.

There are six guards in the room now. Everyone is silent, watching them. Watching their guns.

The first guard looks around the room, sweeping his gun over the crowd. His gaze rests on me. Slowly, I raise my hands, palms out. The barrel of his gun points at my chest, and he stares at my uniform.

The missing epaulets. The space where my name tag should be.

"Corporal Smith?"

My knee starts to shake, and I shift my weight slightly until I'm steady on my feet.

"Corporal Smith!" He shouts again.

"Yes, Sir." My voice is steady, but quiet.

I'm trapped. I'm pinned down. And I still don't know who is pointing the gun.

"Over here, Corporal."

I glance at Bex, and she glances at me, then back at the guard.

Your turn, Bex. This is where you pay me back.

I step forward, hands raised. I keep walking, until I'm standing in front of the guard. He lowers his gun.

For a moment, I think I'm safe. I think the fight isn't over. That this is my side, saving me.

But then the guard pulls out handcuffs and shouts at me to hold my hands out in front of me. I look at him, as if he's Conrad, taunting me. As if he's a disobedient recruit. But he gestures with the cuffs until I hold out my hands.

I can feel the eyes of everyone in the room, watching me. Watching him, snapping the cuffs onto my wrists. I give the room a defiant look, but all I see is Elizabeth, staring at me, a cold smile on her face.

Come on Bex. Speak up.

But she stays silent. And I realise that she's going to betray me after all.

Promise

Bex

Everything happens so quickly. They take Ketty away, and before I can speak up, they're moving into the room, patting everyone down and taking our weapons. Pushing us back to the far end of the space. I glance at Dan, and he shrugs. I make my way over to Mum, and stand with her, her hand in mine.

One of the guards steps forward.

"Ladies and gentlemen. Thank you for your cooperation. In a few minutes, the King will be arriving at Belmarsh." There's a murmur from the people around me. "He would like to personally congratulate the Face of the Resistance, and to formally release the prisoners from their detention." I glance at Dan, and he nods back at me, smiling. "In the meantime, make yourselves comfortable. This is an informal occasion, and His Majesty would like to offer his personal thanks to everyone involved in today's events."

Mum's grip tightens on my hand. "That's you, Bex. He wants to thank you." Her face is white, and her voice is soft, but she's smiling. She shakes my hand in hers. "The King wants to thank you!"

I smile at her, but I can't stop thinking about Ketty. I've screwed up. I've let them take her away.

"Bex?" I'm watching the guards. I pull my hand away from Mum. "What is it?"

"Ketty." I say, into the silence, and there's surprise in my voice. "I didn't save her."

Locks

Ketty

The soldiers lead me out of the waiting room, and up the stairs. They wait for the door to open, and surround me as we walk to the entrance hall. There's a prison van waiting outside, and they open the door and push me up the steps. Two of them step in behind me, dragging me onto a bench and sitting, one on each side, as the driver starts the engine.

A flickering blue-white light stutters to life on the ceiling. Someone slams the door closed, and I hear the locks turning. There's an icy feeling in my spine as the van starts to move.

Bex hasn't spoken up. My last chance to walk away vanished with the closing door.

I'm on the wrong side. I'm in the wrong uniform, and the one person who could save me has broken her promise.

I'm on the losing side.

Everything you've done. Everything you've worked for. It wasn't enough.

The van jolts and shudders as the driver pulls out onto the main road. I've made this journey enough times to know where we are, but I have no idea where we're going.

I try to feel something, as we drive. I try to feel angry, or hurt. I try to feel fear.

But I'm numb. I wasn't expecting this. I wasn't expecting Bex to break her promise.

I've been counting on Bex. Counting on her as my last chance. Counting on her honesty.

And I was wrong.

I should have run. I should have walked away. I should have used the trial as my cover, and walked into the crowd. I could have been one face in thousands, heading home by tube. Catching a bus across the country. I could have walked away with a hundred thousand people as my shields.

I made the wrong choice, and I'm in handcuffs.

Bad situations don't have to end badly.

Maybe you can still talk your way out.

Discussion

Bex

They've taken Ketty. They've taken her away, after I promised to protect her. She kept her word. She brought me to Mum. She stood with me in the conference room.

We both have blood on our hands.

I need to keep my end of the deal.

I take a step towards the guards, but Mum's there, next to me. She puts her hand on my arm.

"Leave it, Bex. It's not your problem." She looks up at me. "You know what she's done. Let the soldiers deal with her. She's not worth your time."

I look around the room. Dan and Margie. Charlie and Maz. Amy. Mum. We're all here. We're all safe.

But Ketty's gone. And I promised to help. I'm safe, and there is still something I can do.

Charlie crosses the room as I step towards the guards. She stands in front of me, hands on my shoulders.

"Bex. Stop. You don't have to do this. I know what Ketty did to you. I know what she did to your mother." She glances over my shoulder, to where Mum is waiting. "You're getting involved again. Take a step back. This isn't your fight."

I shake my head. "I promised."

Charlie hangs her head. "I know, Bex, but sometimes …"

"I promised."

Charlie steps back, throwing her hands up. She looks over my shoulder again.

"Mrs Ellman?"

I look back. Mum shrugs. "I've done what I can, but I think my daughter is a better person than I am."

Charlie smiles, shaking her head.

I catch Dan's eye across the room and he whispers something to Margie, then walks over and puts a hand on my shoulder.

"Which is it, Bex? Am I wrestling you into a chair, or picking up a gun and standing with you? What's the crazy plan?"

"I made a promise, Dan. I need to save Ketty."

The colour has gone from Dan's face. He's angry, and he's hurt. His eyes search my face, and he's trying to understand.

"You have got to be joking, Bex."

I shake my head.

"After what she's done? After what she did to Margie? To Jake? To *your mother*?" He runs a hand through his hair. "After what she did to you, Bex?"

"I know." My voice is small and quiet after Dan's shouting. "But she brought me back to Mum." I glance round the room. "To all the prisoners. And I promised."

"She was desperate, Bex! She's using you to get out of being punished! You were an easy target, and she pounced on you." He raises his voice. "You don't owe her *anything*!"

"She deserves what's coming, Bex. Let her go." Charlie puts her hand on Dan's arm.

I look down at the floor. I can't meet their eyes. My voice is a whisper.

"We killed someone. Together."

"You and Ketty?" Dan and Charlie exchange a glance. "In the conference room?"

I nod.

"Bex, you can't …"

"That doesn't make you …"

I look up at Charlie. "Yes, it does. We're as bad as each other." My voice is stronger now. "I'm safe. I'm on the winning side. But I've done something terrible."

Charlie shakes her head, watching me. "Why do I get to walk away?"

Dan takes my hand and looks me in the eye.

"Because you're the good guy, Bex. You've done the right thing, over and over." I shake my head and try to pull my hand away, but he tightens his grip. "The things you've done – they weren't the easy things, or the things you were supposed to do – but they were the right things."

Charlie glances back at Mum, and then at me. "You haven't tortured anyone, Bex. You haven't locked anyone up. You haven't hurt people for fun."

"No. But I killed someone. Someone important. And Ketty was standing beside me. We took the shot together."

Somehow that's the death that hurts the most. I can still see the firing squad guards falling to the stage, their armour failing under my bullets. But that was self-defence. That was protecting my friends. In the conference room, I fired because I was angry.

"That doesn't make you the bad guy!" Dan is shouting again. "Everything you've done has been right and good. Dangerous, stupid, crazy – yes, but also brave and honest and caring." He grips my shoulders and turns me to face him. "You're not like her, Bex. You're not like Ketty."

"Are you wrestling me into a chair, Dan?"

He leans on my shoulders, bowing his head.

"If you make me, I will." He looks up, pointing with one hand at the people around me. "And your friends will help me."

Cell

Ketty

I'm behind bars. I'm locked up, and I'm alone.

The prison van brought us to a police station, somewhere in London. I'm in a cell, and I'm waiting.

I have no idea what they're planning to do.

The cell is tiny, with a flickering strip light and no window. There's a sleeping platform, and a thin, plastic-covered mattress.

I'm sitting on the mattress, my head in my hands.

I can't see any other cells through the bars on my cell door, but I can hear other prisoners arriving, and I can hear people being taken away. This is only a holding cell. They're keeping us here until – what? I think it over. Are they sending us to prison? To instant trials?

To firing squads?

My hands are shaking. I've done everything I can, and it's not enough.

I pulled Bracken out of the conference room. I took Bex back to her mother. I let the Belmarsh prisoners walk out of their cells. I'm out of options.

Everything we've done – Bracken and me, Conrad and Lee – it ends here. This is where my actions catch up with me. This is where I'm held accountable.

This is where I fall.

And this is fear.

I'm expecting interrogation. I'm expecting to sit, chained to a table, while the cameras watch and someone asks me to justify what we've done.

Could I make a deal? Could I give them Bracken? Or Conrad?

And I think about the other interrogation room. The one without cameras. The two trained men in black

157

jumpsuits. The Enhanced Interrogations that I've witnessed.

That I've run.

And Jake, at Camp Bishop, begging me to stop the pain. Bex, outside the fence, Jackson's fists flying into her. Margaret Watson, looking through me as the blows landed.

Am I brave, like Margaret? Or will I beg? Will I stand tall and let them hurt me? Or will I break?

Will they enjoy it? Will they mock me as they serve out pain? Will they smile when they break my bones?

I did. I smiled. I enjoyed it – watching people break. Hearing them beg and plead. I enjoyed the power, and I enjoyed their weakness.

I run my hands over my face and hair, staring at the floor between my feet.

How will I stand, between the men in black? Tall and unbroken? Or cowed and fearful? Pitiful. Falling to the worst place in the world.

I shake my head. There's nothing I can do. I'll find out who I am when they take me away.

I'll find out what I've become.

Bully

Bex

The King arrives, and thanks us, and shakes our hands. He talks to Mum, and the other prisoners. He congratulates us for saving our friends. He talks to Margie for a long time. Dan stands next to me as the King puts his hand on my shoulder and thanks me for my speech, and I know he's ready to stop me if I ask about Ketty.

The King moves on, talking to everyone in turn. The atmosphere in the room is awkward, but excited. Everyone is on their best behaviour, but we're all looking at each other, trying to believe that this is real.

And all I can think about is the promise I've broken.

Margie puts a hand on my arm. I give her a smile, and another hug. I still can't believe she's OK.

"You don't have to help her, Bex." I look at her in surprise. "Dan told me what happened."

"But …"

"She used you. She saw that she was on the losing side, and she saw that you could help."

I shake my head. "That's no excuse. I promised."

She puts a hand on my elbow, and leads me to the chairs at the edge of the room. She sits down, and I sit next to her.

She takes a deep breath, her eyes closed.

"Shall I tell you who Ketty is?" She looks at me again, and her hands are shaking.

"I'm sorry, Margie. I didn't mean …"

"Just listen, Bex."

I nod, and wait for her to talk. She clasps her hands together in front of her, and she's shivering as she starts to speak.

"She's a bully, Bex. She's cruel, and she's violent, and she's only looking out for herself." Her voice shakes, and I reach out to hold her hand, but she shrugs me away.

"In that room, just there," she points to a door, behind us. "In that room, she tried to make me talk. She tried to make me tell her things – about you. About Dan."

I nod. "I've been in the interrogation room."

She shakes her head. "That room is different. There are no cameras. They can do what they want to us, in there."

I rest my hand on the arm of her chair, waiting. She closes her eyes, and waits for a moment. When she speaks again, it's in a whisper.

"They have men. Men in black uniforms. They're trained to hurt the prisoners."

I shake my head, and I can feel tears in my eyes.

"Margie. I'm so sorry."

"And Ketty? She was in there with them. Telling them what to do. Telling them when to punch me, and kick me, and hold me down." Her voice trails off, and she covers her face with her hands.

"The bruises?"

She nods. I can feel tears, spilling onto my face.

"And she told them what to do?"

She drops her hands from her face, looking at the ceiling. She blinks back her own tears, and looks at me again.

"Worse than that. When I wouldn't talk ..." She shakes her head. "When I wouldn't talk, she used her own fists."

She looks up, and I realise that Dan is standing next to me, watching her. He kneels down, and takes her hand in his, lifting the other to her face and pushing a stray wisp of hair back behind her ear. He doesn't speak, but they stay like that for a long moment, his hand on her shoulder.

I feel sick. I know this. I know about Ketty. I know what she's done to Mum, and to Jake. I know what she did to me, with Jackson.

And I know she's used me.

Dan turns to me, and there's a look in his eyes that I've never seen before.

"Do you get it now, Bex?" He sounds choked. He sounds as if he's holding back tears.

I nod, slowly.

I want to do the honourable thing. I want to do the right thing. I want to keep my side of the bargain that brought me back to Mum.

But I can't let Ketty go free. I can't let her walk away from this.

"Do I have to wrestle you into a chair, Bex?" He asks, in the same tone of voice, and I realise he's not joking. "Because I will, if I have to."

I need to remember whose side I'm on. Who has my back. Who stood with me, through everything.

This is a promise I have to break. This is the right thing to do.

I look at Margie, remembering the bruises on her face. Her expression, as she faced the firing squad.

I try to answer, but my voice has gone. I shake my head, and he nods, turning back to Margie.

The coalition can have Ketty. Let them decide how this ends.

I'm done helping her.

Conrad

Ketty

There are voices in the corridor. Someone arriving. And someone leaving.

"Where are you taking me?"

It's Conrad. He's shouting, but there's an edge of fear to his words.

"Take your hands off me."

I'm on my feet and at the door before I can think.

"David!"

The corridor is quiet for a moment. There's a scuffling sound as someone is dragged from their cell, and then the soldiers are marching past, Conrad between them, his hands in handcuffs.

"Conrad!"

He looks at me as he passes my cell.

"Ketty." He sounds disappointed. "You're here."

"Where are they taking you?"

He laughs, shaking his head.

"Where's Bracken, David? Is he here?"

Conrad stops, and his guards start to drag him forwards. He looks back at me.

"Haven't you heard? Bracken shot himself. Made a mess of some clerk's office, back at Horse Guard's. Bracken's gone."

I watch as the guards pull him away, out of sight down the corridor.

"You're on your own, Ketty. You're on your own."

I stagger back, away from the door, and sit down again on the mattress.

Bracken's gone.

I took his hip flask. I tried to help. I tried to keep him safe.

162

But I killed him.

I took his whisky. I took what he needed, and I left him alone. And he couldn't handle it.

I *killed* him.

I shake my head. All those years at Camp Bishop, working together. All those months of keeping him sober. Keeping him in his job. Threats and anger and fear. Allowing his weakness to shape my life.

And what for? I protected him, but he couldn't protect me. He was weak, and his weakness broke him. Everything I worked to protect, lost with a single bullet.

My fists are clenched, my nails digging into my palms. Conrad is right. I'm on my own. And I'm falling.

Cars

Bex

The King shakes my hand again, one more time before he leaves.

"You should be very proud of yourself, Miss Ellman," he says, smiling. "We couldn't have done this without you."

I nod, and thank him for his support.

I can't tell him how I really feel. How angry I am with myself, and with Ketty. How sorry I am for forgetting my friends.

How much I want to turn back the clock, and not allow Ketty to manipulate me.

Charlie puts her hand on my shoulder, and we watch as the King and his guards leave the room.

"You've done the right thing, Bex." I nod. "Not the easy thing. The right thing." She pulls me into a hug, but I can't hug her back. I'm too angry with myself. I don't deserve kindness like this.

"You OK?" She says, pulling back.

I shrug. "Not really. I've been stupid. I wish …"

She shakes her head. "No wishing, Bex. Look around. Everyone's here because of you. Because you made a deal with Fiona, and you stuck to that deal." She smiles. "*The King* just thanked you, Bex. The King wouldn't be free, and in charge, if you hadn't spoken up." She watches my face, waiting for a smile, but I stare back at her. She points across the room at Margie. "Your friend is alive. She's safe, and she's here with you, because of what you did today. The Home Forces didn't get their execution. PIN didn't get their show." She shakes her head again. "At least – not the one they were planning."

"I think we gave them a show." And I can't help smiling, thinking about how Margie's trial must have looked to anyone watching on TV.

"I think we did."

There are tears in my eyes, but Charlie's right. We saved Margie. I hope we saved Dr Richards.

For the first time, I wonder where Fiona is.

*****

The door opens, and a prison guard walks in. She looks nervous, faced with a room full of people in amour, and orange jumpsuits. The room falls silent.

She clears her throat.

"There's a fleet of cars outside. I'm supposed to bring you all up. They're here for you. And you can pick up your weapons in the entrance hall."

We all start talking at once, and she holds her hands up for quiet.

"Where are they taking us?" Maz shouts.

She shakes her head, and holds her hand up. "I don't know. But they're diplomatic cars. They've all got flags flying at the front, like you see on TV."

"Whose flags?" Dan and Maz shout together.

She shakes her head again. "All different, as far as I could see."

"Any Dutch flags?" Charlie says, her eyebrows raised.

"I don't know. But there are black motorbikes, and armed guards, so I think you'll be safe."

Charlie looks at me, and smiles. I look back at the guard.

"Who sent them?"

She smiles. "They told me it was the King."

Pride

Ketty

There's a shout from the end of the corridor.

"Katrina Smith!"

When I raise my head, my hands are shaking.

This is it, Ketty. Who will you be?

Slowly, as if I'm carrying a heavy load, I pull myself to my feet. I can hear footsteps approaching.

I think of the first prisoner I put through Enhanced Interrogation. The man who owned the car Bex used at the nursing home. How he begged and pleaded with us, before anyone had laid a hand on him. How he knew what was coming, and how the fear gripped him and pushed him to his knees.

And I think of Margaret Watson and Sheena Richards on the execution platform. Facing their firing squad, heads held high. Proud, confident, and unbroken in the face of a public death.

You're on your own, Ketty. Can you do this?

I shake my head, and think about the bad situations I've faced. Fighting off Dad. Knocking Jackson to the floor. Keeping the recruits safe during the raid on the coach. Walking, again and again on my shattered knee. Losing Jackson. Standing up to Lee, and to Bracken. Standing up to Conrad.

I've been working with Bracken for too long. We've been a team, and he's made me forget how to be myself. How to be strong.

I know who I need to be.

When the guards reach my door, I'm standing in the middle of the cell. At ease, feet a shoulder width apart, hands clasped smartly behind my back. I've straightened my uniform and pulled my pony tail tight. I fix my gaze at a spot above the door and face the guard who unlocks the cell, my head held high.

There's nothing else left for me to do.

Motorcade

Bex

We pile into the cars. Black limousines with diplomatic plates and flags flying from the fronts of their bonnets. And a London taxi, for Mum, and her wheelchair. The driver helps her into the car, and I climb inside with Charlie and Maz. Dan waves to us as he follows Margie into the car in front, a chauffeur in a uniform holding the door for him. He looks as if he's just landed from Mars, in his armour, and I can't help laughing.

I sit down next to the wheelchair.

"Are you OK, Mum?"

She gives me a huge smile.

"I'm fine, Bex." She leans over and puts her arm round my shoulders. "I'm free, and I've got you back. Everything else can wait."

The taxi moves off, following the cars in front. There's a motorbike, matching our speed outside the window, blue lights flashing.

Charlie takes Maz's hand. "Welcome to the UK, Maz Ainsley."

He looks out at the motorbike, dropping back to drive behind us as we pick up speed.

"I assume this is normal for public transport in your fair country?" He grins.

Charlie grins back, and shakes her head. "Oh, no. This is just for me."

"Oh, well. I'll just have to make sure I travel with you in future, won't I? Anyway," he winks at me, " I think Bex had something to do with this. Face of the …"

I shake my head, catching his eye. "Don't even think about it."

Charlie punches his shoulder, and he laughs. "OK, OK."

He leans forward, past Mum, and knocks on the glass. "Driver? Where are we going?"

The driver slides the partition across.

"Mayfair, Sir. The Royal Hotel."

Charlie raises her eyebrows.

Mum holds up her arms and looks down at her prison jumpsuit.

"I feel a bit underdressed," she says, smiling.

Walk

Ketty

"Katrina Smith."

"Yes, Sir."

The guard looks me up and down, and makes a note on his clipboard. He stands back as two women in blue prison uniforms walk into the cell. I keep my eyes fixed on the point above the door.

"Arms," says one of the women, unclipping handcuffs from her belt.

I hold out my hands, not moving my gaze.

I've heard others being pulled from their cells. I've heard them shouting.

I will not be dragged away.

I close my eyes as the handcuffs lock round my wrists, hard and cold against my skin. I force myself to breathe. To push away the fear.

Discipline, determination, backbone, Ketty.

Don't let them win.

The man at the door marks his clipboard, and walks out into the corridor.

One of the women takes hold of my elbow, but I shrug her away.

"I can walk."

She shrugs, and puts a hand against my back.

"So walk."

The guards escort me out into the corridor.

*****

There's another prison van. Another journey, cuffed between my guards.

But this time, I don't know where I am.

I keep my eyes fixed on the wall opposite my bench, and make myself take slow, calming breaths.

I don't know where they're taking me.

I sit up straight, pushing away thoughts of trials and executions, and Elizabeth's voice comes back to me.

"If you ask me, you deserve a firing squad, Ketty."

My hands are shaking, and the pain in my knee is growing. I fix my eyes on the opposite wall, and wait.

Dressed

Bex

The taxi pulls up outside a tall red-brick building on a street lined with trees. A man in a hotel uniform opens the door, and helps the driver pull down the ramp for Mum. We follow her out, into an evening lit with street lamps.

"This way, please."

The Doorman leads us through the front doors, and into a reception lounge. There are velvet sofas and chandeliers, and polished wood panelling.

It's beautiful.

I think of the safe house – the empty hotel we left this morning. And I think of the cells at Belmarsh. It's hard to remember that there are places like this in the world.

The Doorman leads us to a sofa, and asks for our names. We sit, waiting, our armour and guns out of place on the plush fabric.

He returns with four keys, and three rucksacks.

"These are your bags?"

It's my bag, from the safe house. Someone's brought it here, and there's a label with my name on. I take it from him, and Charlie and Maz take theirs. I'm starting to understand what Fiona's been doing, behind the scenes.

He hands us each a room key, and I shake my head.

"I'm sharing with Mum."

He looks doubtful. "Are you sure? The OIE has reserved rooms for each of you."

I look at Mum, and she's watching me. "Take it, Bex. You might want it."

I shake my head. Charlie taps my shoulder and whispers in my ear. "Take it as a group room, Bex. There's no common room here."

I can't help grinning as I reach for the key. "OK. Thanks."

*****

We're all on a corridor together – me and Mum in the accessible room. My room next door, and Charlie and Maz next door to that. Dan. Margie. Amy.

Amy comes running down the corridor as we open our room.

"Bex!" She gives me an excited hug. "There's a party tonight, in the ballroom. But Margie doesn't have anything to wear," she looks over my shoulder, "and neither does your Mum."

I nod, trying to keep up.

"So I thought – let's unpack our bags, and see what we've got. We must have something to fit everyone. What do you think?"

"Sounds good." I look over my shoulder. "Mum?"

She smiles. "Thank you, Amy. That sounds good to me."

I hand Amy my room key, and point to the door. "Get everyone in there. I'll be in in a moment."

She grins. "Thanks, Bex!"

*****

Mum's room is enormous. There's a giant bathroom, set up for a wheelchair, two leather sofas and two double beds. The TV is the size of a cinema screen.

I drop my bag, and my helmet and gun, onto one of the beds, and sit down next to them, letting myself fall onto the clean, white sheets.

I can't believe we're here. I can't believe we've made it.

And I can't wait to get out of my armour. I sit up, and start tearing at the laces on my boots. I pull them off, and my socks, and start unclipping the plastic panels.

Mum sits, watching me.

"Can I help?"

"I'm good," I shout, throwing the dented chest plate onto the bed and stretching my arms. It feels good to stand on a soft carpet, in bare feet and my base layers.

But I need to get dressed. And I need to find clothes for Mum.

"Ready?" She nods. I pick up my bag, and head next door, Mum pushing herself behind me.

*****

My room is smaller, but there's still plenty of space. I unpack my bag onto a corner of the bed, sorting through jeans, tops, and underwear. Amy does the same, and Charlie joins us, tipping out her clothes on the end of the bed.

I stuff everything that needs washing back into the bag, and take a look at what's left.

There's a pair of black jeans and a purple shirt that will do for tonight, so I fold those up and put them to one side.

Margie puts her head round the door.

"Are you guys serious? Do you have clothes?"

Amy waves her in, and Margie stares at the piles on the bed.

"Oh my god, give me jeans. Give me skinny jeans! And a decent bra!" She winks at me. "I have a handsome man to impress, after all!" I can feel the colour in my cheeks as I smile back.

It takes a few minutes to work out what Mum and Margie need, and then we're sorting through the piles on the bed.

"Mum?"

"Anything that fits. I'm happy with anything."

Charlie holds up a patterned blouse and a long black skirt. Mum smiles.

"That's perfect. Thank you."

And we go on, digging out jeans and tops and underwear until everyone has a bundle of clothes in a size that fits.

Pockets

Ketty

The van pulls up. I hear the front doors slamming, and someone unlocks the door at the back. The guards stand up, and help me to my feet.

When I step outside, I'm in a cage. Heavy metal gates behind me, bars overhead, and tall, red-brick walls on three sides. There's a door ahead of me, and the guard puts her hand on my shoulder, pushing me towards it.

I stand up straight, and walk ahead of her, trying to hide the pain in my knee.

Inside, we walk past a reception desk and through another metal gate. One of the guards hands a folder to the woman at the desk, and picks up a clipboard and two plastic bags.

Keep walking, Ketty. Don't let them win.

We stop in the corridor. The guard unlocks a door, and pushes me through.

I'm in a small cell. There's a table, and a bench. Posters on the walls warn me to declare everything in my pockets, and list the punishments for carrying knives, or drugs.

And on the bench, neatly folded, is an orange prison jumpsuit.

I feel sick. I can feel my knee shaking. I feel myself falling, and I force myself to stand.

Discipline, determination, backbone.

"Pockets," says the guard behind me, holding out the smaller plastic bag. It takes all my effort to fix her with a recruit-scaring stare while I hold out my hands. She nods, and the other guard pulls a bunch of keys from her belt and unlocks my handcuffs.

I stare at my wrists, turning my hands and stretching my fingers. It's a small victory, but it feels immense.

"Pockets," she says again, shaking the bag. I nod, and work through the pockets of my uniform, pulling out my ID card, my backstage pass, my access card for Belmarsh, the keys to my flat. I unclip the empty holster from my belt and take the watch from my wrist, dropping each item into the bag.

"Anything we should know about?" Asks the other guard, pointing at the posters on the walls. I shake my head, and take out my wallet. I hold it for a moment, over the bag, and then force myself to let it go.

It feels like surrendering the last of my independence. It feels like losing myself.

The last thing I hand over is the bottle of painkillers. The guard takes the bottle from my hand, and stares at the label.

I hold out my hand.

I can't believe I have to ask.

"Could I take a couple? Before you put them away?"

She shakes her head, reading the back of the bottle.

"Not allowed." She drops the bottle into the bag. "You'll have to see the nurse, for anything like this." She seals the bag, and puts it out of reach on the table.

The pain in my knee peaks with every heartbeat.

She steps towards me.

"Arms out."

I hold my arms out straight as the guard pats me down, searching for anything I haven't declared. I stare at a poster on the wall, trying to stop my knee from shaking.

She nods, satisfied, and the other guard makes a note on her clipboard.

Then she turns to the table and picks up the second bag.

"Clothes," she says.

I can't help rolling my eyes.

She looks down, pointing. "Shoes first."

I walk to the bench, and untie the laces on my boots. I pull them from my feet, and place them neatly next to me on the floor.

I will give them my clothes with military precision. Neatly folded. Neatly stacked.

I take off my socks, and fold them into the tops of my boots, then I stand up, and pull my shirt over my head. I fold it, carefully, straightening the creases on the sleeves, and place it on top of the boots. I do the same with my trousers, and my T-shirt. With everything.

When I'm done, she points at the jumpsuit.

"Get dressed."

It's new. The fabric is stiff, and there are sharp creases where it's been folded. I realise it must have come from the government stores.

A jumpsuit for a terrorist. And now it's mine.

I almost laugh.

There's a faint chemical smell as I pull the jumpsuit up, and shrug it over my shoulders. The material is rough against my skin. I pull up the zip and turn to the guards, standing smartly at ease again, eyes fixed on the door.

This is it, Ketty. The prison, the cell, the orange jumpsuit.

This is everything you feared.

But I'm alive. I've beaten Lee, and I've beaten Bracken.

You can do this, Ketty. One step at a time.

Party

Bex

The cheer as we walk into the ballroom is so loud it hurts my ears.

Neesh is here, and Caroline. Gail. Fiona. Jo. All the prisoners from the cells, and all the fighters from the bunker.

And Jake, sitting on a sofa, his arms round two girls in camouflage T-shirts.

I can't take it in. Mum takes my hand, and when I look at her she's smiling. Charlie takes the other hand, and lifts it above my head. The cheering begins again.

Jo runs out from the crowd, and throws her arms round Margie. And then Gail is hugging me, and Neesh. Jo asks me about Dr Richards, and I tell her I'm sorry about Will. Someone puts a drink in my hand and pulls me into the room. Everyone wants to shake my hand, and ask me what happened, or tell me what happened to them.

It's exhilarating.

And it's too much.

I put my drink down and push my way to the edge of the room, past buffet tables and trays of champagne, and slip through a door into a service corridor.

I lean against the rough concrete wall, trying to catch my breath.

Margie's safe. Dr Richards is in hospital. Mum's safe.

That's all I need to know.

And in making it happen, I killed people, and I betrayed the person who saved my life.

I can feel the weight of the rifle in my hands, pointed at the man in the conference room. Shooting the guards as they fired their useless bullets back at me.

I don't deserve a party. I deserve a prison cell.

The door opens, and the sound of the celebration bursts into the corridor. A waiter walks through, carrying an empty tray.

He stops, staring at me.

"You're the Face …"

I nod. "Yeah."

"I saw you on the screens today! You were wild!"

I shake my head. He looks back over his shoulder.

"Isn't this party for you?"

I shrug. "I don't feel like celebrating."

He steps back. "You just saved the country, and you don't feel like celebrating?"

I shake my head. He leans the tray against the wall and plants his hands on his hips.

"What does it take to get you to party?" He's grinning at me.

"Some bad stuff happened today," I say, and I can't meet his eyes.

He steps forward, and touches my arm, gently.

"Yeah. I know it did." He points back at the door. "But some good stuff happened, too. There are people out there who wouldn't be here, if it wasn't for the bad stuff."

I nod. "I wouldn't be here if it wasn't for the bad stuff." I don't mean to say it out loud, but I can't stop myself.

"Then I think we should drink to that." He holds up a finger. "Don't move." And he pushes through the door.

I lean my head back against the wall.

Bad things happened. But he's right. Good things happened, too.

We went to war today. We fought. We did everything we've been trained to do.

And we won.

We *won*.

It's over. I don't need to train any more. I don't need to fight. I don't need to hold a gun, or run in my armour. I don't need to hide my face.

I don't need to do what Fiona wants, or Caroline, or the RTS.

I'm free. And so are the people who trained with me.

I'm smiling when the waiter comes back with two glasses of champagne. I take one, and hold it out. He clinks his glass against mine, and we drink.

"Cheers!" He says. "And thank you, Bex Ellman." I can't help smiling, and he smiles back. "Now get out there, and celebrate the good stuff."

He holds the door open, and I walk back into the party.

Cellmate

Ketty

My prison-issue essentials are waiting on the top bunk when the guards bring me to my cell. Towel, toothbrush, hairbrush, and soap, along with shorts and a T-shirt for sleeping in, and a change of underwear. The bottom bunk is already occupied, by a woman I recognise. One of the Privates from the document drop at the Home Forces Building. She can't be more than eighteen. She's pretty, and she's quiet. She's been crying, tears staining her cheeks.

I roll my eyes. I'm not climbing to the top bunk while the guards have my painkillers.

I wait until I hear the door lock behind me, then step over to the bed. My pulse is hammering in my knee, and I make myself stand up straight.

"Bottom bunk's mine," I say, calmly.

She looks up, surprise in her voice. "Corporal Smith?"

Right first time, Private. Now get out of my way.

I nod, smirking. "I don't want any trouble, but the bottom bunk is mine."

She stares at me for a moment, and I wait, meeting her gaze.

She nods. "Yes. Of course."

She stands up. I wait while she moves my things from the top bunk onto a shelf, then sit down on the bottom bunk, relieved to take the weight off my knee.

"I'm Penny," she says, holding out her hand.

"Ketty," I say, lying down on the bed and staring at the slats of the bunk above me.

She drops her hand to her side, disappointment showing on her face.

Shopping

Bex

We're outside. We're walking along Oxford Street in the middle of the day, and I don't have to hide my face.

Our Wanted posters are still on display, on bus shelters and billboards. On a side street, I glimpse a wall of resistance posters – my face staring out, and the flag waving behind me.

Someone put those there. Someone brave. Someone who knew they might get caught.

I hope they're safe. I hope they got away.

Amy's hand is gripped in mine as we walk towards the department store, our armed escorts clearing a path through the crowds. It's only a short walk from the hotel, but everyone seems to know that we're here.

"Have you decided what you're buying?" She sounds nervous, glancing around at the people watching us.

I shake my head. "Something smart. Something for parties." She nods. "Whatever's on Fiona's list."

They've closed the store for us. The guards have to push their way through the crowds outside, and two men in smart suits hold the doors open, watching for anyone trying to walk in behind us. There are photographers in the crowd, holding up cameras and shouting our names. There's at least one TV camera. A woman with a microphone is shouting at me, trying to ask a question. One of the escorts puts a hand on her shoulder and turns her away.

It's a relief to walk through the doors.

A woman in a suit is waiting in front of the perfume counters. She waits for the doors to close behind us, then steps forward.

"Welcome! It's an honour to be able to assist the Face of the Resistance," she nods at me, "and your friends. Please, Ladies, step this way. Gentlemen – please follow my colleague." Dan squeezes Margie's hand before letting go and following his Liaison Officer towards the back of the shop. Maz follows, turning back and grinning at Charlie as he walks away.

"This way, Ladies." We follow her towards the lifts.

*****

We've each been assigned a personal shopper, and Gail is here, making sure I buy the items on Fiona's list. They walk me round the womenswear department, picking out smart suits and blouses and dresses. It's overwhelming.

I don't want any of this. I don't want to go on television, or meet the King again, or go to any more parties. I want to stop. I want to enjoy my freedom.

I thought I'd done everything I needed to do, but I was wrong. I still have to do as Fiona tells me, if I'm going to make it through the next few weeks. The whole country wants to hear our stories, and Fiona is making sure they don't all come after us at once. She's put guards on the hotel, and she's negotiating with newspapers and TV stations.

But we need to be dressed for TV. Dressed for receptions and parties and royalty, and all we have is the clothes in our rucksacks. Margie and Mum have nothing.

So Fiona has sent us shopping, with lists and requirements and assistants.

And I hate it.

The personal shopper pulls back the curtain on another changing room, and sends me inside with an armful of clothes. I pull off my fleece and jeans, pull another party dress over my head, and look at my reflection in the mirror.

I look tired. I look pale, and exhausted.

And I look ridiculous, in the bright pink sequined ballgown Gail picked for me.

*****

"What have you got?" Amy bounces up to me, shrugging off her assistants. I'm searching through a table of long-sleeved T-shirts for the colours Gail thinks I need.

I shrug. "Nothing I like."

"I've got the most amazing dress!" She's grinning, and I realise that she's actually enjoying this. I make myself smile back.

"That's great, Amy. You can be our party queen."

Her Liaison Officer calls her over, and she hurries away, still grinning.

I turn back to the T-shirts, and find Margie, watching me from across the table. She's dressed in one of Charlie's T-shirts, and the skinny jeans she wore last night.

"No luck, Bex?" I shake my head. "What are you looking for?"

I tell her what I need, and we search together.

"I wanted to talk to you ..." she says, eventually, and catches her breath. "I want you to know how much I appreciate what you did yesterday."

I shake my head. "It wasn't just me."

"No, but you're the one who made the broadcast. You're the one who put your face on the screens." She shudders, putting both hands on the table in front of her.

"I wanted you to know how it felt, seeing you. Hearing your voice. Hearing the crowd, cheering your name, in the middle of their show trial. I thought …" She shakes her head. "I thought they were going to shoot me, Bex. I thought that was it." She looks up, meeting my gaze. "And then you were there. You were talking, and you were telling them that it was all over."

I think back to the conference room. The director's shout as they hacked us out of the feed.

"But they stopped us. They carried on …"

"I know. But the crowd changed, after you spoke. They didn't want to see a firing squad. They wanted to see victory." She closes her eyes. "Even when I thought it was over. Even when I was looking at the firing squad, and they were raising their guns, I knew that you'd made a difference. And then you were there, and Dan, and I knew their bullets couldn't touch me." She shakes her head again. "So thank you. Thank you for being the Face of the Resistance, and inspiring people, and making all this happen. And thank you for being brave."

"But Will …"

She nods. "I know. Will saved his daughter. He did the only thing he could."

"I couldn't stop him."

"Don't beat yourself up. Will chose to do what he did."

"But …"

She stares at me.

"Bex. You were amazing yesterday. You stormed the stage. You wiped out the firing squad. You spoke to the crowd and you told them to start a revolution. The *King* said you were a hard act to follow." She reaches out and puts her hand on mine. "You were born for this stuff. You're good at it. Keep going out there and inspiring people. OK?"

I don't know what to say, but there's a tight feeling in my chest.

This isn't over. I don't get to walk away.

The TV interviews, the parties – this is all part of the job. I need these outfits as much as I needed my armour.

"Have you heard any more about Dr Richards?" My voice is quiet as I think about the medics on the stage. The bandages as they carried her away.

She shakes her head. "She's stable." She shrugs. "They think she'll be OK." She looks up at me. "Don't blame yourself, Bex. It wasn't your fault. You did everything you could out there."

I nod. Margie hands me two T-shirts in the right colours. I make myself smile, and thank her.

Then I step round the table and wrap my arms round her shoulders. She hugs me back, but there's something cold, something distant about her. As I pull her closer, I realise she's shaking.

"You OK?" I whisper. She shakes her head, and pushes me back. She turns, and I watch her walk away, her head bowed.

I turn towards the changing rooms, and I can't shake the feeling that this is the rest of my life. That I'll always be the brave schoolgirl on the resistance posters, Margie will always be the prisoner on the stage, and Dr Richards will be the person I couldn't save. That the others will always be my loyal supporters, and no one will want to hear our real stories. That we're all slipping into the roles we'll be expected to play forever, whether we want to or not.

Prison

Ketty

The morning alarm sounds, and I sit up, throwing my legs over the edge of the bunk. In the bunk above me I hear Penny yawning.

I take my jumpsuit from the shelf, limping as I cross the room. I need painkillers, and I need to stay out of trouble. I need to be a model prisoner.

I smile. This is like Camp Bishop all over again. Be the first up in the morning. Be the smartest, be the best. Earn some favours. I pick up my pile of belongings – underwear, towel, toothbrush, hairbrush and soap – and I'm waiting at the door when the guard comes to let us out. Penny is only just climbing down from her bunk, and I hear the guard shouting at her as I join the queue for the showers.

Discipline, determination, backbone.

You can do this.

Breakfast is toast and weak tea. I sit at a table by myself, looking around at the other prisoners. Wherever we are, this wing of the prison is all Home Forces women. Most of us arrived yesterday, but there are more prisoners arriving this morning, disoriented in their brand new uniforms.

But it's all lower-ranking staff, here. There's no one of Bracken's level, or Lee's. Major General Franks isn't here.

I drink my tea, watching the sea of orange jumpsuits.

No one tries to join me at my table, and we're back in our cells by nine, doors locked.

*****

"Ketty?"

"Penny."

She's sitting on the floor, watching me as I lie on my bunk. She sounds scared.

"How long do you think they'll keep us here?"

A heart-to-heart with my cellmate? I don't need this right now.

I shrug.

"They can't lock us up forever, can they?"

"Maybe."

She takes a sharp breath. "You don't mean that, do you? I mean, they need to give us a trial, or something?"

I stifle a yawn. "Probably."

She shuffles closer to the bunk, and lowers her voice.

"You worked with Bracken, locking people up. How does it work?"

I roll my eyes.

You have no idea what I've worked on.

I stare up at the top bunk.

"It works like this, Penny. Cells. Crappy food. Orange jumpsuits."

"But how do we know ...?"

I turn to face her, and I can't help raising my voice.

"We don't know, Penny. That's the point. That's what being locked up *is*." She moves back, a shocked look on her face. "We know nothing. We have no power. And we have to get up every morning and eat the food and wear the jumpsuit and do as we're told, and *they don't have to tell us anything*."

"But I thought ..."

"Then stop thinking." She shrinks away from me as I push myself up on one elbow. "You're a Private, Penny. You were a glorified postman. You haven't done anything, and this," I point around the cell, "is probably the worst that could happen to you."

She nods, curling up against the wall and pulling her knees up in front of her. I realise there are tears on her cheeks.

"I'm a *glorified postman*? What have *you* done, that's so much worse?"

I lie back on the bed and shake my head. I can't help laughing.

"None of your business, *Private* Penny. Leave me alone."

She wipes her eyes on her sleeves and glares at me before standing up and climbing back to the top bunk.

*****

I lie on my bed, thinking about the other prisoners. The Privates. The secretaries. The nobodies.

Who are they bringing here?

Are we the inconvenient ones? The ones without responsibilities?

Are we the ones they can't put through show trials?

Maybe the prison hasn't worked out who I am. Maybe they don't know about my connection to Bracken. To Conrad and Lee. To Franks.

Keep your head down, Ketty. Keep quiet. Maybe this is as bad as it gets.

Studio

Bex

"We'll be live in a moment. Are you comfortable?"

I nod at the presenter, looking out at the cameras, and the audience.

"Thank you for coming in, all of you. I'm very excited to hear your stories." And she turns away, waiting for the light on the camera to go live.

I'm sitting on a bright red sofa, dressed in one of the suits Gail bought for me yesterday. Mum is beside me, in her wheelchair, and Dan sits next to me. He looks like a bank manager, in his black suit and a pinstriped shirt. He glances at me, and raises his eyebrows in a silent question. I nod.

This is our first TV interview.

Everyone is expecting me to smile. To talk.

To be as brave as my photo on the poster.

I clasp my hands in my lap, and try to stop them from shaking.

*****

"Welcome back! And welcome to my very special guests. Joining me on the sofa this morning is the Face of the Resistance herself, Bex Ellman; hero of the hour Dan Pearce; and Bex's mum, Elizabeth. Welcome, all of you."

I nod, and try to smile. I can feel the makeup stiffening my face. The heat from the studio lights. Sweat, beading on my palms.

We're here to share our story, and we're here to make Fiona look good.

I'm terrified.

"We are very honoured to have you on the show. I understand that this is your first public appearance, after what everyone is calling the Horse Guard's Revolution?"

We all nod.

"Dan. If I can start with you? Tell us how it felt to invade the execution platform. We all watched the PIN coverage, and your courageous actions touched everyone." She turns to the audience, who start to cheer and clap.

And I'm back in the crowd again, in front of the stage. People shouting. People chanting. People cheering for Margie's firing squad.

Dan answers the question, but I don't hear what he says.

My heart is thundering. I'm wondering how many of these people were in that crowd.

"Bex?"

Mum reaches across and takes my hand, and I realise that the presenter is waiting for me to say something.

"I was asking about the Recruit Training Service. How you ended up at Camp Bishop."

I try to clear my head. She wants an answer. She wants to know what happened to us.

My throat tightens.

I glance at Dan, and he nods at me again.

I take a breath.

"The recruiters. They turned up at school." Dan's nodding, encouraging me. "They told us to pack our bags, and they marched us out of the door."

"That was it? They didn't tell you where you were going?"

"No."

"So you walked across the country, with no idea where you were heading?"

We both nod.

"And when you reached Camp Bishop? What was it like?"

"It was tough." Dan shakes his head as he speaks. "They were training us to fight."

"What was the training like?"

He shrugs. "Guns. Armour. Assault courses."

I'm shaking my head. These are empty words. The audience needs to understand what we went through.

"Bullies," I say, before I can stop myself. "Beatings." I can feel Jackson's fists slamming into my ribs. Ketty, pinning my arms to the ground.

The presenter nods.

"But you didn't stay at Camp Bishop, did you?" Dan shakes his head. "You broke out. I gather that was a dramatic moment."

She smiles at me.

"We stole a truck." It's all I can think of to say. The real story is too messy, too complicated. I don't know how to explain.

The audience gasps.

"You didn't just steal the truck. You drove it out of the gates in front of the entire camp, and got yourselves and your friends away for good."

"Yeah." I think about Jake, and what he'll be saying about me if he's watching. Reminding everyone that I left him at the gates, Commander Bracken's gun to his head. My hands are shaking. I can't speak.

"So what made you leave? What made you take that risk?"

Dan turns to me, and I can feel the heat from the lights. The glass eyes of the cameras, watching. I close my eyes, and I can see the road into Leominster. The crashed cars. A handbag. A glove. A pink teddy bear.

"Bex?"

I force myself to open my eyes.

This is what the audience needs to hear. This is what they need to focus on – not us. Not the heroes. They need to know what was done to keep them afraid.

The audience is silent, waiting for me to speak.

This is it. This is why I'm here.

"I saw what happened in Leominster." The presenter nods, waiting for me to continue. I glance at Mum, and she squeezes my hand.

"I saw the rubble of the buildings. I saw lines of crashed cars. I saw …"

But I can't tell them about the belongings, scattered on the ground. It's too much.

I shake my head, and take a breath.

"I saw the government weapons, and the government soldiers making them safe after the attack." I grip Mum's hand a little tighter. "I saw Senior Recruits from Camp Bishop, picking up the weapons and clearing them away."

I remember hiding, crouching in the ruins of a shop, while Ketty and Jackson laughed and joked in the middle of the destruction.

I remember crawling along the road in my armour. Hiding under the car. Waiting for the soldiers to find me.

I remember fear, and anger.

"So you were sure it was the government who attacked Leominster?"

"Yes." I'm nodding, my voice tight. "Absolutely certain."

"We couldn't stay," Dan says, watching me. "We couldn't keep training when we knew what had happened." He grins at the presenter. "We didn't want to be the bad guys."

The audience laughs, and I feel sick. I don't think they've heard me. I don't think they've understood.

I can see the handbag, the glove, the teddy bear.

I don't think they'll ever understand.

The presenter gives Mum a bright smile.

"And Elizabeth. You were locked up by the Home Forces?" Mum nods. "We've all seen the footage of your interrogations. Of the way you stood up for your daughter." She looks out at the audience, and there's a scattering of applause. "How does it feel to be the mother of the Face of the Resistance?"

Mum smiles, and tightens her grip on my hand.

"I've always known my daughter is a hero. This is just one more reason to be proud."

I close my eyes as my face starts to burn with embarrassment and frustration.

The audience is cheering.

I want to be anywhere but here.

Talk

Ketty

"Katrina Smith!" A guard throws open the door to the cell. "With me. Now."

I stand up and try to hide my limp as I walk to the door. There's a second guard in the corridor, waiting, handcuffs in her hand. She holds them up and glares at me until I hold out my arms. She pushes back the sleeves of my jumpsuit, and the metal is cold as it clamps round my wrists.

I look back as the cell door closes; at Penny, watching from the top bunk. She meets my eyes, and doesn't bother hiding a smile.

*****

The guards bring me to a waiting room. Strip lights on the ceiling, a row of blue plastic chairs against the wall, and the smell of antiseptic. One of them opens a door, and pushes me inside.

It's an interrogation room.

Bright lights. A metal table. A chair, screwed down to the floor.

And a one-way mirror, in front of me.

I stumble, and the guards pick me up by my elbows, dropping me into the chair. They take the handcuffs from one arm and pass the chain through the loop on the table. The cuff closes again round my wrist, and I'm trapped. Cuffed to the table in a room that looks just like the one at Belmarsh.

But now I'm on the other side.

I take a breath, and make myself sit up straight, watching myself in the mirror.

Wondering who is on the far side. Who is looking back at me.

What do they see?

I look at my reflection, and all I can see is my orange jumpsuit, and my handcuffs. I see what I always see in the interrogation room. I see weakness, and defeat. A victim to push until they break.

I force myself to look again.

My face is pale, and the bruises round my neck stand out under the bright lights. My hair is in a neat pony tail, and I'm sitting up, shoulders square, head high. I can see myself, and the look of defiance in my eyes.

Good enough, Ketty.

The door opens, and a tall man in an olive uniform walks in, pulling out the chair opposite me and dragging it to one side before he sits down.

My stomach sinks. He's making sure the cameras can see me.

This is it, Ketty. This is the interrogation.

"Katrina Smith," he says, watching me, his eyes flicking to the bruises on my neck.

Cooperate, Ketty. Buy yourself some time. There's no one else left to protect.

"Yes, Sir."

"I'm Colonel Ryan, British Rebel Forces."

I glance at his sleeve, and there's a stripe at the top. Half Union Jack, half Dutch flag. I raise my eyebrows, but he doesn't respond.

"You were Colonel Bracken's assistant?"

"Yes, Sir."

His voice is flat and cold.

"And before that, you were his Lead Recruit at RTS Camp Bishop?"

"Yes, Sir."

He doesn't nod. He doesn't acknowledge my answers.

"And you were in Leominster, for the attack."

It's not a question. There's a knot growing in my stomach.

Careful, Ketty. Don't give them an excuse for a firing squad.

He watches me, waiting for me to speak.

"Leominster, Miss Smith. You were there."

Miss Smith. I've lost my rank, as well as my freedom. Everything I've worked for.

"I was, Sir."

"Did you participate?"

Is this about what happened? Or is this about me?

I shake my head. I need to say the right thing.

"I was sent to assist the drone operators. I was told it was a weapons test."

"And you believed what you were told?"

"Of course, Sir." I can't help raising my voice.

"And did you see anything to convince you otherwise?"

"Not on the day of the attack, no. Sir."

He nods, and it's as if he's hearing me for the first time. As if my answers finally matter.

"Were there any precautions in place, Miss Smith? Any Personal Protective Equipment you had to use, during the test?"

The knot in my stomach tightens, and I nod.

"Protective suits, Sir. Nuclear-Biological-Chemical. And gas masks." My voice is quiet. I don't want to talk about this.

"And this was explained as part of the test?"

"Yes, Sir."

He nods again, sitting back in his chair. Relaxing.

"And after the attack?"

"Sir?"

"You said you didn't notice anything on the day of the attack. So you saw something afterwards?"

I look at the mirror. At the invisible cameras, recording everything I say.

You didn't do anything wrong, Ketty. You didn't know.

"The next day, Sir."

"Tell me what you saw."

It's a command, not an invitation to speak.

I take a deep breath, and close my eyes. I know what I saw, but I don't want to think about it.

"Bodies, Sir."

"You saw bodies? Where?" He leans forward in his chair.

"In town. We were sent in on clean-up duty. Packing up the weapons and taking them back to base."

"And the Home Forces let you see that? Even though they told you it was a test?"

I shake my head, thinking this through. "I don't think we were supposed to see it."

You're innocent, Ketty. Make sure he knows that.

He waits for me to explain. He's listening. I'm telling him something he doesn't already know.

"We got lost. We went off our route." He nods. "And there was a park, or a sports ground. Behind some houses. Only the houses were rubble, and we could see into the park."

"And what did you see?"

I close my eyes again. "Piles of bodies, Sir." Bright colours, heaped up on the grass. "I thought they were clothes, at first, but then we got closer, and ..."

"And what did you do, Miss Smith?"

What anyone would have done, Sir.

I look at him. What does he expect me to say?

"Nothing, Sir. There was nothing we could do. It was all over. They were about to let the TV cameras in."

"So you didn't tell anyone what you saw?"

I shake my head, thinking about my conversation with Bracken. About his confession. About using the attack to further our own careers.

Bracken's dead. You don't need to know what we talked about.

"No, Sir. We were instructed not to."

He nods.

"And who instructed you?"

"Brigadier Lee ..."

... who I killed ...

"... and Commander Holden."

And it all seems absurd. Lee is dead. Bracken is dead. Conrad is locked up. I'm locked up.

What can they get from me that they can't get from Conrad, or Franks?

I stare at the table in front of me. At my hands, cuffed together.

I think about his cold questions, when he knows what I'm going to say. The glimmer of interest, of connection, when I tell him something new.

This is how it feels to be manipulated. He's making sure I want to talk. That I want to give him something of value.

I want him to see me, not the handcuffs. Not the jumpsuit.

I want to connect. And he has all the power.

Come on, Ketty. You know how this works.

Maybe this doesn't need to be about what he can get from me. Maybe I can turn this round. Make him see that this is about what I can offer him.

I've run interrogations. I know how this works. I know how to use this room.

This is about survival, Ketty.

I turn to Colonel Ryan, shifting my body on the chair until I'm facing him. I'm talking to him, not to the cameras.

I lean towards him, and smile.

"Colonel. I'm as shocked by this conspiracy as you are. I was in Leominster, and I was in the Home Forces. I can help you. I can give you the story from the inside." He raises his eyebrows, watching me. I lift my hands, tugging the chain of the handcuffs. "I'm here. You've got me. So ask me, Colonel. Tell me what you want to know."

I put my hands down on the table, and wait for his next question.

*****

Back in my cell, I lie on my bunk, thinking about what Ryan asked me.

Is he looking for the truth, or is he collecting evidence against me?

Has he manipulated me into condemning myself?

Have I bought myself time, or have I confessed to the murder of an entire town?

How much did you give him, Ketty? How much will it take to find you guilty of a war crime?

I push away thoughts of a firing squad platform. Of crowds, shouting. Of soldiers, taking aim, waiting for the order to execute me.

And I try not to think about spending the rest of my life in a cell like this.

Sixty years, Elizabeth said. Sixty years, with no way out.

I can feel myself choking. I can't take a breath.

This is fear, Ketty. This is how it feels to be on the losing side.

Breathe. The worst hasn't happened yet.

You're still here.

Penny hangs her head over the top bunk.

"Nice outing, Ketty?" There's cold smile on her face. "Drinks with the Major General, was it? Or did the guards need your coffee-making skills?"

I say nothing, staring at the bottom of her bunk, willing myself to breathe. She has no idea what I'm dealing with. How dangerous this is for me. What they could charge me with.

She shakes her head and holds her hands out, wrists together.

"The bracelets suit you. You should wear those more often."

Careful, Ketty. She's not worth it.

It takes all my effort to stay where I am, every muscle tensed, and not drag her off the top bunk by her hair.

Lunch

Bex

"This one? Or this one?"

I hold up my two smart blouses, and Mum studies them.

"That one," she says, pointing at the dark green cowl neck.

"OK."

"And you should wear the silver necklace."

I nod. It feels strange to have all these clothes to choose from. To think about jewellery and shoes after so long wearing jeans and fleeces and uniforms.

"You look smart," she says, as I pull on my jacket. She pushes herself over and straightens my collar.

She's dressed up, too. Fiona's organised a rota of carers to help her get dressed in the morning, and get her to bed at night. She's picked out a navy dress with a smart, buttoned collar, and a necklace with a tiny silver bird.

A symbol of freedom, from Fiona's shopping trip. Mum talked the personal shopper into making it part of the outfit.

I smile at her, and I can't help thinking about the prison jumpsuit. Her wrists, handcuffed in front of her.

How different she looks now.

"You, too."

"Ready?"

I take a deep breath.

"Ready."

*****

The hotel ballroom is laid out with large, round tables, and smart leather dining chairs. There's a table of drinks inside the door, and it's the waiter from the first night's party filling the glasses. I look around, and I'm surprised to see that we're the first guests to arrive.

"Bex Ellman!" He calls out, waving us over. "And Elizabeth." He gives Mum a huge smile. "Another party?"

I roll my eyes and smile back. "Another party."

"You look worried. Is this one important?"

I grimace. "This is 'meet the parents'. This is where we have to convince my friends' Mums and Dads that we're all fine, and totally not suffering any trauma or nightmares from being on the front lines of the revolution."

I don't mean to make him uncomfortable, but he pulls a face. Mum takes my hand, and I realise how tense I am. How much I'm not looking forward to this.

"Tough call." He looks at the glasses in front of him. "I could suggest alcohol, or I could suggest vitamins." He points at the fruit juice. "The fruit punch is pretty good."

I can't help smiling as he hands us both our drinks.

He winks. "Good luck, Bex."

*****

We're on a table with Dan and Margie. Mum sits next to me on one side, and there's a seat for Dan's father on the other.

Dan arrives first, and his parents follow him in.

It's the first time any of my friends have seen their families since we left the UK, and it's as if we've been away forever. I know Dan's parents from school, and I'm surprised at how much older they look. It's less than a year and a half since they last dropped him off at

Rushmere, but they look as if they've aged ten years, waiting for him to come back.

"The lovely Bex!" His dad walks up to the table, power suit and tie just as I remember them. He waits for me to stand up so he can give me his usual smothering hug. It's like being hugged by a bigger, starchier version of Dan, and it makes me smile. "And Mrs Ellman. It's a pleasure to finally meet you." He shakes her hand, a serious look on his face. "We were sorry to hear about your husband, Mrs Ellman. My condolences." She nods, and gives him a quick smile.

I'm busy with introductions when Margie walks in. She's holding the hand of a younger girl, and she's followed by her parents. Her mother wears a sundress in a bold African pattern, a thick cardigan round her shoulders. Her Dad's shirt collar is open, his sleeves rolled up. I glance at Dan. We've never met Margie's family – they've always been busy in Kenya when Margie arrives at school – but we've seen photos. It's clear that they're related.

"Is that her sister?" Dan nods.

Jake and Amy and their families arrive together, parents deep in conversation. It's clear that they're old friends. There are two brothers in the group – the older boy with short black hair is obviously Jake's brother, and the younger is Amy's. They stop and look around the ballroom, nudging each other and grinning.

Fiona invited everyone who escaped from Camp Bishop – everyone with their face on a Wanted poster – so Jake's here, whether he wants to be or not. He glances at our table, but looks away when he sees me watching.

Charlie's invited her brother, but she walks in with Maz. It's only when she's picked up a drink and found her seat that a man walks in, looking lost. Maz taps her on the shoulder, and she runs to the door, wrapping her arms round her brother and crying. He's crying, too, and

I wonder whether he's ever going to let her go. Maz grins, and shakes his hand. Her brother keeps running his hand through his hair, and looking around as if he can't believe he's here.

*****

"Dan tells me you've been looking after him, Bex." Dan's mum smiles at me.

I glance at Dan. "I think we've been looking after each other, Mrs Pearce."

"They've all taken care of each other." Mum reaches out and puts her hand on my arm. "They're lucky to have such good friends."

I look around the table. Everyone's enjoying their lunch, and everyone's joining in the conversation. Even Margie's sister is chatting with Mum about her life in Kenya.

This isn't as awkward as I thought it would be. I'm surprised to find that I'm enjoying myself.

It's better than the newspaper interviews I sat through this morning, with Dan and Margie and Charlie.

Margie catches my eye, and smiles. I smile back, glancing at her family. She rolls her eyes, but I know she's pleased to see them.

"I gather you've spent some time in the Netherlands?" Dan's father asks across the table.

Margie's mother nods. "We couldn't get into the UK. They wouldn't let us get on the plane, in Kenya." She glances at Margie. "They'd put us on a list. No entry, even though we've got UK passports."

"The Terror Prevention Act." Dan's father nods. "The most abused piece of legislation I've ever worked with." His face brightens. "I'm glad to see you've finally made it back."

"So are we." She looks across at Margie. "We had to watch on TV, while …" She stops, and wipes tears from her lashes.

Dan's father coughs, politely.

"Do you have somewhere to stay, in London?" Dan's mother asks, breaking the awkward silence.

Margie's mother smiles. "We do, thank you. Fiona's very kindly rented a flat for us. It's overwhelming, really, how kind everyone has been."

"I think its the least they can do," Margie's father snaps. "After everything."

"Well, if you need a place, we've got plenty of room." Dan's father smiles. "We're not far from here, and we'd be happy to have you." Dan's mother nods, and I realise that this really is Dan and Margie's 'meet the parents' meal. I take a sip of my drink, hiding my smile.

"And you, Bex? You've got a bed for the night?" Dan's father leans his arm against mine, as if he's sharing a secret.

"I have, thank you. I've got a room upstairs."

"Well – any time you need a break from all this," he waves a hand at the grandeur of the ballroom, "you'd be welcome to stay with us."

His Mum leans over, reaching past her husband to put her hand on my arm. "Honestly, Bex. Any time. You'd be very welcome."

I nod, smiling.

"Thank you. I'll keep that in mind."

*****

There's dessert, and coffee, and Fiona pulls up a chair to join the conversation.

"You should all be very proud," she says, raising her coffee cup. "We wouldn't be here if it wasn't for your children."

Mum puts her hand on my arm, and gives Fiona a smile.

"What this lot have done – escaping from Camp Bishop, getting themselves through the last year – I'm constantly amazed by their courage, and their resilience." She looks round the table. "Not to mention the care they've shown for each other."

I'm blushing now, and so is Dan.

"And as for this past week?" She shakes her head. "I can't tell you how important they've been."

Dan's mum puts her arm round his shoulders, and Margie's dad wraps her in a hug. She hugs him back, tight, hiding her face in his shoulder.

And I realise how much I miss my Dad. I wish he could have been here. Alive, well, laughing with us.

Mum follows my gaze, and squeezes my arm.

"He'd be proud," she says quietly, smiling.

Whispers

Ketty

I carry my lunch tray to an empty table and sit down against the wall, facing the room. I look around at the prisoners. The group of Privates at the next table – Penny among them. Knots of people, eating lunch together. Women in orange jumpsuits, laughing and joking as if this is normal.

Who are we? And where are the officers?

Is it a good sign that I'm here, with them – with the people who don't matter? Will I stay here, after what I told Ryan yesterday?

Or will they move me on? Put me on trial?

I eat the tasteless stew, listening to the conversation at the next table. Something about haircuts, and how they want to dye their hair orange, to match the jumpsuits.

I roll my eyes, and finish my lunch.

I take my tray to the clean-up racks, shafts of pain flashing through my knee. As I walk past Penny's table, the conversation falls quiet. Penny watches me as I force myself to walk without limping, and her friends huddle together, giggling, and whispering.

It's worse than being back at school.

There's a prison guard, watching us as we eat. She's standing next to the security gate, a bored expression on her face. She looks up as I walk over.

"Smith, isn't it?" I nod. "What are you after?"

"I need to see the nurse," I say, as calmly as I can.

She looks me up and down. "Do you?" She asks, her voice flat.

"I need painkillers. I was told to ask the nurse."

She laughs. "I'm sure we'd all like some painkillers, Miss Smith. Why should you be special?"

I close my eyes. I can't believe I have to fight for this. I think of the bottle of tablets I've kept in my pocket, handing out comfort to Bracken, and to myself, whenever we needed them.

"My knee …"

She stares at me, as if this is the worst excuse she's ever heard.

I meet her eyes, but she shakes her head.

"Give it a rest, Smith."

I glare at her for a moment longer, then bend down and roll up the leg of my jumpsuit, pulling it up to my thigh. I hold it there, and look back at the guard.

She stares, taking in the criss-crossing scars, red against my skin.

"What …?"

I can't help smirking. "Gunshot wound." She nods, still staring. "Constant pain. I'd like to see the nurse now, please."

She nods again, pulling the radio from her belt.

"Escort for a prisoner to medical, please. Non-emergency."

I unroll the jumpsuit, and let it drop. "Thank you," I say, as politely as I can.

*****

We sit at a table, waiting for the escort to arrive.

"So who shot you?"

I shrug. "A terrorist."

Her eyes widen. "Which attack?"

I can't help smiling. "Not a public one. I was in uniform. They shot me for protecting a coach load of kids."

"Really?"

210

I nod.

Close enough.

"So what happened?"

"I kept the kids safe."

She gives me an appraising look. "Good job, prisoner. Sounds dangerous."

"It was. The person with me was killed." I'm surprised when I choke on the last word.

"*Killed?*"

I nod.

She shakes her head. "You were lucky."

I was used. I was bait.

"I was lucky."

Her radio crackles, and there's a shout from behind the gate.

"That's your escort," she says, standing up.

I push myself to my feet, glancing back at the dining room.

Everyone on Penny's table is watching me, laughing, as I walk out of the room.

*****

The nurse pokes my knee, her gloved fingers cold against the scars. She looks up as I take a sharp breath.

"This looks painful." I nod. "Everything's swollen. Have you twisted it?"

"I think so." She looks at my face, and my clenched fists, and peels the gloves from her hands.

"So what have you been using? Something on prescription?"

I shake my head. "Something from the chemist."

She nods. "I think we can do better than that."

She pulls a key from her pocket, and unlocks a metal cupboard. She pulls out a plastic bottle, and shakes four tablets onto a tray.

"Two now. Two before bed." She tips two into my hand, and two into a red ziplock bag. She signs the bag with a permanent marker, and hands it to me. "Come back tomorrow, after breakfast, and I'll give you the next dose."

She fills a plastic cup with water and passes it to me. I swallow the tablets and take a drink.

"Do you want to wait here while it takes effect?"

I shake my head, standing up from the bed. "I'll be fine. Thank you."

"Suit yourself," she says, watching me walk out to the waiting guard.

*****

"Friendly with the guards, now, are we, Ketty?"

Penny is sitting on the top bunk when the guard brings me back to the cell.

"Best buddies," I say, lying down. "Jealous?"

There's a pause, and then her head appears over the side of the bed.

"No need to be sarcastic."

I smile, staring up at the slats of her bed.

"Why do you always sit on your own, Ketty?" She actually sounds concerned. I try not to laugh.

Giggles and hair dye? Give me a break.

She watches me, and I realise that she's trying to help. She's trying to be friendly.

"Leave it, Penny," I say, quietly.

"But ..."

I prop myself up on my elbows.

"Let me spell this out for you. I'm a Corporal. I worked for Colonel Bracken. I worked with some of the most wanted members of the Home Forces. When the government works out where I am, I'm going to be in a lot of trouble." She nods. "You," I say, pointing up at her, "are a Private. You were the bottom rung of the ladder. You fetched and carried and smiled and saluted and you had *no idea* what was going on in the conference rooms upstairs."

She stares down at me, horrified, as if I've just punched her. I roll my eyes.

"I did, Penny. I knew. I'm involved, and I've done things that you're better off not knowing about." I lie back on the pillows, one hand over my eyes. "So forgive me if I choose not to sit with you and your friends, and talk about hair dye and prison gossip, and whatever else you find to giggle about. I don't need that, and I don't need you."

There's a pause, and then the bunk shakes as she pulls her head back and throws herself onto the mattress.

Getting the message now, Private? Leave me alone.

Park

Bex

"We can't do this, Fiona. We can't just keep going out there and facing the cameras. You need to give us some time to figure out where we are."

Fiona frowns, and glares at Dan.

"Is that so, Mr Pearce?"

He nods.

We're standing in the lobby of the hotel. The taxi that dropped us off from our third interview this morning is still outside, and Fiona is waiting to tell us what's next on our publicity tour.

"We need to stop. We need a break. We did this yesterday, and the day before, and you want us to keep going all day today. One of our friends was killed on that execution platform, and one of them is in hospital. We need a moment to take everything in."

She looks at Dan, and then at me, one eyebrow raised.

I nod. "I can't do another interview. I can't keep talking about all this."

She pulls a sheet of paper out of the folder she's holding against her chest.

"This afternoon is a photoshoot – you're going to be in your armour for this one – and an interview for the Revolution newspaper. It's for their first edition, and they're very excited to meet you."

"No." She looks up at us, and she's about to protest. "No, Fiona." I'm surprised at how forceful my voice sounds.

"Right," she says, pushing the sheet of paper back into the folder, her voice tight. "So what would you like to do this afternoon? A trip to the seaside? A picnic in the park?"

I know she's joking, but I can't help shrugging. "Sounds good."

Fiona glares. Dan stifles a laugh.

"Maybe I can send Amy to see the newspaper. And Charlie to have her photo taken?"

I shrug again. "I don't care any more, Fiona. I need a break. I need to talk to Mum, and Margie. I need to do something normal, just for an afternoon." Dan's nodding, next to me.

Her shoulders slump.

"Fine. Fine – I'll reschedule. But I need you back and working again tomorrow. This is a limited-time story, and we need to make sure people understand what happened this week. We can't afford to let you drop out of sight."

I make myself smile. "Thanks, Fiona. We'll be ready for tomorrow."

*****

The guards insist on calling taxis to take us into Hyde Park. I don't think they want to repeat the walk to Oxford Street – pushing through crowds, and trying to keep the cameras away.

Charlie's had a word with the kitchen staff, and they've packed us a picnic in old-fashioned wicker baskets. Dan and I have changed out of our smart clothes, and into jeans and trainers. It feels great to be going somewhere by ourselves. Somewhere Fiona hasn't chosen for us.

It's a gorgeous spring day, and there are people walking and jogging beside the lake. We find a spot on the grass, next to the water, and spread out the blankets from the picnic hampers. It doesn't matter that we're wearing fleeces and coats – we're outside, and we're safe. The guards stand in a loose circle around us, protecting us from interruptions, and we're finally alone, and free.

"When did we last do this?" Dan lies back on the blanket, his head on Margie's knees.

Margie looks around, and down at Dan. "I don't think we've ever done this, Pearce," she says. "First time for everything."

He waves his hands. "Not this, exactly. I mean when did we last go outside, and sit around, and do nothing important?"

Margie looks at me, and we're both thinking the same thing.

"School," she says.

"Sitting on the school field." I think about it. "I think we were supposed to be revising, but I don't think we got much work done."

"Do you think they'll have us back?"

"Rushmere?" Margie shakes her head. "Do you want to go back?"

Dan shrugs. "I need to go somewhere. I need to finish educating this exceptional brain." He points to his forehead, and Margie rolls her eyes.

I can't help smiling. Dan's right – it's been too long. We've spent so long hiding our faces and staying out of sight. It's wonderful to sit down on a blanket on the grass and talk about nothing.

"Is he always like this?" Mum's laughing, watching us.

"Yes!"

Dan sits up, surprised by the chorus of voices. Even Maz is laughing at the hurt expression on his face.

"Come on, Dan," he says. "It's true."

He lies back down, pouting. Margie strokes his hair.

"Who wants lunch?" Maz pulls one of the baskets towards him. "I'm starving."

Charlie opens the baskets, and pulls out sandwiches, wrapped in greaseproof paper. Quiches. Carrot sticks and bowls of dips. Punnets of strawberries. Bottles of lemonade and orange juice. There are plates, and plastic wine glasses, and real linen napkins.

"These are for you," she says, smiling, as she throws a packet of sandwiches onto Dan's chest. He picks it up and squints at his name, written in neat handwriting on a sticky label.

"What have you got, Dan?" I glance at Charlie, and she winks at me as Dan sits up and unwraps the parcel.

A grin spreads over his face, and he holds up one of his sandwiches on both palms, like an offering.

"Peanut butter and banana, Bex! Peanut butter and banana!"

Amy grins. Mum leans down and whispers in my ear.

"Is this something I should know about?" She's smiling, and waiting for me to explain.

"It's the first sandwich Dan made for me, when I arrived at Rushmere. It's … kind of important."

She puts her hand on my shoulder, and I realise that she didn't know about Dan, and his sandwiches, and how he made me feel welcome on my first day at boarding school. That she's only just finding out how important my friends have been to me.

We all take our pick from the sandwich pile. Charlie passes out food and plates and napkins, and Maz pours the drinks.

"Do the sandwiches meet with madam's satisfaction?" He asks, as he hands me a glass of lemonade. I give him a wide grin.

"They're amazing, Maz. This is a proper lunch." He nods, and grins back.

We sit and eat, talking and drinking and watching the swans on the water. Charlie and Maz take Mum for a walk round the lake, two guards with guns walking behind them, and I lie back on a blanket and watch the people walking past. Margie and Dan feed each other strawberries, and Amy gathers up the plates and napkins.

Margie moves over on the blanket and sits down next to me. Dan stretches, and stands up, stepping over to help Amy load everything into the baskets.

"You did a good job, Bex."

I don't want to talk about the execution platform again. I don't want to think about Dr Richards, and Will. I don't want to think about the bullets, and the guards.

I nod, looking up at the sunlight through the trees.

"Dan says you kept him going."

I look up at her. This isn't what I was expecting.

She looks out at the lake for a moment, hugging her knees.

"He says you were there for him, when he needed someone to talk to."

I shake my head. "He was there for me, too."

I glance at Dan and Amy, arguing about how to stack plates in the basket.

"I know."

"We had a pact," I say, pushing myself up on my elbows. "Any time we needed to talk, we'd be there for each other."

She nods.

"He got me through what happened with Mum. He talked me out of feeling bad about some really stupid things. He reminded me what was important."

"And you did the same for him."

We both look out at the swans on the water. When she speaks again, her voice is a whisper.

"Am I coming between you?"

I look round at her, and I'm sure I've misunderstood. I sit up, and turn to face her. She looks at me, and there are tears on her cheeks.

"Are you coming between …?" I meet her gaze, and she looks back, tears brimming. "No!"

"I wondered. After all that time …" I shake my head. "It's just … when we're alone …" She closes her eyes. "He's so careful. There are things he won't talk about. Things he won't say, in front of me. It's as if he thinks I'll break, if he does. As if I'm made of glass."

I look at my friend. At the person we saved from the firing squad. At the person I nearly lost, again.

And I think about Dan, in the common room. Dan at the safe house in London, so close to giving up.

"He's hurting too, Margie," I say, quietly. "We were terrified that we wouldn't reach you in time. He's played your execution in his head so many times." She shakes her head, eyes shut tight against her tears. "And now you're here, and part of him doesn't really believe it. He's terrified of losing you again."

She nods, and opens her eyes, brushing the tears away from her cheeks with her fingers.

"You're sure? You're sure he wants to be with me?"

I look across at Dan, doing his best to distract Amy. To give us some time alone. He points at something on the path, laughing with her.

I shake my head. "Dan adores you, Margie. There's no way he wants to be with anyone else."

She gives me a brief smile through her tears. "And what about you, Bex? Am I stealing him from you?"

I stare at her, shaking my head. Trying to find the right words.

"You know Dan. You know *us*, Margie. He's like a crazy twin brother to me. I'd take a bullet for him, and he'd take one for me, but I'm not … We're not …" I screw up my face, and push against her shoulder. "Eeeuuw!"

She smiles, and puts out a hand to steady herself. She pushes the tears from her face.

"Thank you," she whispers. "I had to make sure."

Dan shouts as Amy punches his shoulder. He falls to his knees, clutching his arm, clowning around and making her laugh.

I pull a face. "He's all yours, Margie," I say, pulling her into a hug. "And I'm really glad you're back. We missed you."

She hugs me back, tightly, and there are tears in my eyes when she lets me go.

*****

It's nearly five when we pack up our blankets and the guards escort us back to the taxis. Mum chatters to Charlie as we drive away, and I lean back in my seat and look out of the window, watching the trees, and the light on the water.

I can't believe the afternoon is over already. I have to go back to Fiona, and whatever she has planned for tomorrow.

"You OK?" Maz says, watching me.

I shrug, and he nods, following my gaze out of the window.

Back at the hotel, there's a message waiting for us at reception. Fiona wants to see me and Dan and Amy.

She's set up an office in one of the meeting rooms. There's a TV and a laptop in front of her on the table, along with two phones, and piles of folders and paperwork.

"Come in," she calls, looking up. "I trust you've all had a lovely day in the park." She doesn't smile.

We file into the room, Dan closing the door behind us.

"I have your schedules for tomorrow." She hands us each a sheet of paper. "I need you all ready, and smart, for a nine o'clock start." She looks at me. "I trust that meets with your approval."

I nod, and she gives me a tight smile. "Good. I'll see you all in the lobby at nine."

We thank her, and walk out of the room. As I turn to leave, the image on the laptop screen catches my eye.

It's Ketty. Ketty, in an orange jumpsuit, sitting in an interrogation room. She's handcuffed to the table, and the freeze-frame catches her as she's tugging at her handcuffs, saying something to the man with his back to the camera.

Ketty, sitting where Mum sat. Where Margie sat.

Ketty in handcuffs.

I can't hide my smile as I walk out, wondering what they're charging her with.

Where they'll begin with the list of her crimes.

Revenge

Ketty

Penny's out of bed before the alarm in the morning, and I wake up to the sound of my possessions hitting the floor.

"Oops." She says, sliding her hand back along the empty shelf, silhouetted by the emergency light above the door.

The painkillers have worn off, and I'm about to drag myself out of bed when the alarm sounds. The cell lights come on, catching Penny in the act of kicking my hairbrush under the bed. It hits the wall behind me, and I know I don't have time to pick it up before the guard arrives.

I kneel down, gritting my teeth against the pain in my knee, and pick up my toothbrush, soap, and underwear, untangling everything from my towel and jumpsuit. Penny smirks, watching me.

I fold everything carefully into my towel, then wrap my jumpsuit round it, ignoring her. I pull myself up and step over to the door to wait for the guard.

And just before the door opens, I reach across and take Penny's hairbrush, pushing it into a pocket of my jumpsuit before she can react.

Her face is a mask of fury.

I do my best to hide a smile.

Don't underestimate me, Private.

*****

We wait in line for the showers. Penny pushes her way forward and stands with her friends, whispering and glancing back at me. I stand up straight, ignoring the prisoners around me.

Discipline, determination, backbone. You're better than this.

We file in. I drop my jumpsuit bundle on the changing bench and pull out my towel and soap. I hang my towel and pyjamas on the hook above the bench, and step into the shower.

There's no privacy in here. There's a guard on the door, and there are twenty of us in here at a time. I shower as fast as I can, and then run the soap through my hair, eyes closed as I rinse it out.

When I open my eyes, mine is the only shower running. I turn round, wringing the water from my hair, and my stomach sinks.

Everyone else is dressed.

The guard is gone from the door – I don't know how they've distracted her. Everyone else is sitting on the bench, watching me.

I stand up straight, ignoring the giggling from Penny and her friends, and step out of the shower.

My towel is gone.

My clothes are gone.

The giggling gets louder.

I stare at the space on the bench. There are nineteen women, watching me. Waiting for me to make a move.

And I don't know what else they're planning.

I think of Elizabeth, falling in the shower. I think of Margaret, hugging her knees, her skin painted with bruises.

I could start a fight. Nineteen of them against one of me.

I could give up. I could ask for my clothes.

And they could refuse.

Or I could do something they're not expecting.

Choose, Ketty. Make a decision.

I pull myself up. I straighten my back, and imagine I'm on the field at Camp Bishop. I look round at the figures in their orange jumpsuits, and give each of them a recruit-scaring stare.

Penny shrinks back. The giggling stops.

The room is silent.

I turn, naked and wet from the shower, and walk towards the door.

There's some muttering, and someone shouts at me, but I keep walking. Out into the corridor, past the women behind us in the queue, and out into the dining room.

All the conversations stop. Everyone is watching me.

Staring at my scars. Staring at my body.

Keep going, Ketty. This only works if you don't stop.

My heart is pounding, sending jolts of pain through my knee with every beat. My hair is wet – cold and heavy against my neck. Water tracks down my back and drips from my fingers as I walk.

I head for the guard at the door. She's talking to the guard from the showers, and they both look up as I walk over and stand smartly at ease in front of them. I can feel the eyes of everyone in the room on my bare skin.

"Miss Smith," says the dining room guard, and I allow myself a smile. It's the woman who called for my escort to medical, yesterday. "You seem to be missing something."

The shower guard's face turns pale, and she's swearing as she runs across the dining room.

I force myself to stand up straight.

"Can't seem to find my clothes, Sir," I say, trying to keep my face neutral. I can hear shouting as the guard reaches the showers.

The dining room guard looks me up and down, taking in my scars and bruises, watching the water pooling round my feet. She rolls her eyes.

"Did they …?"

I shrug. The shouting grows louder.

She stares at me, and glances towards the showers.

She doesn't know what to do. The dining room is quiet around us. The guard is still shouting at Penny and the others.

No one knows what to do.

It's thrilling, manipulating people like this. Refusing to be humiliated.

I'm the one standing naked in front of everyone, and right now, I have all the power.

I have to hide a smile. I'm starting to enjoy this.

She shakes her head, and puts her hand on my elbow.

"Come with me."

*****

The guard takes me to my cell, and radios for someone to bring me new clothes. She leans against the door frame, watching me as I sit on my bunk, wrapped in my blanket. Her eyes keep flicking from the fading bruises on my neck to the scars on my knee.

"Made yourself some enemies, Smith?"

"I haven't made any friends, if that's what you mean." I shrug. "Giggling and gossip aren't really my thing."

She rolls her eyes again. "That's a yes, then," she says, looking out at the corridor.

Someone in a cleaners' uniform arrives, carrying a bundle. Everything I need, wrapped in an orange jumpsuit. She gapes at me, and I smile back at her. She hands the bundle over and walks away.

The guard passes it to me, and turns back to the corridor.

"I'll let you get dressed." She looks at me as she's closing the door. "Make some friends, Smith. You're going to need them."

*****

Penny doesn't come back to the cell, and her friends don't show up at lunch. I sit on my own, drinking my bottle of water, and looking round at the other tables.

It's amazing how easy it was to silence a room full of people. How quickly the guard brought me what I needed.

And how good it felt, taking control of a situation where I was supposed to play the victim.

I'm smiling to myself when someone walks past me and stops.

"That was amazing. Well done." Her voice is quiet in my ear. I look round, but she's already walking away.

Someone else sits down beside me for a moment, her back to the table. "Smart move," she says, before she stands up and leaves.

"That was brave. Keep it up." I don't see who says that. When I turn round, she's gone.

I smile again. It might have been brave, but it's nothing I haven't done before. Pushing myself to do what needed to be done.

Gutting chickens. Dealing with Dad. Dealing with Bracken.

Learning to walk again.

I pull this morning's bag of painkillers from my pocket and swallow two, washing them down with the last of the water.

You can do this, Ketty.

226

Until the government decides what's next, you can do this.

*****

Penny has been crying when the guard brings her back to the cell. She's missed lunch and dinner, and it's only a few minutes until lights out. She walks in, her nose in the air, ignoring me as she walks to the bunk.

"Good day, Penny?" I ask, smirking.

The bed frame shudders as she climbs the ladder and slumps down onto the mattress.

I'm grinning now, out of sight on the bottom bunk. "How's the discipline here? Is it tough love, or hard labour?"

There's a sob, and a pause while she takes a breath.

"Shut up, Ketty," she says, spitting the words at me.

I shake my head, still smiling, and keep quiet.

Don't underestimate me, Penny.

Publicity

Bex

We're visiting a hospital this morning – Netherlands fighters and resistance members who were injured in the invasion. Me, Dan, and Amy. Smart suits, Liaison Officers, guards.

And cameras.

Press photographers and TV camera crews follow us through the wards as we stop and talk to the injured fighters. The curtains have been pulled back between the beds, and there's a party atmosphere as we make our way to meet each patient. People are happy to see us. Everyone wants a photo with the Face of the Resistance, and the heroes who pulled Margie from the stage.

There are gunshot wounds from Horse Guards Parade – stray bullets from the stage that hit people in the crowd. And there are injuries from the fighting we didn't see. Soldiers holding off the Home Forces. Holding our positions while the coalition arrived.

So many people who put their lives at risk to help us. To keep us safe. To make sure we had a chance.

I listen to their stories, thinking about the bullets slamming into me as I stood on the stage. I know my armour saved me, and I know that there must be people who didn't make it.

It's a shock, when I realise I'm talking to the lucky ones.

Dr Richards is in a private room, hooked up to machines and drips and monitors. She's awake, but she's groggy, and her injuries are bandaged under her hospital gown. I sit and hold her hand for a few minutes, doing my best to ignore the cameras, but I'm not sure she knows we're here.

I make myself smile for their photos, and wave to the TV crews, but I'm relieved when we say goodbye to the nurses and head back out to the waiting car.

*****

Our next appointment is a photoshoot. The newspaper has tracked down another wall of resistance posters, and they want me to stand in front of my repeated image. They try shots of me smiling, and shots where I'm staring past the photographer, lost in my thoughts.

It feels ridiculous, after the hospital, and I'm wondering again about the person who put the posters up. Who they were, and whether they were caught.

Whether they were executed.

"Bex!" I look up, and the photographer waves at me. "One with your friends?"

He sends Amy and Dan to stand next to me, and we find ourselves laughing. Five days ago we'd have been shot for standing here. For showing our faces on a London street. And here we are, smiling for the camera.

Dan puts his arm round my shoulders, and Amy puts an arm round my waist, and we can't keep straight faces.

I can't believe this is real.

The photographer shows us the photos, afterwards. We look happy, and carefree – completely at odds with the posters behind us. He assures us that the editor will love them.

*****

The rest of the day is packed. Radio interviews, the newspaper interview we skipped yesterday, and a meeting with the OIE's opponents – the people who were in charge before the introduction of Martial Law.

Before Leominster.

The woman who talks to us is friendly and cheerful, and I have to remind myself that she works for the ex-Prime Minister. The person who agreed to hand over power to the Home Forces.

"I'm so pleased to meet you all," she says, showing us to our seats at a long conference table. "We know you're working with Fiona Price, and we understand that she's the one who's been protecting you." We all nod, and I'm wondering what she's going to ask us to do. "We're very keen to make sure that this doesn't stop us from connecting with you."

I stare at her across the table, anger swelling in my chest. This is the party that introduced the emergency powers – stopping elections and stripping people of the right to vote. This is the party that approved the Emergency Armed Forces Act, and allowed the Recruit Training Service to conscript teenagers.

This is the party that allowed our abduction to Camp Bishop, and encouraged everything that happened to us there.

They enabled Jackson's fists and Ketty's cruelty. I can feel the breath, knocked out of my lungs as Jackson threw punches and Ketty pinned me to the ground. I remember sitting with Saunders, outside the gates in the rain.

I'm shaking my head and standing up before she can say any more.

"Bex?" Dan reaches out and takes my hand.

"I can't. I'm not going to sit here with the people who started all this."

"Bex. We should at least listen …"

"To what, Dan? To the people who sent us to Camp Bishop?" I point at the woman across the table, my hands shaking. "If it wasn't for these people, we'd all still be at school. You, me, Margie. Studying for exams.

Our worst nightmares would be about exam questions and revision, not bullets and safe houses and executions." I shake my head, pushing away images of Leominster. Of the City Killer, and the line of empty cars.

And I think about the bunker. About Saunders, lying on the cold gatehouse floor. I can't be polite. I can't hold back my anger.

"Joss would still be alive, if it wasn't for these people." Amy gasps. "Joss Saunders would still be at school. Drawing, taking photos. Making a life." My voice is a harsh whisper. "Joss is dead because these people sent him to Camp Bishop."

I twist out of his grip, and walk out of the room.

As I walk out to the car, I'm brushing tears from my eyes, and I'm relieved to find Amy and Dan behind me as I climb inside.

*****

"How can Fiona do this?" I shake my head. "How can she send us to talk to *them*?"

Dan shrugs. "Fair play, I guess. They're organising elections, and the ex-PM is going up against Fiona to run the country. Fiona needs to look as if she's playing fair."

The others are sitting in my room – on the bed and on the sofa – but I can't sit still. I'm pacing up and down between the door and the window, trying to contain my anger.

"But why did she think we would want to talk to them? How could she send us in there, as if this was just another interview?"

I'm trying to understand. I'm trying to make everything fit together, but this doesn't make sense.

"She probably didn't think about it, Bex." Amy shakes her head. "And they were nice to us."

I want to scream.

"Of course they were nice to us! They want us to support them!" I'm shouting, and Amy shrinks back as I walk past her.

Charlie shrugs.

"Maybe they don't want your support. Maybe they just want to stop you from campaigning against them." She shakes her head. "I don't understand it either, Bex."

I clench my fists and let out a yell.

Dan looks up at me.

"I think I know what they're doing."

I stop pacing and glare at him, waiting for him to explain.

"I think they're trying to use us to promote the elections, not influence the outcome."

I feel as if I've dropped into freezing water.

I have to catch my breath.

Dan's right. It makes sense.

"You think Fiona wants us to stop fighting the bad guys, and tell everyone what a good thing it is that they get to vote again?"

He nods.

I hold my hands up, shaking my head. "But why wouldn't Fiona want us to support her? To support the OIE?"

Dan bows his head.

"I don't know, Bex," he says, softly.

The room is quiet. No one has anything to say.

Maz coughs.

"I don't think she needs you to support her."

"Then what …?"

He shrugs. "Sorry, Bex, but as much as you hate it, everyone knows who you are. And everyone knows who's been protecting you." He waves a hand. "That's what all these interviews are about. Reminding the voters that it was Fiona and the OIE who got you out of the UK, and Fiona who got you back in, with her coalition at your backs."

I nod, thinking about all the publicity we're giving Fiona and her party, just by telling our stories.

"So she's already got our support, as far as the public can see?"

He smiles. "Absolutely. She doesn't need to have you campaigning for her, as long as you're not campaigning against her."

I stare at him, shaking my head.

Charlie nods.

"I think Dan's right. I reckon they're going to use you all as the Faces of the Election. Use your stories to make sure people vote. They need to get people excited about democracy again." She points at me. "And you're the most exciting news they've seen in years."

I throw up my hands in frustration.

"She's never going to stop using us, is she?"

Margie raises an eyebrow.

"What do you mean?"

I can feel the fight going out of me. There's nothing I can do to stop this. I pull the chair out from the desk and sit down, my elbows on my knees.

"She's the one who put my face on the resistance posters. She's the one who tried to package our stories without understanding what we've been through." I roll my eyes. "She's the one who put me on the OIE Committee, to keep reminding them why they needed to fight." I look up, at everyone watching me. I'm finally piecing this together. "But that's not why I was there."

"Bex?"

I think it through. Asking to observe the committee. Taking Fiona's offer of a seat at the table. Believing her when she promised they would listen.

And the coalition. The list of their requirements to justify the invasion.

"I was there as the figurehead. I was there to sweeten the deal for the coalition." I shake my head. "She wasn't planning on listening to me at all. She just needed to show that I was on her side. That the face on the posters was the face of *her* movement."

I feel sick. I feel used.

None of it was real. I worked for the committee. I kept their secrets, and I helped pick the target for the South Bank Bomb. The blood of the victims is on my hands, but none of it was real.

Fiona didn't need my input. She needed my face.

Charlie was wrong. I wasn't a player at the table – I was a playing piece in Fiona's game.

"She needed me, because she needed her invasion. And now she wants to run the country."

I slump back in my chair, staring at the ceiling. I can't believe I didn't see this before.

"And we've done her campaigning for her," Dan says, nodding. "We stormed the execution platform, live on TV. You gave the only election speech she'll ever need.

"Even if we refuse to do anything else, Fiona's already taken everything she needs."

Physical

Ketty

It's after dinner when they come for me. We have some free time in the dining hall after the meal, and I'm walking back from the toilets when the lights go out in the corridor, and someone throws an arm round my neck from behind, dragging me backwards. I'm knocked off my feet, struggling to stand in the sudden darkness. My throat is still sore from Bracken's attack, and I'm choking as I fall, my feet slipping on the tiled floor.

My back hits the ground, smashing the breath from my lungs, and my head cracks against the tiles, pain bursting like a firework in my skull. I try to sit up, but someone I can't see locks their arm across my neck, pushing down hard. I'm flashing back to Bracken, his fingers digging into my throat, and I'm fighting panic. I reach up to push my attacker away, but two more women grab my arms, and pin them to the floor. Someone else locks their hands round my ankles.

I close my eyes, and wait for the punches.

Iron fists and steel toe caps. I know how this goes.

There's a voice, hissing in my ear. I can feel her breath, hot on my face.

"Think you're better than us, Corporal? Not here. We're all the same, here." I nod, carefully, my head and neck still pinned against the floor.

"A bit of respect. That's all we want." Another voice. I nod again. "We know you were Bracken's bitch. We know you ran his interrogations."

"We know about you and Corporal Conrad." The hissing voice is back, next to my cheek. Someone else makes kissing noises, and laughs. "He had some things to say about you, *Ketty*."

Not punches, then. Rumours. Lies.

I roll my eyes, grateful for the darkness.

"Bracken's bitch, and Conrad's bitch. Did you get on your knees for Lee, too?"

I'm fighting. I'm pulling my arms up and kicking and throwing my head forward, but the arm on my neck presses down harder, and the grips on my arms and legs only get stronger. I'm pinned, I'm outnumbered, and I can't fight them off.

I make myself relax.

It's just words.

Get through this. Wait for them to leave.

The breath on my face fades as the person behind me sits up.

"She has a weak point." It's a statement, not a question. "Which knee was it, Penny?"

I can't breathe. Panic locks my muscles and my pulse slams through my body. I can feel my hands, shaking against the floor.

They've seen me without my jumpsuit. They've seen the scars. They've seen me limping.

They were there in the showers. They were there in the dining room, when I showed the guard.

"The right knee," says Penny, calmly.

I want to shout, but the arm is still against my throat. I throw my head to one side, dislodging the choke hold.

"No no no no NO NO NO!" I shout as loud as I can, until someone claps a hand across my mouth.

I'm begging. I'm pleading with my captors. This is the weakness I've enjoyed, in my prisoners.

This is who I am.

This is fear.

My whole body is shaking as I feel the grip on my arms shift. Someone swaps their hand for a knee, pressing into the bone, just below my elbow. I try to twist out of her grip, but she leans on my leg, pinning me to the floor. I pull one arm free, and reach up to grab the person behind me by her hair.

But it's too late.

The world explodes into pain. Something smashes into my knee. Something hard and unforgiving, and I feel bone, breaking. All the pain of the bullet, all the pain of learning to walk again, all the pain of the PowerGel, failing, crashes into me, and I'm screaming.

The hands let go. The arm lifts from my throat, but I don't feel it. All I can feel is the hot, shrieking pain in my knee.

When I open my eyes, I'm curled up on the floor. The lights are on in the corridor, and my attackers have gone.

The pain is everywhere.

I'm alone, and I'm still screaming.

Fiona

Bex

"That's it. I'm going to go and talk to her. I want to know what's going on."

Dan jumps out of his seat at the breakfast table, catching my elbow and slowing me down.

The conversation from last night is still going. I've been thinking about all the ways Fiona has used me, and I want answers.

"Wait, Bex. We don't know what she wants. We're just trying to understand …"

"And that's why I'm going to ask her a straight question." I glare at him. "Coming?"

He drops my elbow, shaking his head. When I turn back at the door, he's still standing, watching me, Margie's hand against his back.

*****

"Bex." Fiona looks up from her laptop as I walk into her conference room. "I'm a little busy …"

I don't let her finish. I'm not going to let her send me away.

"I want to know what I'm doing here."

She blinks, staring at me, and shakes her head. "I don't have time for this."

I stand in front of her, my hands shaking. I know I should walk away. I know I should leave her alone. Come back later.

Do what she wants.

I know Dan should be here, holding me back, but I'm too angry to leave.

I pull out the chair next to hers, and sit down. She closes her laptop and sits back in her chair, folding her arms.

"What is it, Miss Ellman? What's so important that you have to talk about it now?"

I force myself to meet her gaze. I need an answer. I need her to be honest with me.

"What are you expecting from me, Fiona?"

She shakes her head again, shrugging her shoulders.

"I don't know what you mean."

I take a deep breath. I need to make her understand.

"You saved us, Fiona. I know that." She nods. "You had us picked up, after the bunker raid. You got us out of the UK. You protected us, in Edinburgh. And you got us back here, with an army behind us." She starts to speak, but I cut her off. "You got us where we needed to be, and our friends are alive. Mum's free. We couldn't have done all that without you."

My hands are still shaking, and Fiona is waiting for me to continue. I need to think clearly about this. I need to explain.

"I was your Face of the Resistance. I let you use my photo, on all those posters." I can't help pulling a face. "And I hate that photo." She laughs, once. "I made your videos. I made your speeches. I let you put me on your committee."

She raises an eyebrow. "As I recall, you demanded a seat on the OIE Committee."

"You didn't need to give it to me." I throw my hands up in frustration. "I mean, what was I doing there? A seventeen-year-old girl, with the rest of you? With all your experience? Casting votes and debating with you?"

"A seventeen-year-old with combat experience, Bex. A seventeen-year-old with inside knowledge of the Home Forces, and the resistance. Don't sell yourself short."

I nod. I haven't thought about it that way. "OK. So there were some things I could help you with."

"And so we asked you to join us."

I'm staring at my hands in my lap. I need to make my accusation. I need to say what I came here to say.

I look up at her.

"I think I was there to convince the coalition to support you."

She watches me, a smile spreading over her face. I can feel the colour rising in my cheeks.

"You're right, Bex. That was part of the deal. I told you they needed a figurehead, and putting you on the committee showed them that we were serious."

This is too easy. I came here to argue. I came here to make my case, and she's agreeing with me.

"So you planned that?"

She laughs again. "Of course I planned it." She looks around the room, pointing at the black and white photos of London on the walls. "And it got us here, didn't it?" I nod. "It got you here. It got your mother out of the cells, and saved your friends from execution."

She's using Mum. She's using Margie.

She's trying to justify everything she's done.

But she's right. Putting me on the committee did help us to get here.

"And what about now? All these interviews and photos and parties?"

She looks down at the table, and back up at me.

"I know this is hard, Bex. I know all you wanted to do was save your friend, and your mother. But we still need you."

I stare at her, the anger building in my chest. "To do *what*?"

She clasps her hands together on the table in front of her.

"You're the Face of the Resistance, Bex. You're the person who made the speech at Horse Guards Parade." I nod, clenching my fists. "You're still the figurehead. You're still the symbol everyone's looking up to."

"I don't want …"

"I know. But please, Bex, just for a bit longer. You're making people feel good about all the changes we're making. About having the King in charge while we arrange the elections. This is all new to the people out there, Bex. They're used to bombings and firing squads and the Home Forces. We're asking them to adjust to democracy again. To freedom. And we're using foreign soldiers to do it."

She smiles at me, waiting for an answer. Waiting for me to say yes.

I let her wait.

She shakes her head. "It's scary for people, watching Polish soldiers patrolling their streets. French soldiers. Spanish, Dutch. German. They need to know that there's a plan. That we haven't been invaded. That the fight was with the military government, not with the people of the UK."

I close my eyes. I can see what she's saying, but she's not listening to me.

"Think about what could happen, if you walked away. If the Face of the Resistance stopped supporting the coalition."

I shrug. "What?"

"The situation is delicate. People don't like seeing coalition soldiers in their towns. What if they stopped trusting us? What if they started fighting back?" She shakes her head. "We could lose everything, Bex. Everything we've fought for. We could find ourselves with a proper civil war on our hands." She looks at me. "Do you know how destructive that would be?"

And I realise that she's right. There's no Prime Minister. No government to blame for all this. There's no focus for people's fear and anger.

But there is a focus for their hope. There's a focus for their struggle.

There's someone who knows what they've been through.

And that's me.

I'm the figurehead. I'm the Face of the UK.

I'm the person holding this together.

I shake my head, and force myself to breathe. To stay calm.

"And what about the other side? Your political opponents. What am I supposed to do for them?"

She looks down. "I heard about that. You didn't stay long enough to find out, did you?"

I shake my head, and try to stop myself from shouting. "How can I work with them, after they handed us over to the RTS? And how does it help anyone if we're working for both sides?"

She takes a deep breath. "OK. Yes, I'm running against the former Prime Minister, and yes – we both want the job." I nod. "But more than that, we both want a country that isn't tearing itself apart." She looks at me, and she's smiling. "I know what they did, and that's why I'm running against them. But we both need you, Bex. We need you keeping everyone happy. We need you supporting the process of change. We need you on our election broadcasts, because we need people to see a familiar face. We need them to see the Face of the Resistance, the person who told them to resist, leading the way back to democracy."

I roll my eyes. Dan was right – I'm the Face of the Election. The Face of the UK.

"How long do you need me, Fiona?"

She shrugs. "At least until the elections. After that, people will feel as if they've got their country back."

I stare at her. "That could be months!"

She looks back at me, calmly. "It will be months."

"I can't do this for months! I can barely do it now!" I'm shouting. I feel like crying. "My friends – we're all exhausted. We've been on the run for a year. We need to stop, and figure out who we are, after all the running. We can't be your figureheads. We can't carry on."

"You can, Bex." She puts a hand on my arm, and I feel my muscles stiffen under her fingers. "You need to. We're doing everything we can to make it easy for you." She waves a hand at the room. "We've got the use of the hotel for as long as we need it. You've got your own rooms. You've got guards on the doors, keeping everyone away. We're keeping you safe, and we're giving you a home."

"It's not enough, Fiona," I say eventually. "We need to recover. We need time. We need to remember who we are."

She nods. "OK, Bex. I hear you. I'll bear all that in mind." I start to speak, but she carries on. "Let me know what you need, and I'll do my best to make it happen. And I'll make sure you know what we need. Deal?"

I don't want to agree to this. I don't want her to keep using us. But she's right. She needs us.

This country needs us.

I don't want everything we've done to be wasted.

I nod, slowly. "Deal."

"Thank you, Bex." She says. "I know this is hard. Just … keep going, for now. Keep doing what you're doing."

She smiles, and opens her laptop. I'm standing up to leave when she opens the video again – the one I saw two days ago.

A freeze-frame of Ketty, chained to a table.

I point at the screen.

"What's going to happen to the prisoners?"

She looks up in surprise, and nods. "Katrina Smith. You've got some history, you two, haven't you?" I nod.

She looks at the screen.

"It depends who they are. Some of the ringleaders are looking at life in jail. Others might get shorter sentences. At the moment we're just trying to work out who we've caught, and where they're locked up. There are a lot of prisoners, but not much information. We're trying to find out what people have done. Whether we can build a case for a trial. What we can charge them with, and who to use for the high-profile trials. Who to put on TV."

"I can help you with that one," I say, pointing my finger at the image on the screen. "I can give you a list."

Fiona raises an eyebrow. "Really? I'd be interested to hear your list."

I stare at her, then start talking, counting off Ketty's crimes on my fingers.

It takes a while, and Fiona listens, asking questions and making sure she understands.

And all I can think about is Ketty in court, TV cameras running as she listens to her guilty verdict.

Past

Ketty

The morning alarm sounds, and I struggle to open my eyes. I try to sit up, and swing my legs off the bed, but my leg won't move. I try again, and a bright flash of pain bursts through my knee.

I sink back against the pillows, and it takes me a moment to remember where I am.

Prison. Hospital.

On the losing side.

*****

"Breakfast."

The nurse pushes through the curtains and puts a tray down on the table. I'm pushing myself up on my elbows when she turns to help me, and I wave her away.

I can do this.

I push myself upright on the bed. I lift myself with my arms, ignoring the sting of the needle from the morphine drip, and drag myself backwards until I'm sitting against the pillows. My knee, bandaged and braced with plastic splints, pulses with pain as I move, but the hospital painkillers make it bearable, as if I'm floating above the hammer blows. As if I'm floating above everything. She pushes the table over the bed.

Cereal. Milk. An apple. A pot of yoghurt. A bottle of orange juice. A vitamin tablet. Better than the food in the dining room.

"Eat up," she says, cheerfully. "You've got a visitor."

Another interrogation.

"Colonel Ryan again?"

She shrugs. "No idea." She points at the breakfast tray. "Eat."

She starts to walk away, but I touch her elbow.

"Could I get a hairbrush? And a blanket?" I wave my hands at my bandage, and the shorts I'm wearing. "I don't want to be interrogated like this."

She nods. "Fair enough. I'll see what I can do."

*****

"Someone to see you."

The nurse pulls back the curtain round my bed, and Colonel Ryan steps into the booth. The nurse helped me to wash, and brought me a hospital blanket and a sweatshirt – grey to match my T-shirt and shorts. I've brushed my hair, and pulled it back into a smart pony tail. It's hardly a uniform, but it's not a jumpsuit either. It's the best I can do, in here.

"Miss Smith."

"Yes, Sir."

He puts a heavy folder down on the table.

"That will be all," he tells the nurse. She closes the curtain and walks away.

He sits down on the stool beside my bed, glancing at the blanket over my bandaged leg.

"This is unusual," he says, eventually. "I prefer to have a private room to talk to prisoners." He looks around at the curtained booth. "But this will have to do." He points at my knee. "I gather you're having trouble walking, Miss Smith."

"Yes, Sir."

Nothing I haven't dealt with before.

"Unfortunate."

"Yes, Sir." I keep my voice calm, as if we're talking about the weather. Blocking out thoughts of the dark corridor. The hissing voice in my ear. The hands, gripping my arms and legs. The stretcher to the prison hospital, every step jolting the broken bones and the scar tissue.

"I have some more questions for you."

I nod. This isn't so bad. No cameras, no one-way mirrors. No handcuffs.

He opens the folder, and pulls out a voice recorder. He sets it running, and places it on the table.

Careful, Ketty. This isn't a friendly chat.

"We covered a lot of ground last time we spoke." He picks up the voice recorder, checking the power light, and puts it back on the table. "This time I'd like to talk about the decisions you've made."

I stare at him. I don't understand what he's saying.

"Tell me – what made you join the RTS, Miss Smith?"

More cold questions. I close my eyes, wondering what he wants to know. Thinking back to my life before Camp Bishop. Before Bracken.

Before Jackson.

And I'm telling him about Mum, leaving. Dad, doing his best, but always drunk. About leaving school. About Ken, and my job at the butcher's shop.

About getting out, and getting away, and joining the Recruit Training Service as soon as they'd have me.

My thoughts are foggy. The morphine is choking my mind, and it's like trying to think in slow motion. But I answer his question.

He nods, and listens, the red light on the voice recorder steady as I speak.

"And was the RTS what you hoped it would be?"

"Yes." The word is out of my mouth before I've really thought about it.

It was safety and challenge and structure. It was responsibility and consequences.

It was justice.

I try to explain, but I'm aware that I'm slurring my words. That I'm not making sense.

"One moment, Sir." He nods, and watches, eyebrows raised as I tug on the needle in my arm. I pull out the morphine drip, and push my fingers against my skin to stop the bleeding. I need to be thinking clearly. I need to say the right things.

"Ready, Sir," I say, meeting his eyes. He blinks, and looks away.

Too much for you, Sir?

I can't help smiling.

"Your promotion to London, Miss Smith. How did that come about?"

"Colonel Bracken. He requested me as his assistant."

"And why would he do that?"

I shrug, still thinking through the painkiller fog. "I was his Lead Recruit. I worked with him through Leominster. I helped in the hunt for our lost recruits. I took a *bullet* for his recruits." I'm vaguely aware that I'm hammering a finger on my chest as I say this. "And I worked with him on the raid at Makepeace Farm."

"So he trusted you then."

I think of the whisky bottles on the shelf in his office. The secrets I kept for him.

I try not to smile. "Yes. He trusted me."

"And the Terrorism Committee?"

Wake up, Ketty. Don't say anything stupid.

"What about it?"

"You kept Bracken going. You made sure he could do his job."

I nod. "Every day."

"So you supported the Terrorism Committee?"

I blink, trying to clear my thoughts.

"I didn't know …"

"What did you think they were doing, Miss Smith?"

"I don't know. Catching terrorists."

248

"And are you proud of your decisions?"

"Am I *proud*?"

He nods, watching me. I don't understand what he wants to know.

I think about it. Am I proud?

Have I made good decisions?

Have I done the right thing?

I look around the tiny booth. At the curtains, screening us off from the ward outside. At the morphine drip, and the blanket, and my broken knee. At the limits of my freedom.

And I laugh.

What's the point?

I can't change anything. Everything that happened, happened. I can't go back and undo it.

I made decisions, and they made sense when I made them. Get out of the RTS. Get promoted. Protect me, protect Bracken.

And here I am, in a prison hospital, my knee smashed again, talking to someone who only wants to know about the past.

Part of me knows this is the morphine, messing with my head. And part of me doesn't care.

"Thank you, Miss Smith," he says, reaching to switch off the recorder.

Dark

Bex

"Is this one of those 'any time you need to talk' moments, Bex?"

I nod. Dan's standing outside my door with Margie, waiting to go to breakfast. We've got an hour before Fiona wants us in the lobby, ready to meet another set of journalists.

But I haven't slept. I spent most of the night staring at the ceiling, trying not to wake Mum in the other bed. In the end, I came in here, and curled up in my own bed.

I'm fighting tears as I open the door.

Dan gives Margie a shrug, and she puts her hand on his elbow.

"I'll wait for you downstairs."

He nods, and follows me into the room. I sit down on the bed, and Dan sits next to me.

"What's up, Bex?"

I take a deep breath, but I can't stop the tears from spilling down my face. My voice feels rough and broken.

I need to talk to someone, and I'm pretty sure Dan's the only person who will understand.

"How do you do it?" It's barely more than a whisper.

"How do I do what?"

"Live with it. With the bad stuff."

He leans back on his elbows. "You mean killing people?"

When he says that out loud, it's like throwing a punch.

I nod. "Yeah."

He shrugs. "I don't know, Bex."

I turn to look at him. "But you do, though. You're not awake all night, thinking about it."

"Some nights," he says, looking away.

"But …"

"I'm not a robot, Bex. I know what I've done. And yes, it keeps me awake sometimes."

"Really?"

"Yes."

I crawl back to the pillows and tuck my legs under the covers. I wanted answers. I wanted to know that he has this figured out.

But he's as broken as I am.

"Does it get better? Does it stop?"

He shakes his head. "It gets … less vivid. The memories fade. But I still know what I did."

I look down at my hands, feeling the weight of the rifle again. "Yeah."

He sits up, and turns to face me.

"How do you feel? How does it make you feel?"

I shrug. "Horrible. Like I've done the worst thing I could possibly do."

It feels good to say that out loud.

"Guilty, then?"

"I guess. But worse than that. As if there's something bad inside me. Something dark."

He nods. "As if you could do it again?"

There are tears in my eyes as I look at Dan. At my friend, who has my back. Who knows what I've been through. Who knows what I've done.

"Yeah. As if I *will* do it again."

And that's the part that hurts. Not trusting myself. Knowing how far I'm willing to go.

He closes his eyes. "You're a good person, Bex. You're not going to kill someone unless you have to."

"How can you say that? How can you say I'm a good person?" I can see the man in the conference room, choking as our bullets took his life away. I can see the firing squad, their armour bursting open as I fired my gun. I can see the bodies on the South Bank. The wreckage from the OIE bombs.

He reaches over, and takes my hands in his.

"You're a good person, Bex Ellman." He looks me in the eye. "I know you're a good person, *because* you feel like this."

I shake my head. "I don't know what you mean."

"The people you killed. Were they threatening you? Were they threatening the people you care about?"

I think of the conference room. Listening to those awful comments about Margie. I try not to think about the bombs. The people under the rubble. "No." I shake my head. "Yes. Maybe."

He tugs on my hands. "You killed the *firing squad*, Bex. You shot the people who were about to shoot your friends. You saved Margie, and you saved Dr Richards." He shakes his head. "I don't know how much longer my armour would have lasted. You saved me, Bex."

I nod. I can feel the bullets, slamming into my armour, knocking me backwards.

I can see Dan, his arms round Margie, head down, sheltering her from the guns.

And I can see the back of Will's shirt, turning red with the impacts.

"You did the right thing, Bex. You protected your friends."

"Like you did?"

He nods. "Like I did."

I remember standing in the gatehouse at the bunker, knowing that Dan was outside in the dark. Hearing shots, and watching the door open.

Knowing that he'd killed people to get us out.

My breath catches in my throat, and my voice is a whisper.

"I wouldn't be here if you hadn't."

He looks at the ceiling and back at me. "None of us would be here if I hadn't."

"Does that help? Knowing that we're still alive?"

He smiles. "Of course it does."

I think of Margie, waiting downstairs. I think of Dr Richards, bandaged and cared for in her hospital bed.

"But …"

He pulls his hands away, and fixes me with a stare.

"Bex. You did the right thing. No one blames you for what you did." I nod. "And this? This just shows that you're human. That you understand what you've done, and that you don't want to do it again."

I shake my head. "I don't. But I feel as if I've crossed a line. I feel as if it will be easier next time, and I don't want that. I don't want killing someone to be easy."

He laughs. "It won't be, Bex. You know how it feels, now. You know how hard it is." He shakes his head. "You know that you need to live with it, afterwards."

"But I know I can do it. That dark place inside? That's real, now. I know I can take someone's life away."

He hangs his head, and stares at the white hotel sheets.

"That's not dark, Bex. That's brave. You know you can step into danger to save the people you care about. You know you won't run away. You know you can protect them, no matter what."

I nod, leaning back and staring at the wall behind him.

He's turning the gun in my hands into something positive. Turning shooting people into something good.

I can't see it. I can't accept it.

He looks at me.

"OK. Try this." I sit up straight. "Every time you find yourself thinking about the people you shot, and feeling bad, flip it around."

"How?"

"Don't think about the people you shot. Think about the people you saved."

"I can't …"

"You can. *Make* yourself. When you're lying awake, and you're seeing the bullets, think about Margie instead. Think about the last thing you said to her, yesterday. Think about the last time she hugged you, or laughed with you. Think about finding clothes for her to wear, and eating sandwiches in the park."

It feels too easy. It feels cheap, when people have died because of me.

"Does that work?"

He gives me a serious look. "It works for me."

And I know he means it. I'm one of the people he saved. Thinking of me, of Margie, of the rest of us – that's what's keeping Dan going.

I think of Margie – Dan and his armour protecting her on the stage. I think of Dr Richards. I think of the firing squad, their bullets pushing me back as I tried to stop them. Their armour, useless against my Armour-Piercing rounds.

I shake my head. My rifle taking their lives is all I can see.

I know he's right. I know I need to focus on my friends. On the people who are here, because of me.

Margie. Dr Richards. Dan, his armour cracking and denting under the rain of bullets.

He's watching me. Watching my reaction.

I shake my head, and I can't meet his eyes.

"If that doesn't work, then think about me, Bex. Think about how happy I am that Margie's alive."

I stare at him, trying to push the memories from my mind. He breaks into a grin, and I can't help laughing.

I pull a face. "I'd rather not, Dan!"

His grin widens, and his cheeks start to turn pink.

I hold up my hand. "I don't want to know. I don't want to know!"

I pull the pillow from behind me, and throw it at him.

There's a knock at the door, and Margie's standing there, just in time to see me throw a second pillow.

"Are you guys coming down …?"

She gives us an appraising look, and raises an eyebrow, smiling.

"Oh, I see how it is. Are we torturing Dan?" I nod. "Can anyone join in?"

I pat the other side of the bed. "Absolutely. Just make sure you bring a pillow."

She picks up a cushion from the sofa, slips off her shoes, and crawls into the bed next to me.

"Is this for throwing, or for self defence?" She looks around. "We don't seem to have many pillows left."

Dan is ducking down, the pillows I've thrown stacked in front of him like a fort.

And suddenly I'm laughing, and crying, and Margie has her arms round me, and Dan is stealing all the cushions from the sofa, and I can't believe we're here. We've come from safe houses, and cells, and the cruelty of an execution platform to this gorgeous room. We're here and we're alive.

And Dan's arms are round me, and it's just the three of us – alive, laughing, and half buried under a pile of pillows.

Interview

Ketty

"You're a popular prisoner." The nurse puts down my breakfast tray and checks the drip in my arm. "You've got another visitor booked in later."

I look up at her. "Another interrogation."

She nods. "Let me guess. Bed bath, sweatshirt, blanket, hairbrush?"

I can't help smiling. I feel as if there's someone on my side.

"Yes, please."

She checks her watch. "I'll be back in half an hour."

*****

I wait until she's behind the curtains, then pull the needle from my arm, using the napkin from the tray to clean away the blood.

I can't afford to answer more questions with morphine. I can hardly remember what we talked about yesterday.

I need to be awake. I need to understand what I'm being asked.

What I need to say.

I'm leaning back against the pillows when the nurse comes back. She glares at me, picking up the needle.

"You have *got* to stop doing this, Corporal."

"I don't need …"

"You do. I was here when they brought you in, and no one screams like that over a paper cut. I'll fetch another drip."

I shake my head. "Not until after I've spoken to my visitor."

She folds her arms. "You are one stubborn woman, Katrina Smith."

I give her a smile. "I've heard that before."

"I'm sure you have."

She picks up the breakfast tray and walks out, leaving the curtain open to the corridor outside.

And I realise – there's no one left who knows this about me. There's no one left who knows what I've done. What it's taken to get myself this far.

Bracken's gone. Jackson's gone. Lee's gone. Conrad is … who cares where Conrad is? He's gone.

I'm starting over. Whatever happens next, I'm starting again. There's no shorthand with anyone. No common ground. There's no one who knows what I'm thinking. There's no one who saw me push myself to walk again, after Dan put his bullet in my knee.

And I have to push myself all over again. I have to work up through the wheelchair, the crutches, the painkillers and the limping, and I have to do it here. Behind bars.

I feel sick. I feel angry. All that effort, all that pain, all over again.

And there's no one here who understands.

There's no one left who knows me at all.

I'm crying, suddenly. Big choking sobs. I try to breathe, to calm down, but the tears keep coming.

I'm crying for Bracken. I'm crying for Lee. I'm crying for a life where I knew what was expected of me.

Fetch the coffee, bring the painkillers, keep Bracken on his feet. Argue with Conrad. Try to impress Franks.

But most of all, I'm crying for Jackson.

Jackson, who knew what I could do, and always challenged me to do more. To be better.

My friend, who would sit here and mock me for getting myself beaten up by a bunch of girls. Who would hunt them all down and help me take revenge.

257

Who understood me.

Come on, Ketty. This is pathetic.

When the nurse comes back, I'm still crying, and the top of my T-shirt is wet with tears.

She watches me, arms folded. "This is why you need the morphine."

I look up at her, laughing and crying at the same time. "This *is* the morphine. This is why I don't want it."

*****

She closes the curtain and helps me to wash, and change into clean clothes. She gives me an ice-cold cloth to hold over my eyes, and hands me the hairbrush and a mirror. I pull my hair into a pony tail, and straighten my sweatshirt. She brings me a blanket to cover my legs.

"How do you feel?"

I nod. She doesn't need to know that my knee is pounding with every heartbeat. That I'm clenching my fists to distract me from the pain.

There's the click of high heels in the corridor outside, and someone calls my name.

The nurse turns, and opens the curtains.

"In here."

Next interrogation, Ketty. This time without the painkillers.

*****

A smartly dressed woman walks into the booth, holding out her hand for me to shake. I unclench my fist, and hold my hand up to her. She has a businesslike grip – firm, and confident. She pushes the table away, sits down on the stool, and puts her briefcase on the floor.

"Katrina Smith?" I nod. "I'm Fiona Price. Chairman of the Opposition In Exile."

I raise my eyebrows. This woman, and her organisation, have been at the top of our Wanted list since I came to London. She's been hiding in Edinburgh, and sheltering my escaped recruits. She sent Jake Taylor to the Netherlands to get him out of facing trial in London. She rescued Bex and Dan, and the others, and used the Scottish Government to protect them.

She's part of the coalition, and the invasion. She wants to be the next Prime Minister.

What does she want with you, Ketty?

"It's a pleasure to meet you, Corporal Smith."

I nod again, waiting for her questions. Waiting to find out why she's here. Willing myself to ignore the pain.

She folds her hands on her knees.

"I hear that you're the power behind the Terrorism Committee."

I shake my head. "I don't know what you mean."

"Colonel Bracken. Alcoholic. Should have drunk his way out of a job months ago, but you kept him going."

I nod. I don't know what to say.

"Hiding the bottles. Cleaning his flat. Keeping him in coffee and painkillers. Very commendable, Corporal." She gives me a cold look. "Why did you do it?"

I have no idea how to answer.

Keep it simple, Ketty. Don't give her anything she can use against you.

"That was my job, Madam Chairman."

She nods. "And was it your job to help him with interrogations?"

"Sometimes."

"And what would you say your strengths are, in the interrogation room?"

I'm speechless again. Every question is thrown like a punch. Is she trying to confuse me? Is she trying to push me into a confession?

If so, what is she hoping to hear?

"I suppose I ask the right questions?"

"I think you do more than that." She watches me again, and I try to keep the surprise from my face. "I think you know how to drill down. I think you know how to ask, and keep asking." She leans towards me. "I think you understand how people think, and what they're afraid of."

She sits back on her stool. She hasn't consulted any notes, and I realise she isn't recording our conversation.

What does she want?

She gives me another cold look. "Let's talk about Margaret Watson."

I close my eyes for a moment, shaking my head.

This doesn't end well, Ketty.

"You were coordinating the trial?"

"I was to begin with. I had to hand it over."

She nods. "To Corporal Conrad, I understand?"

How does she know all this?

"Yes."

"And what do you think you brought to the arrangements?"

This is it. This is the confession she wants.

I can't look at her. I can't meet her eyes and incriminate myself. I'd rather take my chances in here than walk into whatever show trial she has lined up for me.

The pain in my knee is growing, a chain of hammer blows in time with my pulse.

She's waiting for an answer.

I shrug. "We wanted to catch people's attention. We wanted to distract them from everything else that was going on. We needed a show, and I worked with PIN to make that happen."

I slump back on my pillows. I've said what she pushed me to say. I need painkillers, and I need to stop talking.

She nods. "That fits with what Conrad told me."

She's spoken to Conrad.

And now she's speaking to me.

And she wants me to confess.

I force myself to sit up straight, fighting to keep my voice calm.

"I'm sorry, Madam Chairman, but I don't understand. What is it you want me to say? What do you want to hear? Is there something I can help you with, or are you just waiting for me to admit to something criminal? I'm in a barely tolerable amount of pain, and I'd like to know where this interrogation is heading."

I sit back again.

This is it. This is where I find out what she's putting me on trial for. What charges I'll have to answer.

She smiles.

"You misunderstand me, Corporal. I've spoken to Corporal Conrad, and I've spoken to Colonel Ryan. I've had access to your previous interrogations, and the ones you ran at Belmarsh.

"This isn't an interrogation. I'm here to offer you a job."

Campaign

Bex

"So. Free day!" Dan leans back on the sofa and grins. "What will we do with ourselves?"

"And Fiona's out all day?" Amy sounds excited.

"All day." I shake my head. "But we can't do anything crazy. She wants us rested and ready for tomorrow."

"How hard can it be, sitting round a table on TV and talking about ourselves?" Dan's grinning again.

"I'm serious, Dan. She really needs this. She needs us to make a good impression."

He nods. "We could go out." He looks around the room. "We could go anywhere!"

"We could go to the cinema! Or we could go shopping again. Or have another picnic!"

Margie looks at Amy. "Have you looked out of the window? You'll have soggy sandwiches if you try that today." A smile creeps across her face, and she turns to Dan. "We should have a party. Your parents are at work today, right?" Dan nods. "Let's go to your house! Let's have a party while they're out!"

Dan holds his hands out. "Why can't we party here? Look at this place. This is asking for the biggest Rock'n'Roll party in history. We could trash the room, and throw the TV out of the window ..."

"Hey! That's my room you're talking about! Trash your own room!"

He grins at me. "Spoilsport!"

"Anyway," I say, thinking this through. "If we go out, we have to take the armed guards with us. And Margie's right – the weather's horrible." I pick up the TV remote from the bedside table. "But Dan's right, too.

This is a great place to spend a rainy day. We've got room service, and the hotel has thousands of movies we can watch."

"Duvet day!" Dan punches the air. "Junk food and movies! Genius, Bex. And Fiona gets to pay the bill."

*****

"Mum?"

She puts down the book she's reading, and pushes herself towards the door. "Bex. Have you worked out what you're doing with your day off?"

I shrug. "Staying here. Watching movies. Calling room service."

"All of you?"

"Pretty much. You can join us, if you want."

She smiles, and takes my hands as the door closes behind me.

"I'm happy here. You and your friends need some time together, without Fiona scheduling everything that happens. Go and enjoy yourselves!"

"We'll be next door, if you need anything."

"I'm fine, Bex. I have a phone." She winks at me. "I can order room service, too."

I nod, but I don't move. I don't let go of her hands. I feel as if there's a weight on my shoulders. As if I'm wasting my day.

I'm so used to being Fiona's puppet – to meeting people and posing for photos and saying all the right things – I don't know what to do when I'm not following her schedule.

"What's wrong, beautiful girl?"

I shake my head. "I don't know."

She squeezes my hands. "You're stopping. You've got a whole day to yourself for the first time since we got here. That's hard, Bex." I nod. "Everything that's

263

happened – it's going to catch up with you. Fiona's been keeping you busy, and that's not just for her benefit. She's keeping you distracted, too. She doesn't want you to have time to think about what happened."

"So what do I do?"

"Go and sit with your friends. Go and watch terrible movies and eat junk food." She pulls my hands towards her. "But do it together, Bex. Do something with your friends that doesn't involve telling your story." She smiles at me. "Enjoy yourself. Allow yourself to enjoy your day. You need this, and your friends need it, too. Go and forget about everything else."

I squeeze her hands, and let go, nodding. "Thanks, Mum. I'll try."

*****

My room feels empty. Everyone's in their own rooms, fetching duvets and pillows. The cushions are back on the sofa, and the bed's been made. It's as if yesterday's pillow fight never happened.

I can't make an impression on this place. Every time I move something, every time I try to make it my own, someone makes the bed and cleans and tidies everything away. Even the notepad and pen on the desk – I find them in exactly the same place, every day, wherever I leave them.

It's as if I'm not supposed to exist. As if Fiona is erasing the real me.

I drop the notepad into the desk drawer, and pull out Joss's drawing.

It's crumpled, and torn around the edges, but we're still there, smiling out of his pencil lines. Arms round each other, dressed in our armour.

Safe.

And we're safe again now – all except Joss. We're protected and we're sheltered. No one's hunting us down.

But we're as trapped here as we were at Camp Bishop. Fiona needs us to stay here – to work for her – for months.

And we owe her for our safety. We owe her for our survival.

We don't have a choice.

"Bex?" Margie stands in the doorway, a duvet draped over her shoulder.

I drop the sketch back into the drawer, and close it.

"Yeah." I force myself to smile.

"Are you OK?"

"Fine." I nod, trying to convince myself. "I'm fine."

"Are we doing this?" She asks, holding up the duvet.

"Yes." I'm really smiling now, and Margie smiles back. "Come in, and get comfortable. These movies won't watch themselves."

*****

We crowd onto the bed, wrapping ourselves in duvets and blankets, leaning on each others' shoulders and knees. And we watch movies.

There's an argument, at first, but Dan's the only one who wants to watch anything violent, so we end up watching dreadful RomComs and kids' movies, Dan groaning through every predictable plot twist, and Margie poking him in the ribs when he complains too loudly.

It's wonderful.

Amy is upset that Jake refused to join us, but she sits back and lets herself get caught up in the romance.

When Charlie and Maz find us after lunch, we're sitting on the floor, surrounded by pizza boxes and huge bags of crisps, arguing over the next film.

Dan grabs the remote, and starts scrolling through the options.

"Back me up here, Maz," he says. "I've been watching chick flicks all morning."

Maz shrugs. "You're outnumbered, mate. Sometimes you've just got to go with the majority." Charlie grins, and gives Maz a kiss on the cheek.

Margie checks her watch. "Isn't Fiona on TV today?" She takes the remote from Dan, and switches back to the TV listings.

She scrolls through to the news channel – what used to be PIN. It's strange to be in London, watching news coverage without the PIN logo.

The newsreader runs through the headlines, and there's Fiona. She's shaking hands with her opponent, smiling at the woman who sent us to Camp Bishop. They stand together on a platform, and announce the beginning of the election campaign.

"So she's the candidate, then." Dan sighs. "It's official."

"It's not as if there was ever any doubt." I think about Fiona in Scotland, running the OIE committee. "She always wanted the top job."

"And she's going to get it." Maz shakes his head. "The other party doesn't stand a chance."

"Good."

And then it's my face on the screen, and Dan's. Footage from Horse Guards Parade. Of Margie, on the platform. Dan, crouching over her. Will, throwing himself in front of the bullets. Me, pumping bullets into the firing squad, every shot as accurate as my practice rounds on the firing range.

Fiona's using us in her speech.

I can't watch. I feel sick, watching everything happen again. Watching her use us for her campaign.

"Oh, she's so winning this." Maz sounds impressed. "Who wouldn't vote for you guys?"

Maz is right. We're winning this for Fiona. She's using footage of people dying – footage of me, taking their lives – to put herself in power.

And the voters will love it.

I close my eyes and hide my face in my hands.

"This is never going to stop, is it?"

Hospital

Ketty

"Paperwork's being approved, Smith." The prison guard smiles. "You're getting out of here."

She hands me a sealed plastic bag. My wallet. My watch. My painkillers.

I stare at the bag. At everything I had in my pockets on my last day in the Home Forces.

And I'm falling again.

Everything's changed. Everything is different. There's been a revolution, and I'm a piece of the past. I don't fit in this new world.

I turn the bag over in my hands.

My ID card. My backstage pass. They used to represent power and entitlement, and now they're meaningless. The Home Forces is disbanded, and we're all in prison, or in hiding.

But Fiona Price wants me to work for her. *Fiona Price* is arranging my freedom.

I shake my head.

This is real, Ketty. This is happening.

"Thank you," I say to the guard.

She smiles again. "Good luck, Katrina," she says.

*****

Two nurses help me to move from my bed to the gurney, hooking my morphine drip to the frame and making sure my knee doesn't twist in its plastic brace. The prison guard puts my boots and my folded clothes next to my feet, and the nurse hands me a folder.

"Medical notes. Make sure you pass them on to the hospital."

I nod, and thank her.

The guard and the nurse push me out of the curtained bay, and into the corridor.

And that's when the anger hits me.

I walked myself in here. I refused to let them drag me from my holding cell, and I refused to show them fear. I held my head high, and I followed their rules. I did not let them break me.

But I can't walk myself out.

It doesn't matter what I did – what I pushed myself to do. Standing tall when they came to take me away. Folding my clothes when they took them from me. Using the interrogation room. Taking control of my humiliations.

None of it matters. My knee is smashed again. I'm broken, and powerless, and they're pushing me to freedom on a gurney.

My fists are clenched as they wheel me through security gates, and out into the rain.

There's an ambulance waiting, and the medics load the gurney inside.

"Stay stubborn, Katrina," says the nurse, quietly, her hand on my arm. "You'll get through this."

There are hot tears on my face as she walks away.

Keep it together, Ketty.

You're free.

*****

"So you were Home Forces?" The nurse checks my morphine drip, and tucks the hospital blanket round my knee.

I nod. He's wearing fatigues, but I don't recognise the flag on his sleeve. His English is good, but he has a strong accent.

They must have arrested the military hospital staff, as well as the rest of us. I'm being treated by the coalition.

"And they're letting you out?" I nod again. "You must be the only Home Forces member who isn't behind bars." He looks at me. "What's so special about you, Katrina Smith?"

I wish I knew.

"Good behaviour?"

He laughs, and points at my knee. "It's either very good behaviour, or very bad. Your notes say this wasn't an accident."

I shrug.

He puts his hand on my shoulder. "Are you comfortable? Is there anything you need?" I shake my head. "TV remote is here, water is here. Your clothes and belongings are in the cupboard."

"Thank you," I say, as he walks away.

What I need is Fiona. I need to know what I'm doing here.

*****

The room is small, but it's larger than my bay at the prison.

And it's mine. One bed.

White walls, blue high-grip floor, institutional furniture, and a large window with a view of the grey sky.

I sit back against the pillows.

No more interrogations. No more handcuffs. No more cellmates. No more watching my back.

Now I just have to learn to walk again. And keep Fiona happy.

I don't know whether to laugh or cry.

I pick up the TV remote, and start scrolling through the channels.

*****

It's Fiona. Fiona, on what used to be PIN, shaking hands with the woman who used to be Prime Minister.

They're announcing the elections. They're announcing the start of the campaign.

I watch as Fiona makes her speech, praising the bravery of the resistance fighters. Praising Bex, and Dan. Making sure we all know that the Face of the Resistance is working with her.

She's praising my recruits. The kids I've been hunting since they broke out of Camp Bishop.

And now we're on the same side?

I shake my head. This isn't making sense.

What does she want from you, Ketty?

*****

"Miss Smith?"

I switch off the TV and turn towards the door. A tall woman in a khaki t-shirt and camouflage trousers is waiting in the corridor.

"I'm Dr Hayes. Battlefield Medicine. Can I come in?"

"Of course."

She walks over to me and shakes my hand, smiling, then looks down at the blanket covering my knee. There's a Dutch flag on her sleeve, but there's no trace of an accent in her voice.

"Can I take a look?"

I nod, and pull back the blanket. She takes a pair of surgical gloves from her pocket, pulls them on, and starts to peel back the bandages.

"There's a lot of scarring here." She looks at me. "And your notes say the kneecap is broken." I nod. "How's the pain?"

I lift my arm, tilting the needle towards her. "Morphine," I say, as if that explains everything.

She nods. "I'm going to put some pressure on it. Tell me if the pain gets too bad."

She pokes and prods, and I can feel the bones, scraping. I close my eyes, clenching my fists and digging my nails into the palms of my hands.

"Does this …?"

"Yeah. That hurts."

"OK," she says, tucking the bandages back into place and peeling her gloves off. "That's a lot of damage. But I think we can help. How soon do you need to be walking?"

I realise I have no idea. I don't know what Fiona has planned for me. Is she expecting me to stay here? Does she need me with her, or can she keep me in a hospital bed, ready to answer whatever questions she comes up with?

I don't want to stay here. I want to be on my feet. I don't want to be helpless and broken for a minute longer than I need to be.

And she's not asking Fiona. She's asking me.

"As soon as possible."

Dr Hayes smiles.

*****

When she comes back, there's a box under her arm.

Plain cardboard. Serial number. And an icon of a running figure.

For a moment, I can't breathe. I can't believe what she's bringing me.

It's a PowerGel.

She smiles, and puts the box on the table.

"Fiona Price asked me to give you this. Don't get too excited – these take a lot of getting used to. But we should have you walking with crutches by the end of the week."

She opens the box, and pulls out the white gel and the black fabric.

"This is going to feel weird when I first put it on, but …"

"I know." She looks at me, taking in the smile on my face, and raises an eyebrow.

"I've used one before." I point at my knee. "The first time. For the bullet wound."

She nods. "Well, then, you know two things. One – that it will stabilise the knee, and block the pain. And two – that when you take it off, you're going to need the morphine."

*****

By the time Fiona arrives, I'm out of bed, and I'm dressed in my fatigues. The swelling means there's a limit to how far I can bend my knee, but I've walked end to end of the corridor on my own, and I've refused to use the crutches the nurse brought for me.

It's harder this time, because of the broken bones, and I'm limping. No obstacle courses for me today.

But I'm walking.

The pain-killing cold of the gel sinks into the joint, and the fabric wrap keeps my leg from buckling. I'm off the morphine drip, and I'm out of my room.

I remember how to do this.

"So you're ready?"

I turn to find Fiona watching me as I limp towards the nurses' station.

I can't help grinning.

*****

"You're going to be my assistant, Katrina. And you're going to bring me Major General Franks."

I stare at her. She's sitting on the chair in my room, and I'm propped up on my pillows. I'm resting my leg in front of me on the bed, the bulge of the PowerGel circling my knee under my uniform.

"You don't have Franks?"

"Oh, we have her." Fiona smiles. "She's in one of your special cells, at Belmarsh."

"Then why do you need me?"

"Because she's not talking."

Of course she's not.

Lee's dead. Bracken's dead. Her plan to distance herself from the Terrorism Committee is working.

"So you want me to do … what, exactly?"

"To start with? I want you to walk with me, into her interrogation room." She leans towards me. "I think she's counting on no one knowing what she did. I've researched the Terrorism Committee. Franks created it, then walked away. She's supposed to look innocent of all the plots and the bombings."

I nod, slowly. Brigadier Lee was supposed to take the blame. If anything happened, all the attention was supposed to be on him.

But I shot Lee. I killed him, in the conference room.

And now he can't protect Franks.

"So you want her to see my face? You want her to know that I'm working with you?"

She nods. "I think you know exactly what she did. I think you know exactly what the Terrorism Committee did. And I think she knows that. I think you can make her talk."

I think about opening the cells at Belmarsh. About cutting the patches from my uniform.

About choosing a side.

I left Franks behind when I killed Lee. When I took Bex to Belmarsh.

When I accepted Fiona's offer.

And now I'm going up against the Head of the Home Forces.

I have no right to be here. No right to be free. And I have no right to a PowerGel, and a bed in a military hospital.

But here I am. This is where Fiona has put me. This is what she wants from me.

And this is what I'm good at.

It feels like finding land under my feet, after weeks of swimming out of my depth.

It feels like safety, for the first time since I came to London.

You can do this, Ketty.

I smile at Fiona. "I think so, too."

TV

Bex

"So tell me what happened when you arrived at Camp Bishop."

We've been asked this question so many times. Dan and I can answer it without thinking, each of us taking a piece of the story, but this time we have to remember to let Jake and Amy talk as well.

The interviewer is a famous journalist. He's been working in the US since the government stepped down and the Home Forces took power, and this is his first appearance in the UK since the revolution.

They're expecting a record-breaking audience for this interview. And they're broadcasting live.

We're all here, sitting round a glass-topped table, surrounded by green screens and cameras. I'm sitting between Mum and Dan. Margie's next to him, then Jake, Amy, and Charlie. And Fiona, sitting on the other side of the interviewer, waiting for her chance to take credit for saving us.

We're all in our smartest suits, and we've all sat through the attentions of the hair and makeup crew. I have to keep stopping myself from touching my hair. I feel ridiculous sitting here, my hair full of hairspray and my face coated in makeup, while we talk about life in the RTS.

"And I know that life wasn't easy, during your training. You experienced bullying, and some physical abuse."

Dan looks at me, and I nod. This is always my question. This is the story I get to tell.

"The Senior Recruits had a lot of power," I say, thinking about Ketty. "They used intimidation and punishment to make sure we behaved."

"And what form did this punishment take?" The interviewer's face is a mask of concern.

I force myself to meet his eyes. "They didn't like us working together. They didn't like anyone trying to form a team. I helped these guys," I point along the table. Amy smiles, and Jake rolls his eyes. "And I helped our friend, when he injured himself on a run. The Senior Recruits didn't like it."

It's like reciting lines from a play. We've told this story so many times, I barely have to think about it.

"What did they do?"

"They grabbed me. One night after dinner. They dragged me outside the fence, and they held me down and punched me." I close my eyes. I can see Jackson, his fists pounding into my ribs. Ketty, pushing my arms into the mud. I can feel each blow, forcing the air from my lungs.

There are some things I can't forget.

"And did the Commander know about this?"

I shrug. "I don't know. If he did, he didn't care. He didn't stop it."

I can see Saunders, slumped on the grass outside the gate. The guards, refusing to let us in. Ketty, telling them to leave us there. I can feel the rain, soaking our base layers. Saunders' sobs, as we waited for help.

The interviewer asks about Leominster, and Margie, piecing together the events that led to our escape. I tell him again what I saw in Leominster. The abandoned cars, the lost belongings. Ketty and Jackson, laughing.

"So you stole a truck?"

We all look at Charlie, and she explains how she got us out of camp.

I glance at Jake, and he's staring at the table. His arms are folded across his chest, and he's the only person leaning back in his chair.

"So *you* broke the Face of the Resistance out of Camp Bishop?" The interviewer smiles at Charlie, and she shakes her head.

"I might have been driving the truck, but it was Bex who got everyone out."

The interviewer turns to me, but I'm too busy watching Jake.

I see his expression change as he turns to Charlie. His crashes his fist onto the table, and Fiona gasps.

I can't help rolling my eyes.

"That's such *bullshit*, Charlie," he shouts. The interviewer looks surprised, and opens his mouth to ask another question, but Jake isn't finished. "You left me there. Me, and Amy. You know you did. And you left me with a gun to my head."

I should be expecting this. Jake, making his point on live TV.

But he's disrupting our story. He's making this all about him.

And he's shouting at Charlie.

Charlie nods. "That's true, Jake, and I'm sorry. There's nothing we could have done."

"*You could have stopped!*" His face is red, and twisted with anger. Amy puts her hand on his arm, but he pushes her away. He points at Charlie. "Have you ever had a gun to your head? A loaded, powered-up rifle, pressed against your skull? Someone's arm, locked round your throat?" She gives him a sympathetic look, but she doesn't answer. "Didn't think so," he says, quietly.

I'm about to say something when Margie leans forward, her hands clasped in front of her on the table.

"I can understand how that felt, Jake." Her voice is quiet and controlled. "You feel completely powerless, and you know there's nothing you can do, if they decide to pull the trigger." She looks at him, and he stares at her.

All I can see is Margie on the platform. Margie facing the guns.

But Jake hasn't finished.

"*You*! You think you can understand? It was all about *you*. Getting you out of camp so you wouldn't get caught. You're the reason I was left behind. You and Bex." He nods at me. "And how did that work out for you, *Margaret*? We went through all that, and you still got yourself arrested."

Margie blinks, and Dan reaches for her hand. She lets him take it, closing her eyes and taking deep breaths.

I can't believe what I'm hearing.

The interviewer isn't saying anything. We're live on TV. Everyone will be watching, and the interviewer isn't stepping in. I look out, past the cameras, and the director gives us a thumbs-up.

And I realise. This is great TV. This is soap-opera-beating, reality-TV-level viewing. They wanted a large audience? They'll get it. People will be phoning their friends, telling them to change the channel. They'll be talking about this for weeks. This is what the interviewer needs to relaunch his career.

And Jake's giving it to them. He's insulting my friends, and he's hurting Margie.

"Jake!" I lean forward, making sure he can see me. "We got you out. You and Amy. And Margie welcomed you at Makepeace Farm. Don't make this her fault."

He points at me, shaking his head. "I blame you, Bex. I blame you."

It's as if we never left Edinburgh. As if we're back in the police station, watching Jake feel sorry for himself. Back in the corridor outside his room, watching him leave for the Netherlands.

I don't have anything left to say to him.

Fiona puts both hands on the table, and we all turn to see what she's going to say.

"That's enough, Jake." He tries to interrupt, but she talks over him. "Bex saved you." She points at me across the table. "Bex got you out of Scotland. I made the arrangements. I got you to the Netherlands, but it was Bex who persuaded me to try."

He sits back in his chair, and there's a smirk on his face.

"You're all under her spell, aren't you?"

No one moves. Jake looks round the table, waiting for someone to speak.

And I've had enough.

This isn't about Jake. This is about all of us.

I'm on my feet, pointing at him. "There is no spell, Jake! There's just us. Just the people who worked together, and got ourselves out of Camp Bishop." He laughs. "You, too, Jake. We got you out, too. And then we got out of the bunker. And then Fiona got us to Newcastle, and Scotland, and we worked together to stop you from being deported."

I look round the table. Mum, looking up at me, concern on her face. Dan, his arm round Margie as she fights to stay calm. Amy, tears smudging her makeup. Charlie, shaking her head. And Jake, red-faced and angry, as he stands up, facing me.

"You love this, don't you?" He asks, still smirking. "You love having people in your debt. You want me to be grateful. You want me to be your friend."

I shake my head, blinking back tears.

"That's not what I want at all, Jake." He raises his eyebrows, and I realise it's true. I miss him. I wish that none of this had ever happened. And I wish he didn't hate me so much. But I don't need him to like me. I close my eyes, and my voice is quiet in the silent studio. "I just want you to forgive me."

Mum puts her hand on my back. Charlie reaches across the table towards me. "Bex …"

I shake my head, watching Jake.

And he laughs.

He pushes his chair back, and starts to unclip his microphone.

"I don't need to be here. I don't need to join the Bex Fan Club." He looks round the table, tugging the battery pack from his belt. "I don't need any of you."

He throws the microphone and the belt pack onto the table and walks away, pushing his chair over as he goes. Someone with a clipboard hurries towards him and guides him away, between the cameras.

Mum takes my hand, and pulls me back into my chair. Everyone's watching me. Everyone's waiting for my reaction.

I can let this get to me, or I can shrug it off. I catch Fiona's eye across the table.

And I remember her warning.

"We could lose everything. Everything we've fought for. We could find ourselves with a proper civil war on our hands."

She's counting on me. On the Face of the Resistance. She needs me to hold the country together.

I make myself shrug, as if watching Jake laugh at me means nothing.

"I guess I can't please everyone," I say, forcing myself to smile.

Fiona's face lights up, and she smiles at me, nodding. Behind her, the director gives us another thumbs-up.

Honesty

Ketty

I'm watching on the screen in the make-up room. The kids tell their story as someone works on my hair and someone else dabs foundation onto my face. I'm wearing a roll-neck sweater under my suit jacket, so they don't have to disguise my bruises.

Fiona picked me up from the hospital this morning, and took me shopping. I have a wardrobe of smart suits, wide-legged trousers, high-necked tops, and flat shoes. The loose trousers hide the PowerGel, and the necklines hide the bruises. She doesn't want me looking weak, standing beside her.

She wasn't planning to put me on screen, but when the director found out who I am, he insisted.

I watch as Jake and Bex shout at each other, and Jake storms out. I can't help smiling.

She left me behind, too, Jake.

I know how it feels to be betrayed by Bex Ellman.

*****

Bex pretends that she doesn't care about Jake, and the interviewer moves on to ask about Makepeace Farm. Bex talks about friendship, and working with Will and Sheena.

And then they're talking about the raid on the coach.

Someone touches my elbow, and the makeup woman gives me a final inspection.

"You're on. This way." A woman with a clipboard pins a microphone to my collar, and hands me a box. "Clip that to your belt." And she waves me towards the door.

I push myself out of the chair, and follow her into the studio. I'm still limping, but I'm walking better than I was yesterday. I follow her to the line of cameras.

"Let me stop you there, Dan," the interviewer says. "I think we have someone else here who was on the coach." He looks round at me, and watches as the woman pushes me towards the table. There's an empty chair, next to Fiona.

It takes all my effort to hide my limp for the six steps to the chair. I sit down, and the interviewer smiles.

Dan glares at me. Bex looks from me to Fiona and back, her face reddening under her makeup. And Elizabeth shakes her head.

What am I doing here, Fiona?

"Corporal Ketty Smith." I nod, and turn to him. "You were in charge of the recruits on the coach?"

"I was."

"And what did that mean, when you found yourselves under attack?"

I keep my eyes on the interviewer. I can feel the stares from across the table, but this isn't about them. This is about keeping Fiona happy.

"It meant that it was my responsibility to keep them safe."

"So they were in danger?"

I think about the men in the road, guns trained on the coach. I think about Bex and Dan in their armour, bringing the fight to us.

"The resistance fighters were armed. I had to protect the kids."

"And you did. You put yourself in the line of fire."

I nod again, avoiding Dan's gaze. "I took a bullet, to protect them."

"And it worked?"

I shrug. "Jake and Amy walked away with their friends, but we got the rest of the kids to safety."

"You were never in any danger!" Dan shouts across the table. "You took a bullet because you were threatening Bex. All you had to do was stay in your seats, and we would have left you alone."

I can see the coach. I can see Jackson, refusing to sit still. I can feel the bullet, knocking me down. I can feel myself falling.

And I can hear the shots from outside. The shots that killed my friend.

Shots that came from Dan's rifle.

I can't let him rewrite history on live TV.

"Tell that to Jackson." My voice is a growl as I glare at Dan.

"He didn't make it, then?"

I can't speak. There is nothing I can say that would make him understand. I shake my head, my fists clenched on the table in front of me.

Hold it together, Ketty. You're here for Fiona.

"I'm sorry, Ketty. That was never meant to happen."

I make myself take a breath. I feel as if he's shot me again.

"You're sorry? You killed my best friend, and you're *sorry*?"

Fiona puts her hand on my arm, and I sit back in my chair.

Focus, Ketty. Don't let them get to you.

"So back at Makepeace, your troubles weren't over?"

Charlotte shakes her head. "They came after us. They would have gassed us all in the bunker, if Bex hadn't realised what was happening."

"They tried to kill you with poison gas?"

Charlotte nods. The interviewer looks shocked.

I can't help rolling my eyes. "You were shacked up with a terrorist. What did you expect?"

"You were there, Corporal?"

Really? We're doing this live on TV?

I keep my eyes fixed on Bex, and she glares back at me.

"I was."

Shouting

Bex

How can she do this? How can she sit there so calmly and tell everyone what she did?

"I was," Ketty says, her eyes never leaving mine. "In fact, I was the first into the gatehouse." She shrugs. "We tried to open the bunker. We tried to let you out, but your guard was too devoted."

Amy gasps. "You did it? *You* killed Joss?"

Ketty shrugs, still staring at me. "He was in my way. I gave you all a chance, and he refused to cooperate."

She's still talking, but I can't hear her. I can't hear anything.

She was in prison. She was chained to a table, wearing a prison jumpsuit. What's she doing here?

I look from Ketty to Fiona, and back. Fiona has her hand on Ketty's arm.

And she's wearing a suit like mine. A jacket, that matches mine. A dark green top, that matches my T-shirt.

Fiona. Fiona got her out.

Fiona is working with Ketty. She's taken her shopping, and she's putting her on TV.

After everything I told her, she's using Ketty, and she's using me.

I glance at the director, and he's grinning. The interviewer watches us, waiting for me to react. Ketty's eyes don't leave my face.

I take a breath. Fiona needs me. She needs us. She needs stability and confidence.

She needs the Face of the Resistance.

But this is too much.

This is *too much*.

I'm on my feet again. Dan's trying to pull me down, back into my chair, but I drag my arm free and lean both hands on the table.

"I will not do this." It's all I can do to keep my anger under control. I should leave. I should walk away, but I need Fiona to understand.

"Bex?" The interviewer wants me to explain. He wants to hear the whole story.

Fine.

"I will not work with *her*!" I point at Ketty, glaring at Fiona across the table. "I will not sit here and exchange small talk with the Senior Recruit who assaulted me. Who tried to put me on an execution platform. I will not sit here and play nice with the person who *tortured my mother*." Ketty smirks, and Mum puts her hand on my arm.

My hands are shaking, on the table. My knees are shaking. My pulse is drumming in my chest, and I feel as if I can't breathe.

I need to decide. Am I working for Fiona? Am I working for the country? For the elections?

Am I still the Face of the Resistance?

Or am I done?

Ketty leans her elbows on the table, watching me. I stare back, too furious to speak.

"It was war, Bex," she says. "That's what happens when you choose a side."

She's blaming us. She's blaming Saunders and Mum for everything that happened to them. She's blaming me.

She shot Saunders. *She* tortured Mum. And she's making it *my* fault.

I need backup. I need support. I need someone to tell her she's wrong.

I watch as Fiona turns to Ketty. I wait for her to argue – but instead, she nods and smiles.

She *smiles*.

And I know what to do.

I'm pulling the box from my belt, and unclipping my microphone before anyone can stop me. Mum and Dan reach out towards me, but I lift my hands in the air out of reach and step back, pushing my chair out of the way.

"I'm done, Fiona." I shout. "I'm done. I quit."

And I turn, and walk away. Past the cameras, past the director, past the woman with her clipboard.

But I can still see Fiona's face. Her jaw dropping as she realises that I mean it.

That she's lost the Face of the Resistance.

Meltdown

Ketty

Bex marches away from the table. Fiona's grip tightens on my arm, and the studio is silent.

I don't know what I've done.

Is this what you wanted, Fiona?

The interviewer turns to Fiona, but it's Margaret who speaks first, shrugging Dan's arm from her shoulders.

"You're right." She looks at me, and her gaze is steady. "This was war. We chose a side, and so did you." She shakes her head. "What you're doing at this table, I have no idea. You were my torturer, and my interrogator. You should be behind bars. What Fiona is doing? What Bex is doing? They're trying to build a new country. They're trying to get rid of your cruelty, and your hate. They're trying to make things better."

I force myself to hold her gaze. There's an icy feeling in my spine, and I can feel myself shivering.

She wants me back in my cell. She wants to see me humiliated and broken.

Fiona's hand stays on my arm, pushing me back in my chair.

Don't react. Don't say anything.

Margaret turns to Fiona, and I let out the breath I've been holding. My hands are shaking, and I clasp them together on the table.

"And you. Dan told me what you wanted. You tried to use his story to promote the Opposition In Exile. You wanted to package what happened to him, and to the others, and use it as propaganda." She shakes her head. "You don't see us as real people, do you? You see

289

photos. Posters. Images you can use for your campaign."
Fiona tries to interrupt, but Margaret talks over her.

"And now? Now you're using us all over again."
She leans forward, spreading her hands. "We're hurting,
Fiona. We're people, not puppets, and we need time. We
need to understand what happened to us, and we need
time to work out how we feel." She shakes her head.
"This is all academic to you, isn't it? Pictures on a
screen." She closes her eyes, and takes a breath. Dan
reaches out his hand, and she takes it in hers, glancing at
him. "But it was real. It happened to us. Real, messy,
life-and-death situations. Real, paralysing fear. Real
pain. And all you could think about, watching us on your
screens, was how we could help you."

Fiona tries to respond, but Margaret holds up her
hands.

"Do you know what? Bex was right. We don't have
to work with you." She looks at Dan, and he nods. They
stand up together, carefully placing their microphones
and belt packs on the table.

"Elizabeth?" Margaret holds out a hand. Elizabeth
nods, and looks at me. She smiles, unclips her
microphone, and puts it in front of her on the table. Then
she turns her wheelchair, and pushes herself away from
the table. Someone hurries in from behind the cameras,
and helps her push the chair over the cables and out of
shot. Margaret and Dan walk behind her. Amy starts to
stand up, but Charlotte puts a hand on her arm and
shakes her head.

Fiona sighs, and releases her grip on my arm.

"Fiona Price," says the interviewer, turning towards
us. "Would you care to respond?"

Debt

Bex

"Bex!"

Maz jumps to his feet as I walk through the waiting area. There's a TV on the wall, and the interview is moving on without me. He looks from me to the screen and back. I keep walking.

"Bex – wait up." He reaches out, and I twist away from him.

"Don't."

He drops his hand. "Where are you going?"

"Don't try to stop me."

"I'm not."

I stop, and turn back to him. He's holding his hands up in front of him, watching me.

I'm too angry to stay here. I'm too angry to talk about this. I turn away, and keep walking.

He follows me. Down a long corridor, and out into the foyer of the building. Someone shouts at me from behind the reception desk, but I keep going. Out through the glass doors, and onto the street beyond.

I stop. It's early evening, and the street lights are competing with the sunset.

I look around, searching for something I recognise. I don't know where I am.

I needed to get out of the studio. I needed to get away from Fiona and Ketty, and here I am.

I'm shaking as I realise what I've done. I've walked out on Fiona. I've walked out on my friends.

And I've walked out on Mum.

Maz takes my arm. "Bex? You OK?"

I shake my head.

"Do you want to go back inside?"

291

I stare at him. "Why …?"

He nods. "Back to the hotel, then?"

I nod, slowly, shivering as the anger starts to fade. He puts his arm round my shoulders, and hails a taxi.

"Come on," he says. "Let's get you home."

*****

We sit in the taxi, Maz watching me as I lean my head back and stare at the ceiling.

"So, what's your plan?"

I can't help laughing. "I don't have one. I just … I couldn't stay there."

"You did the right thing, Bex," he says, quietly.

I sit up and look at him. "How can you say that? I just left Mum in the studio with Ketty. I just left Dan and Margie and Amy behind. We left Charlie." I brush tears from my eyes, and my hands come away smeared with makeup. "I gave up, Maz. I quit. I left them all behind."

"Good." He says.

I shake my head. "What do you mean?"

"I mean that you did the right thing." He smiles. "It's about time, Bex."

I'm staring, and I can't think of anything to say.

"I've worked for the OIE for long enough to know how Fiona works. She's been using you – all of you – for months. She used you to get her coalition. She used you to make your speech, when you should have been saving Margie. You had to fight to get her to agree to make Margie a priority."

"But she saved us …"

He waves a hand, dismissively. "Sure. And she's been collecting on that debt ever since."

"We owe her …"

"You owe her nothing. She saved you. As the Chairman of the OIE, that should have been her job. She

292

should have been saving everyone she could, and getting them to Scotland. She should have been sending lines of refugees to the Scottish government. But she didn't."

"So why did she save us?"

"Because you're useful. You're young, and you've done some pretty incredible things. You come with your own ready-made inspiring story." He shrugs. "You're photogenic, and there's just enough heroism, and just enough tragedy in your story to catch people's imaginations."

"But the hotel … the clothes …"

"Her choice. You needed somewhere to stay, and she needed you to look good for her photo shoots. She could have put you up anywhere, but she chose the Royal Hotel. Why do you think she did that?"

I shake my head. "Because it's close to all the TV studios?"

He grins. "There's that. But she chose it because it's *nice*. She chose it to make sure you feel special, and grateful, and that you'll do what she wants you to do."

I think about it. He's right. We don't need to be staying at the Royal. Dan could be at home, with his parents. Margie could be with her family. After everything we've done, we don't need luxury. We need a roof over our heads.

But we're enjoying the luxury.

"So I'm paying for the hotel, every time I do what Fiona needs me to do?" He nods. "Every time I go on TV, or talk to a journalist, I'm paying for my rescue. I'm paying for being alive."

He nods again. "All of you. You're all playing Fiona's game, and she's going to win the election, because of you."

I stare at him, trying to make sense of everything he's saying.

"Why are you telling me this? Isn't she using you, too?"

He shrugs. "Fiona's stuck with me, because I volunteered to come to London and fight with the rest of you. Charlie's the one she needs."

"And Charlie's OK with this?"

He smiles. "Charlie cares about you, Rugrat. She's not going anywhere until she's sure you're OK."

"So I'm keeping Charlie here." I can hear the defeat in my voice.

I look at Maz. I can feel the tears on my face, but I don't care.

"I have to get out. I have to get away."

He raises an eyebrow. "Anywhere in particular?"

I think about the places I've lived. I can't go back to school. I have no idea whether Mum has any money left, or whether she can go back to the nursing home. I can't go back to Camp Bishop, or the safe houses.

I have nowhere to go.

Response

Ketty

Fiona sits back in her chair and turns to the interviewer. One of the cameras moves closer to the table to catch her reaction. I sit up straight and watch as she speaks.

"I'm sorry," she says. "I'm sorry that we can't have a calm conversation about what's happened to our country." She waves her hand at the empty seats in front of her. "I think this shows what we're dealing with."

I glance at Amy and Charlotte, and they're both staring at Fiona.

"You see, Bex is right. We have been through a war. And war is hard on everyone." She folds her hands on the table. "People suffer. People choose sides. We turn against each other." The interviewer nods.

Where are you going with this, Fiona?

And what do you want from me?

"But we need to end this. We need to put this – all these experiences, all this hurt – we need to put them behind us." She smiles. "We need to work together. We need to build a better country."

She turns to the camera. "This is what I want for the UK. I want peace. I want safety and security. And I want us to build these things together." She points again at the empty seats. "These amazing young people have been through so much. They inspired us and they showed us what we can do if we work together." She shakes her head, her smile fading. "But they should never have been sent to Camp Bishop in the first place. We don't need child soldiers to keep us safe. We don't need bullying and conscription in this country. We need schools and hospitals and freedom."

I force myself to stay calm. I'm sitting next to Fiona, on live TV, and she's condemning me. She's telling everyone that what I did was wrong. That people like me have no place in her new country.

Don't react, Ketty. Don't screw up.

I make myself watch as she delivers her speech.

"That's what I want. That's what I promise to deliver. My opponents are the party who introduced conscription. They allowed this to happen. They made these kids into fighters and refugees." She pauses, smiling. "I will abolish the Recruit Training Service. I will not allow any more school children to be sent to fight. I will make sure that this can't happen to anyone else in this country, ever again."

She's using the RTS to score political points. I have to stop myself from rolling my eyes.

"Thank you, Fiona. I'm sure our audience is interested to hear your plans for government. But can we talk for a moment about how this unity will come about? People have been divided by recent events. How do you propose to bring them together?"

Fiona's smile falters, but she composes herself.

"I think that has to be down to individuals. Don't you?" She shakes her head. "I don't think I can command people to work together. I don't think anything short of real change, and real forgiveness, will help to fix our country. But hopefully people will see that working together is better than breaking apart. Hopefully we can find ways to work alongside our neighbours, whichever side they were on."

She puts a hand on my shoulder, and I have to force myself not to pull away. I have no idea what she's going to say next.

Stay calm. Keep Fiona happy.

"This is why Katrina, who was a Corporal in the Home Forces, is working with me. People like Katrina, and people like Bex, need to use their skills to build a better country for all of us. We need to move past being angry and blaming each other. We need to stop pointing fingers, and we need to start asking what we can do to help."

Amy's fist hits the table, and everyone turns to look at her. She lifts a finger, and points at me.

"You want me to *forgive* her? You want me to say it doesn't matter that she *killed my friend*?"

Careful, Ketty. This is live. Everyone's watching.

Fiona shakes her head. "I'm not saying it's going to be easy."

"Easy?" Amy shakes her head. "It's not as if she shot a stranger in self-defence. Ketty killed my friend – one of her own recruits from Camp Bishop – because he refused to let her open the bunker and arrest us." She's crying now, tears blurring her makeup. "She shot one of the kindest, bravest people I've ever met, because she could. Because she had a gun, and he didn't." She looks at me again, and I can see the anger in her eyes. "Isn't that right, Ketty?"

I stare at her. I don't know what to say. I don't know what Fiona is expecting from me.

I'm here. I'm alive. Fiona needs me, for now. But if I say the wrong thing?

Prison. Crutches. Interrogations. Jumpsuit.

Don't screw this up, Ketty.

I think about Colonel Ryan, asking me whether I'm proud of my decisions. I think about Brigadier Lee, using me at the bunker to undermine Bracken. I think about the pressure to arrest the missing recruits.

Every decision I've made was made for good reasons. I kept myself safe. I earned my rank, and my authority. I did what needed to be done.

I glance at Fiona. She's watching me, carefully.

What do you want? Forgiveness? Or another story?

I turn back to Amy and take a breath.

Stay calm. State the facts.

"I had no choice. Just like you, at Horse Guards Parade. You stormed the stage. You shot the soldiers. You did what you had to do to rescue your friends." I shrug. "I did what I had to do."

"That doesn't make it right." She spits the words across the table at me. Charlotte puts a hand on her shoulder.

"No." I shake my head. "But it doesn't make it wrong, either."

I think about Saunders, sitting in the gatehouse, refusing to open the door.

He challenged me. He told me he'd die before he let me through.

Simple. What did he expect?

Amy glares at me for a moment. Her voice is quiet, but when she speaks, she makes herself heard.

"Jackson was calling your name, you know. In the road."

No one speaks. The studio is silent. My pulse hammers in my ears.

Stay calm. Breathe.

I shake my head. I'm sure I've misheard her. My hands are shaking. My voice is a whisper and my heart is pounding, but I make myself respond.

"What did you say?"

"After Dan shot him. He could hardly breathe, but he was calling for you."

And I can feel myself falling, backwards, into the footwell of the coach, pain flaring in my knee.

I remember shouting for Jackson. Screaming his name.

And he was calling for me. He was calling for me, and I didn't know.

I'm not ready for tears. Not here. I push them away with the back of my hand.

Amy watches me, a sad smile on her face.

Charlotte leans across the table.

"Do you get it now, Ketty? Do you understand what you did?"

But I can't speak. I can't say anything.

All I can think about is Jackson.

Packing

Bex

"Do you know where you're going yet?"

I shake my head. Maz is passing me handfuls of clothes from the wardrobe, and I'm stuffing them into my rucksack.

"I'm getting out of here."

He nods. "OK. Good plan."

He hands me a pair of smart shoes, and there's a smile on his face.

"What?"

"I see what Dan means."

"About …?"

"About you, Bex." He kneels down and pulls two more pairs of shoes from the bottom of the wardrobe. "You're always going to do something brave, or something stupid."

I can't help laughing. This doesn't feel brave. It doesn't feel stupid, either. It's just something I have to do.

"And he's right. You keep people guessing. I don't know whether to help you, or stop you."

"You're helping me, Maz." I take the shoes, and push them into the top of the bag.

He glances round the room. "It does look that way."

I give him a smile, and pull the bag shut.

"I think I need another bag. There's more stuff in the drawers." I look around. "Is there a carrier bag anywhere? A bin bag?"

He stands up, and looks at me. "You're really leaving." He gestures at the empty wardrobe. "This isn't just a tantrum? You're not going to calm down later and unpack?"

"I'm really leaving."

"OK then. Wait here." And he walks out of the room.

*****

There are piles of clothes on the bed when he comes back, holding a black rucksack in his hands.

"Is that big enough?"

"Yeah. Where did you get it?"

"It's mine." He shrugs. "I figure you're not going to disappear. You can give it back to me when you've unpacked. Wherever it is that you're going."

I give him a smile. "Thanks, Maz. That's really kind."

"About that …" he says, watching me stuff clothes into his bag. "I can't let you go if I don't know where you're going." He runs his hands over his hair, and looks at me.

"I thought you were helping. I thought you wanted me to get out."

"I do, Bex. I just … what am I supposed to say to your mother, if I let you walk out without a plan?" He makes a face. "What am I supposed to say to Charlie?"

I can't help laughing. I'm not sure who he's more afraid of – Mum, or Charlie.

"I see your point. You should probably go into hiding, after I leave."

"I mean it, Bex. Figure out where you're going, and I'll take you there myself. But if you don't know …" He shrugs. "What is it that Dan always threatens you with? Wrestling you into a chair?" I nod. "Well, I guess I'll have to do that."

I want to laugh. I want him to stop being serious. I want him to let me leave.

But he's right. I don't know where I'm going.

I sit down on the bed and put my head in my hands.

I don't have any money. I don't have a home to go to. Everyone I know in London is staying here, at the hotel.

And I'm safe, here. There are guards on the door. Mum has carers to look after her. My friends are all here.

Dan is here.

Dan is here … and his parents are in London.

I remember Dan's dad, inviting me to stay. His mum, repeating the invitation.

I check my watch. They'll be home from work.

I stand up, and throw the last few items into the bag. I take Saunders' sketch from the drawer, and slide it carefully into a book before packing it.

"I know where I'm going. Are you coming?"

Maz grins. "I'm right behind you."

Taxi

Ketty

"Well, that could have been better."

Fiona sits next to me in the taxi, her voice clipped and angry. I keep quiet. I don't want to know what she thinks about me.

I've washed my face, but the smeared eyeliner is still on my cheeks. And I'm still fighting back tears.

Now I know. I know that the last thing Jackson said was my name.

He could hardly breathe, with Dan's bullets in his lungs, but he was calling out to me.

And I couldn't get to him.

And now Amy knows what I did at the gatehouse. Dan knows, Bex knows.

I killed a member of their tribe, and they killed mine.

And Fiona wants us all to forgive each other.

"I think we rescued it, though. Don't you?" She looks at me, waiting for an answer.

Give her what she wants, Ketty. Keep her happy.

I nod.

"You did well." She smiles. "Playing the victim. You gave me something to work with. Thank you."

Victim?

"I think the gatehouse stuff was really helpful. Playing up the fact that you had your orders, and they had theirs." She nods to herself. "I think that made my point, about healing from a war. That we all have to come to terms with what happened, whatever side we were on."

I look at her, and I can't help myself.

"You really don't get it, do you?"

She gives me a surprised look. "Get what?"

"That this is all real. That people really died. People really got killed." I can't believe I'm talking back to Fiona.

Careful, Ketty.

"We're not just stories, Fiona. We're real people. We've hurt each other, and we've been hurt. We can't just fix everything overnight."

"I know that …"

I shake my head. "I don't think you do. Not really."

Shut up, Ketty. Stop talking.

She stares at me. "OK, Katrina. What if you're right? What if this is all too complicated to fix? What am I supposed to do? What am I supposed to tell people?"

I close my eyes. I don't want to be here. I don't want to be helping Fiona win the election. I don't want to be on her front line, on TV, making her look good.

I shrug. "I don't know. Tell people whatever you need to tell them. Tell them what they need to hear."

She gives me a tight smile. "Exactly, Katrina. Exactly."

Refuge

Bex

"Bex! Is everything OK?"

Dan's mother stands at the door, staring out at me. She looks over my shoulder at Maz.

"What's happened? Is Dan OK?"

I nod. "Dan's fine. I'm sorry, Mrs Pearce. I was wondering – could I take you up on your invitation?"

She takes in my suit, and the rucksacks. She nods and steps back, holding the door open. "Yes. Yes, of course. Come in."

I take the rucksacks from Maz and put them down in the porch, then pull him into a hug.

"Tell Mum I love her, won't you?" He nods. "And make sure Fiona looks after her."

"I will, Bex. Shall I tell them where you are?"

I look round at Mrs Pearce, and she nods. "Yeah. Stop them worrying about me."

He turns away, back to the waiting taxi.

"Thanks, Maz!" I call after him. He waves a hand as he walks away.

"One of your friends?"

"Yeah. He wanted to make sure I was safe."

She picks up one of my bags, and I take the other.

"You'd better come inside, and tell us what's going on."

*****

"And you quit? On TV?"

I nod. Dan's parents didn't watch the interview, but his dad is already scrolling through the channels on the kitchen TV, trying to find a repeat. It makes me smile to

305

see his expensive shirt, sleeves rolled up past his elbows, just like Dan.

"Was that a good idea?"

"I don't know, Mrs Pearce. I just couldn't sit there any more."

She puts a bowl of soup in front of me, and sits down at the table.

Dan's dad stops searching for a second. "What's your plan?"

"I really don't know. I had to get away from Fiona, but I don't know what to do now." I shake my head. "I'm sorry. I've landed you in the middle of all this."

Dan's mum puts her hand on my arm. "Don't worry, Bex. I'm glad we can help."

The soup warms me up, and it's lovely to be sitting in my friend's kitchen. No one's looking for me. No one wants to arrest me, or put me on TV again. I'm here because this is where I want to be, and no one is asking for anything in return.

"There's a bed made up in the guest room upstairs. There are towels in the en suite, and plenty of soaps and smellies."

"Thank you." I make myself smile, but I'm close to tears. All this kindness, when I've just walked out on everyone I care about. I know I don't deserve it.

"We'll be leaving early in the morning, but you're welcome to stay. I'll leave a front door key on the hall table. And there's plenty of food in the fridge – help yourself. We'll be back by seven, and we'll fix something to eat."

I nod, hiding a yawn.

"Go on," Dan's mum says, clearing the empty soup bowl away. "Go and get some sleep."

"Thank you," I say, through another yawn. "For everything."

"Second door on the right, top of the stairs. Let me know if there's anything else you need."

I pick up the rucksacks and carry them up to the guest room. It's huge, with turquoise throws and pillows, and dark wood furniture. I've never been to Dan's house. I've written to him during the holidays, so I know the address, but I've never visited. I'm not surprised that everything is beautiful, and neat, and expensive.

I tip Maz's rucksack up and shake out the clothes in a corner of the room. I pull out a pair of pyjamas, and grab my toothbrush from the other bag.

The bed is enormous, with a huge duvet and piles of pillows. I crawl in, and stare at the ceiling, wrapping the duvet round me.

I really did it. I told Fiona to carry on without me.

I can't help smiling to myself in the dark.

I'm free. And I have no idea what I'm going to do next.

Morphine

Ketty

Fiona drops me at the hospital, and I walk myself inside. It seems strange to be walking in, pain-free, knowing that I'm going to need the morphine drip when I take off the PowerGel.

The nurse smiles when I check into my ward. I head back to my room, and change out of my smart clothes. I pull on shorts and a T-shirt, and sit down on the bed.

I'm sorry, Jackson. I let them use you. I let Fiona use you.

And I let her use me.

*****

The nurse hooks me up to the morphine drip, and leaves me with a tray of food. I sit back against the pillows, and wait for the painkiller to take effect.

I don't feel like eating, but I pick at my meal, trying to forget what happened today.

The Face of the Resistance quit, live on TV. Fiona's big symbol, her figurehead for the resistance, walked out in front of the entire country.

And it would be funny, if it wasn't my fault.

But Bex blamed me, in front of all the cameras. Bex told them who Fiona is working with.

I'm supposed to symbolise everything they were fighting against, but here I am. In Fiona's hospital room, wearing Fiona's PowerGel.

What do you want from me, Fiona?

Dr Hayes knocks on the door. "Are you ready?"

I nod. She moves the table away, and pulls on the surgical gloves.

She reaches for the power switch, but I pull my knee up and flick the switch myself. I lower the knee gently back to the bed as the cold sensation starts to fade. She gives me an approving look.

"You don't need me, do you?" She smiles, and starts to pull back the fastening strip.

I'm bracing myself for the pain, but when she takes away the gel pack the morphine has kicked in. It hurts, but not as much as it should.

She leans over, and pulls the brace from the end of the bed. She slides it gently under my foot, pulls it up until it sits over my knee, and straps it in place.

"OK, soldier?" She asks, and I can't help smiling.

"OK. Thank you."

She packs the PowerGel away and leaves the box on the table.

"I'll be back in the morning to get you walking again," she says, pulling her gloves off as she leaves.

I lean back against the pillows.

I need Fiona. I need the PowerGel, and I need the morphine.

I can't go back to prison.

Fiona needs me, to make Franks talk. She needs me to tell her what happened in the Home Forces.

But after today? After losing the Face of the Resistance? How much longer will she need me?

And what happens when my usefulness runs out?

Am I free, when Fiona decides I'm not useful any more? Or is that when they put me back behind bars?

I shake my head. I've done this before. I need to figure out what she needs from me, and keep delivering.

You can do this, Ketty.

PART 2

MAY

Gift

Bex

I unlock the front door and step back to let Mum push herself into the flat. I look out for a moment, over the lawns and the parkland to the flats on the far side. I still can't believe this is ours. That we have somewhere of our own to live, after everything that's happened.

I pick up the shopping bags and follow her inside.

*****

The keys arrived in the post, addressed to me at Dan's parents' house. A set of keys, a map, and an address. Maz and Charlie came with me on the bus, and I followed the directions. I had no idea what to expect.

It's a ground-floor flat on the old Olympic park. Wheelchair accessible, three bedrooms, and a view of grass and trees, in London.

Inside, we found a huge bunch of flowers, and a note.

For Miss Ellman, who gave a better speech than I did at Horse Guard's Parade. Thank you for your dedication, and your bravery.

Handwritten, on Buckingham Palace stationery, and signed by the King.

Charlie threw her arms round me, and Maz grinned. We explored the flat together.

There was a folder of legal papers, and a voucher and catalogue for a furniture store. Mum and I spent hours in meetings with banks and lawyers, getting paperwork signed and restoring her bank accounts. We spent weeks, buying furniture and setting up the kitchen.

And it's ours, now. Our own home.

I have my own room. It's not a hotel room – no one tidies and resets it every day. And it's not Fiona's, or the OIE's. It's mine.

I found a frame for Saunders' sketch. It was the first thing on the wall in my room, over my desk where I can see it. And I have bookshelves, and books, and cushions, and clothes that I've chosen in the wardrobe. Mum's carers come twice a day, and she's even hired a cleaner. She doesn't want me to spend my time looking after her.

But we still go shopping together, in the supermarket round the corner. And we take it in turns to cook.

It's as far from orange jumpsuits and armour as I can get, and I love it.

*****

"Fiona misses you, you know." Dan helps himself to another sandwich. "And what did you say to my mother? She keeps asking how you are!"

I laugh, and lean back on the picnic rug. It's a gorgeous day, and we're sitting in the park outside the flat – Margie, Dan, and me.

"Number one: I don't care what Fiona thinks."

"After everything she's done for you?" Dan laughs.

"Did she buy me a house?" I point across the lawns at my own front door. "No. Does she listen to me? No. And does she *really* care about me? Or does she want the Face of the Resistance back to make people vote for her?"

He shrugs. "Fair points."

"And number two: I think your mum liked having me around. She did say several times that I'm more house trained than you or your dad."

Dan gives me a hurt look, and then grins. "Also a fair point."

"So what's it like, at the Royal, now that Fiona's campaigning?"

"Same old," says Dan. "Lots of interviews and photos. I'm a total TV celebrity now, you know."

Margie laughs. "She is working Dan pretty hard, now that she can't put you on screen. And she's giving Amy lots of interviews, too."

"And you? Did she listen to you?"

Margie nods. "Yeah. She's been good about what we said. She's mostly leaving me alone." Dan takes her hand, and she smiles at him. "I think telling her what we thought on live TV made her understand that we meant it."

"Useful to know." She nods. "And Ketty?" My voice is quiet, and I'm staring at the blanket. I'm not sure I want to know the answer.

Dan shrugs. "She's turned into Fiona's shadow. She follows her everywhere. But she mostly stays away from us."

"Does she live at the Royal?" I have a sudden vision of Ketty, sleeping in my old room, her wardrobe full of Fiona's uniform, identical to mine.

"No idea." Dan grins again. "Don't care."

"How are you, Bex? How's life in the Olympic Park?" Margie looks round at the grass and the trees. "It is gorgeous here."

I'm smiling as I tell them.

Belmarsh

Ketty

The drive to Belmarsh takes more than an hour, without the Military lanes. Fiona sorts through papers, a pile of reports and transcripts growing on the seat between us.

She waves at the folders. "Find me the Terrorism Committee briefing, would you, Katrina?"

I pick up the files and start working through them.

A career profile for Brigadier Lee. A report on the Home Forces command structure, Major General Franks at the top of the list. A thick file on the Recruit Training Service. Transcripts of interrogations.

And a career profile for David Conrad.

My breath catches in my throat. Everything is here. The date he signed up. His training and promotions. His transfer to act as Lee's assistant.

And his Terrorism Committee duties.

What he did for Lee: contacting the resistance groups, co-ordinating the bombings – that was all official, and it's noted in his file.

What he did to me, and to Jackson. There are records.

I'm smiling as I realise that he will suffer for this. He will pay for Jackson's death. And he will pay for the South Bank bomb.

"Katrina?"

I stare at the page in front of me. "Is Corporal Conrad at Belmarsh?"

She leans across and glances at the report. "I think so. He was Lee's Assistant?" I nod. "Yes. I think he's there."

"Miss Price." Colonel Ryan meets us at the door to the waiting room. "And Miss Smith."

Fiona shakes his hand. "Thank you for meeting with us, Colonel. Is everything ready?"

He smiles. "Your prisoner is waiting."

I look round the room, and there's an icy feeling at the back of my neck. Everything looks the same. The chairs, the tables, the coffee machine. Even the smell – coffee and disinfectant. All my muscles tense, and I realise I'm expecting Lee or Bracken to walk in. I'm expecting to have to explain myself.

Breathe, Ketty.

But I'm not in uniform today. I'm wearing one of Fiona's smart suits, and I'm carrying her document bag. I'm here with the OIE. With the coalition.

With the winning side.

And I'm standing where I stood when the soldiers put me in handcuffs.

Breathe.

My hands are shaking as Fiona takes the bag from me, and Colonel Ryan leads us towards the interrogation room.

"Just one thing, Colonel." He looks back at Fiona. "We've been waiting for weeks for the chance to talk to Franks. Why now?"

"We've tried everything else. You and Miss Smith are the next weapons in our armoury." He watches her for a moment. "I know you want to be the person who cracks Jane Franks. I know you think it will help your election campaign, but this isn't about you. This is about building a case against the person who ran the Home Forces, and the RTS, and the Terrorism Committee. That's the connection we need to make, before we put her on trial. We need to confirm what she knew about the activities of the Terrorism Committee."

I'm really doing this. I'm really taking Fiona's side, against Franks.

Breathe.

*****

Ryan opens the door, and Fiona walks into the interrogation room, her heels clicking on the tiled floor. Franks looks up, glancing between Ryan and Fiona. She's handcuffed to the table, but she sits up straight, and there's an air of authority about her in spite of the orange jumpsuit.

It's a shock to see her here, on the wrong side of the table. She might be in handcuffs, but she looks confident and self-assured.

She looks as if she's the one in charge.

"Good morning, Colonel Ryan," she says, as if she's welcoming him into her private office. She looks at Fiona, and raises her eyebrows. "And Fiona Price. To what do I owe the honour of a visit from the OIE?"

Ryan pulls out a chair for Fiona, and steps away to stand against the wall, arms folded. Fiona looks up at me, and holds out her hand to the other chair.

I take a breath, and walk into the room.

I should know what to expect. I've been here so many times before, but that was always to question terrorists. To get soundbites from Elizabeth Ellman, or Craig Dewar, or Margaret Watson. I wore a uniform, and my authority was clear.

But today is different. There's no uniform to protect me. And this isn't a terrorist behind the table – this is Major General Franks. This is the head of the Home Forces, who wanted to promote me. Who overlooked my unauthorised knowledge of the Terrorism Committee, because she wanted to give me a career.

I can't hide from Franks. I can't pretend I wasn't part of what she did. She knows exactly how much I know.

And that's why I'm here.

And I realise – this is my price. This is what I have to give them, to save myself. Not just the head of the Home Forces – I agreed to that – but my mentor. I have to hand over the person who believed in me, for a PowerGel and a ticket out of prison.

I didn't expect to feel this way.

This is it, Ketty. This is where you choose.

I know what Franks did. She deserves to be here. But I also know what she did for me. She stopped Lee from sending me home. She protected me when I knew too much.

And now she's my ticket to freedom. All I have to do is make sure she confesses to her crimes.

All I have to do is bring down the only person who had my back in London.

I had no idea this would be so hard.

I sit down, and turn to Franks. I realise I'm mirroring her body language: back straight, chin high. Looking as if I'm in charge.

She looks at me, and I see her shoulders slump. She looks down at the table, and across at Colonel Ryan, shaking her head.

She turns back to me.

"Corporal Smith."

I nod. "Major General."

I sit up straight, but inside I'm screaming.

I'm here to make sure she spends the rest of her life in the cells.

I don't want to do this.

I could refuse to co-operate. I could walk away.

And I would lose my freedom.

I remember the panic I felt in prison. The idea of spending sixty years behind bars.

I can feel myself fighting for breath.

Come on, Ketty. This is how you survive.

I don't want to be here. I don't want to betray her.

But it's my only way out.

She looks at my suit. At the Belmarsh visitor pass clipped to my pocket.

"Have you bought your way out of detention, Smith?"

I shake my head. I don't trust myself to speak. I can't answer her. I can't tell her that *she's* the price I'm paying.

She looks around the room. "And do these people know what you've done? Who you worked for?"

I nod. She looks down at the table again.

Don't let her get to you. You can do this.

"So what's the point of this meeting, Colonel?" She says, eventually.

Ryan shrugs. "We're just curious about the Terrorism Committee, Jane. We thought a familiar face might persuade you to talk."

She smiles, closing her eyes. "I'm sure Corporal Smith can tell you everything you need to know."

Ryan smiles. "Oh, she already has. She's told us about the Terrorism Committee. And Jane? She was in Leominster. In the town, after the attack." Franks looks up at Ryan. Her smile is gone, and the colour is draining from her face.

I look away, fixing my gaze on the wall behind Franks. I can't meet her eyes.

This is it. This is where I bring her down.

"Miss Smith helped with what she was told was a weapons test. She's an eyewitness to your greatest atrocity, and to everything that went on in the Home

Forces." Franks closes her eyes and shakes her head. "She's here to make sure you confess. She's here to tell us when you miss something out, or embellish the truth. She's here to keep you honest." He walks over to the table, leaning on it with both hands and looking down at Franks. "Last chance, Jane. Next time we ask you these questions, you'll be live on TV. If you want any protection, any sympathy, you'll start talking now."

*****

"Thank you, Katrina." Fiona is smiling as Colonel Ryan closes the door and leads us back into the waiting room. "That's what we needed."

We left Franks hunched over her handcuffs, head bowed. She hasn't confessed to everything, but she knows that I'm working with Ryan. She knows she can't hide forever.

I'm safe. I'm on the winning side.

And I've paid my price.

I'm not sure how I feel. Franks was in charge of the Home Forces. She set up the Terrorism Committee, and she gave Lee the freedom to do whatever he needed to do to keep the country afraid. She didn't order the bombings, or the raid on the coach, but she knew who was responsible, and she didn't stop them. She needed the Terrorism Committee, and she approved of what they did.

She let Conrad kill Jackson. She's the reason Bracken came to London, and the reason he died.

But she saw something in me. She promised me a career, even when I misjudged my actions. Even when I injured Elizabeth, and attacked Margaret. Even when she discovered that I had access to classified information.

And I've just destroyed her. I've just made sure she stays in prison for life.

Careful, Ketty. This is who you work for now. Don't get sentimental.

But walking out of the interrogation room, I feel cold. I feel abandoned. I feel as if the last person who cared about me has walked away.

Like Dad.

Like Bracken.

Like Mum.

I need to shout, and scream. I need to think about something else.

I need to distract myself.

I glance over at the door to the cells.

"Sir." Ryan looks at me. "I was wondering … is David Conrad in the cells?"

He raises an eyebrow. "He is."

There's your distraction, Ketty. Take it.

"Could I have a moment to talk to him?"

"I don't think that's appropriate, Katrina." Fiona sounds upset.

Ryan watches me, ignoring Fiona.

He smiles. "Why not?"

I have to catch my breath. I wasn't expecting him to agree.

I nod. I don't trust myself to speak. I'm fighting panic.

I don't have a plan. I don't know what I'm going to say to David.

I can feel his hands in my hair. Past midnight on the South Bank, the lights of the city reflected in the black water.

I can feel his lips on mine, electricity between us.

Your place or mine?

My skin crawls. I can see him smirking. Mocking me.

I can see his cruel smile as he mimes picking up the phone to Will. Telling him where to find us. Where to ambush the coach.

His voice, calling us an easy target.

And I can see Jackson, in his hospital bed. Jackson, who called out to me in the road as he fought for breath. As Conrad's lies killed him.

My hands are shaking as Ryan leads me to the cells.

*****

"Oh my god. Ketty!" He stands up from the mattress and runs a hand through his hair. I catch myself smiling as I recognise the gesture – it's what he does when he doesn't know what to say.

"Conrad."

I stand inside the door to his cell. The door is open, and Ryan is waiting in the corridor. I have five minutes, but I don't think I need that long.

He looks at my suit. At my visitor pass.

He shakes his head. "You're not locked up."

I give him a cold smile. For the first time, I know more than he does. I'm in control here, and I'm enjoying his confusion.

"It looks that way."

He stares at me, trying to understand what I'm doing here. He looks smaller, out of uniform. Frightened, but still beautiful. His hair is longer, framing his face. Part of me wants to kiss him again, to feel the lightning in his touch. And part of me wants to make sure he understands how much he hurt me.

Part of me wants him. Electricity and desire. Excitement and danger.

And part of me wants to win. To beat him. To make him pay.

This is your chance, Ketty. Take it.

I look him up and down. His feet are bare, and the jumpsuit hangs off his slim frame. "Nice outfit, David."

His expression changes, and he clenches his fists.

"You were behind bars. You were at the Police Station. How did you get out?" There's anger in his voice.

I point at his jumpsuit. "Oh, I wore one of those for a while." I shrug. "Inconvenient, isn't it? Being locked in here?"

He stares at me, shaking his head. I find myself smiling as I watch him take this in.

"Why did they let you go, Ketty?" He narrows his eyes. "What did they get from you? What did you give them?"

I look down at my suit. "It seems that I'm valuable to the government, David." I shake my head, still smiling. I watch him for a moment, anger twisting his face.

He glares at me, waiting.

I shrug. "But apparently you're not. It seems that you're more useful as a prisoner."

His voice is desperate now. Pleading.

"Tell me what you did, Ketty."

And give you a chance at freedom? Not today, David.

I give him a recruit-scaring stare. "I don't think so." He steps back, shaking his head.

"Enjoy your show trial, David. And get used to this." I wave at the cell. "I think you're going to be here for a long time."

I turn to leave, and he steps towards me, his voice breaking. "Ketty! Ketty, please. Get me out of here."

I turn back. There are tears in his eyes, and he's begging.

He's beautiful, and he's begging me.

His touch on my skin, at midnight.

That kiss.

Jackson, calling out to me in the road.

I take a breath, willing myself to stay calm.

I have the power here. *I* choose what happens next.

Hurt him, Ketty. Make him understand.

"Oh, if this was just about you and me, I might." I shrug. "I could probably get you out. Colonel Ryan might listen to me."

"Ketty. Please. I tried to help you, before …"

I watch as he reaches out to me. As he begs for my help. Posh-shabby-gorgeous, trying to manipulate me again.

Not today, David.

And I know what to say.

This is for you, Jackson.

I step towards him. "This isn't about me, David. You used me. You manipulated me." I shrug again. "I know you tried to help. You tried to warn me about the Terrorism Committee. And maybe I could forgive you everything else, for that."

He nods, waiting for me to change my mind. There's hope in his eyes as he watches my face.

"But the thing I can't forgive, David, is what happened to Jackson."

He shakes his head. "Ketty …"

"*You* did that. You told Will where to find us. You sent the resistance fighters onto my coach, and you killed my friend. *You* killed the person I loved."

I freeze, catching my breath.

The person I loved.

My own words take me by surprise. I hadn't meant to say that. I've never said that, to anyone. Not even to Jackson.

Not even to myself.

Jackson was the person I loved.

I clench my fists, to keep my hands from shaking.

Conrad holds his hands up in front of him. "I was doing my job, Ketty. I was only doing my job."

I can't believe that's all he has to say.

"So was Jackson." I stare at him, and he takes a step back. "Jackson died, because you did your job. Jackson *died*." I wave a hand at the cell again, willing myself not to cry. "So get used to this. Enjoy the jumpsuit and the handcuffs. Enjoy your televised trial." I shake my head. "I can't bring Jackson back, but I can make sure that you pay for what happened. For what you took from me."

"Ketty!"

But I'm already walking out, closing the door behind me and ignoring the look of amusement on Colonel Ryan's face.

And it feels good.

Funeral

Bex

It's raining when we get off the train. It's a tiny station – one building and a bus shelter – and there's a wheelchair taxi waiting for us in the car park.

"So this is where you stayed, when you left Camp Bishop?" Mum looks out over the fields as we drive towards the church.

"Somewhere over there," I say, pointing towards the hills in the distance. "Makepeace Farm is that way."

She nods, and takes my hand. "How are you doing, beautiful girl?"

"I'm OK." I push away thoughts of Will, blocking the bullets that were meant for his daughter. Today isn't about how he died – it's about how he lived. And I'm here because he kept me safe. He gave us a home when we needed somewhere to hide. He took us in, and he trusted us – and he wasn't shy about telling us when we'd done something wrong.

He saved my life. And I'm here to say goodbye.

*****

The church is small, in a graveyard full of leaning headstones and mossy stone slabs. There's a war memorial on the street outside, and a view towards the river and the hills beyond.

There's a line of police in the road, keeping the TV cameras and the photographers away. Mum and I make our way along the path to the church – Mum pushing herself, and me holding the black umbrella we bought at the station in Birmingham. Dan stands up as I walk in, striding up the aisle and wrapping me in a tight hug.

"You OK?" I whisper, and he shakes his head against my shoulder.

"You?" I shake mine, and it's everything I can do not to cry.

"Come on," he says, pulling away and taking my hand. There's a seat for me in the second row, and a space for Mum on the end, and by the time I sit down I've been hugged by all my friends. I glance along the row of wooden seats, and I can't help smiling. We're all wearing black suits and tops, picked out by Fiona for her campaign appearances. She didn't know she was preparing us for this.

I glance behind me. The church is full, and I recognise most of the faces. Will's fighters from the bunker. Jo gives me a smile, and I smile back.

Dr Richards follows the coffin into the church, pushed in a wheelchair by one of the funeral directors. She's in the front row, in front of Mum. Margie sits next to her, holding her hand.

I don't pay much attention to the service. I'm too busy thinking about Makepeace Farm. About meeting Will, and showing him our armour. Training his fighters. The raid on the coach, and his fury when we brought back Jake and Amy.

The minister mentions Will's temper, and people behind me laugh.

But his anger was the reason we didn't go with him to raid the supply convoy. It's the reason we're still alive.

I close my eyes, but I can't stop the tears. Next to me, Charlie pulls a packet of tissues from her pocket and offers them to me. She takes my hand, and holds it tightly as we listen to the eulogy.

*****

The rain has cleared when we walk out into the graveyard. We stand round the newly dug grave as the coffin is lowered in. Dr Richards watches, Margie on one side and Jo on the other, both kneeling on the wet grass, holding her hands.

There's a pub across the road from the church, and in a back room there are tables and chairs, and a buffet for the funeral guests. I don't feel like eating, but I fill a plate for Mum, and leave her talking to Charlie and Maz.

I find Dr Richards with Margie and Dan. She holds out a hand, and I kneel down and give her a hug. Her shoulder is still padded with bandages, and she doesn't move her injured arm.

"Thank you, Bex," she says, one arm round my shoulders. "I wouldn't be here if you hadn't been so brave."

I pull away, shaking my head. "It wasn't just me …"

"I've seen the footage, Bex. If you hadn't gone after the firing squad, I wouldn't have made it off the platform." She reaches up and takes my hand. "You made Dad's sacrifice count. He'd want you to know that."

I nod, blinking away tears. "I'm alive because of him," I say, making myself smile. "I guess I've paid him back, for looking after us at Makepeace."

She smiles, too. "I guess you have, Bex."

*****

"So you're coming, right?" Dan looks up from his plate of food.

I shake my head, "I don't know."

"You have to come, Bex! We can't have Victory Day without you!"

"I quit, Dan. You remember. You were there."

"I know, I know – but it's *Victory Day*. It's the big party. It wouldn't feel right to celebrate without you."

I fix him with a stare. "And is Fiona going to be there? Is Fiona going to be in all the photos, and talking to all the important guests?"

"Well, yes …"

"Then no, Dan. I'm not going."

Margie puts a hand on my arm. "Fiona will be there. Of course she will. But it's not about her – it's about us. We're the guests of honour – all of us." She glances at Dan. "And we want you to be there."

"Come on, Bex," Amy leans across the table. "It won't be the same without you."

I roll my eyes. I don't want anything to do with Fiona, or Ketty, or the Face of the Resistance. I walked out. I got away.

And now my friends want me to go back.

Charlie pulls up a chair and sits down next to me.

"What are we talking about? And why does Bex look as if you've all been picking on her?"

"Victory Day," says Dan, round a mouthful of sausage roll.

"You're coming, right?" Charlie smiles at me. "Tell me you're coming."

I shake my head, slowly, and Charlie frowns. She tilts her head down, as if she's looking at me over a pair of glasses.

"Rebecca Ellman," she says, as if she's a teacher telling me off. There's a sharp intake of breath from Dan, and I can't help smiling. "We will not accept 'no' for an answer. You are coming to the Victory Day celebrations, if we have to kidnap you and drag you there ourselves." She looks up again. "Anyway. Don't you have an amazing dress to wear? A dress you haven't worn yet?" She watches me, waiting for my answer.

I don't want to go to the celebrations. London will be full of people. There will be huge crowds in Hyde Park and Trafalgar Square. There will be speeches and big screens.

I've been in a crowd in London. I've watched on the screens while they put my friend through a show trial. I know how frightening it is to be surrounded by shouting strangers.

This feels too much like Horse Guard's Parade.

I look at Margie, and she's nodding, watching me. "Come on, Bex. Let's all get dressed up and have one more brilliant night." She glances at Dan. "Fiona won't need us for much longer, and then we'll all be going to different places. We won't be just down the road if you want to meet up."

She's right. I hadn't thought about what happens next. About what happens after the election, and Victory Day.

Dan and Margie are going back to Rushmere. Jake and Amy are going home. For the first time in more than a year, I won't be close to my friends.

I've already left. I've already walked away, and this is my last chance to see them all. To spend time with them all, for one more night.

And if Margie can handle the crowds, and the screens, and the people …

I shake my head. If Margie's going, I can't back out. If she's being brave, then I can be brave.

I hide my face in my hands. I don't want to do this, but I don't want to miss it, either.

And everyone's waiting for my answer.

"OK. Fine. I'll come."

I look up at Charlie, and she grins. "You won't regret it. I promise."

Flowers

Ketty

"I'm so sorry, Katrina." Fiona sits down next to me at the conference table. "I've only just found out."

I nod. I know I should feel something, but my head feels like a blank page. A white space, numb.

"There's a charity, that organises funerals for homeless people. They've been trying to contact you. Someone put them in touch with me."

I should care. I should say something.

This is it. This is the last connection to my life before Camp Bishop. And it's gone.

Dad.

"They held a funeral, at the crematorium. His ashes are scattered in the grounds."

I nod again, trying to decide how I feel. I can see him, sitting in the kitchen, the knife he'd threatened me with next to him on the table.

I can hear him, begging me to stay. Calling me his little girl.

And I can hear the door, slamming behind me as I walked away.

"Thank you, Fiona," I say, standing up. "Will you excuse me?"

"Of course. Take all the time you need."

*****

I walk up the stairs to my hotel room, still thinking about the day I left home. The day I took myself to safety, from my home and my job to the security of Camp Bishop. From one alcoholic old man to another.

When she discharged me from hospital, Dr Hayes told me not to run while the bones in my knee are still healing, and I've followed her instructions. But today I pull trainers and running kit from my wardrobe and change into them without thinking. I shake two painkillers from the bottle next to the bed, and swallow them. I check the battery in the PowerGel, and put a spare in my pocket. I take my room key, and a bottle of water, and I take the stairs to the lobby.

Outside, I start to run. I don't have a plan in mind. I don't know where I'm going. But I need to run, and I need time to think.

I follow the road to Hyde Park, and turn to run along Park Lane, past big hotels and expensive cars.

And I wonder how long it took Dad to stop paying the rent. How long he spent sleeping on the street, without me to pay the bills.

I wonder who was with him when he died.

And I think about Jackson, lying in the road outside the coach. Calling my name as he fought for breath, as Recruit Mitchell and the coach driver tried to save his life.

And Bracken, ending his own life when he realised we'd lost. Leaving me and Conrad and Franks to take the blame, and the consequences.

Franks, slumped over her handcuffs in the interrogation room.

All the people I cared about, leaving me to go on without them.

Come on, Ketty. Self-pity doesn't suit you.

I think about Fiona, and what she wants from me now that Franks has given a full confession. How much longer will she need my help? How much longer can she keep me out of prison? Am I free, now that Franks has confessed, or is my name on a coalition list? If I walk away from Fiona's protection, will they arrest me again?

I haven't seen my release papers. I don't know the terms of my freedom. Is this a permanent release, or am I only free until Fiona can't use me any more?

Survive, Ketty. Keep giving Fiona what she wants.

I feel the tightness of the PowerGel round my leg. The freedom of running, after weeks of prison and hospital and working on Fiona's campaign. It's a warm, bright day, and I feel as if I could go on running forever.

I find myself running through Green Park, and out onto the Mall.

I'm following my old running route, back towards the flat. Back towards the Home Forces and the South Bank bomb.

Back towards my old life.

But the flat has been confiscated, the locks changed. It belonged to the Home Forces, so now it belongs to the coalition. Disgraced former Corporals are not welcome.

I can't face running down Whitehall. Past the place I hailed the taxi for Bracken, the night I took him home. Past the buildings where I worked for the losing side. Past the building where everything ended – where Lee and Bracken died.

I turn to run along Horse Guard's Road. Horse Guard's Parade is empty, fenced off from the pavement.

And there are flowers, heaped up against the barriers. Piles of them, spilling across my path.

I stop, and crouch down to look at the cards.

'Remembering William Richards.'

'In memory of a resistance hero.'

'For Will, who saved his daughter.'

There are hundreds of them. Hundreds of bunches of flowers. Hundreds of people, paying tribute to the resistance fighter who betrayed his people to protect his daughter. Who took the bullets that were meant for her.

Who redeemed himself, in the only way he could.

And there are more, remembering everyone we sent to the firing squads.

'For all the victims of the Home Forces.'
'For everyone who died to keep us afraid.'
'Thank you for your resistance.'

I kneel on the ground, reading card after card on the bunches of flowers.

This is what it means to be on the losing side. This is how it feels to see your fellow soldiers locked up, and your enemies become heroes.

The orange jumpsuit might be a mark of shame for Franks and Conrad, and everyone else they've locked away, but out here it's a mark of sacrifice. Out here it's the mark of heroes, standing in their handcuffs on PIN, watching the firing squads turn towards them and lift their guns.

Where do you fit in this new world, Ketty? Where's your place in the coalition's UK?

I shake my head.

Dad taught me to survive, whatever happened. Whoever was against me. And I used what I learnt – with Jackson, at Camp Bishop. With Bracken, through his weakness and his anger. With Conrad. With Jake and Saunders, at the farm. With Penny and her friends, in prison.

I'm still here. Dad's gone, Jackson's gone, Bracken's gone. But I'm still here.

And I'm free, for now.

I stand up, and start the run back to the hotel.

I need to talk to Fiona.

*****

She's waiting in the lobby when I walk through the doors, and Colonel Ryan is with her. They look up as I walk past.

337

"Katrina!"

I turn, my T-shirt soaked with sweat and my hair clinging to my neck.

"Fiona. Could I have a moment to get changed?"

Ryan smiles. "This won't take long."

My breath catches in my throat.

This is it, Ketty. This is where they send you back to prison.

To sixty years, or a firing squad.

I make myself stand up straight, and wait for Colonel Ryan to take away my freedom.

"I'm sorry to do this, Fiona," he says, and I force myself to stand at ease. I lift my chin, and focus on the wall behind him.

I will not let him see my fear.

Discipline. Determination. Backbone.

"I know Miss Smith has been useful to you, and we appreciate her help with getting Franks to talk."

Fiona nods, and glances at me.

"But I think it's time to move on. Don't you?"

Fiona opens her mouth to speak, but before she can say anything, Ryan turns to me. I think of Conrad in his cell, begging me to get him out. I think of Penny and her friends, waiting for me behind the prison walls. I think of Elizabeth. Of spending sixty years in a cage.

Here it comes. Enjoy your final moments of freedom.

"You were a soldier, Katrina," he says. I nod. I don't trust myself to speak.

He smiles. "Do you want to be a soldier again?"

I can't help staring at him. "Sir?"

"You're good at what you do, Katrina. I've seen your interrogations – the way you persuade people to talk. And I've seen your record from Camp Bishop. I know you saved yourself from a difficult situation at home, and that you worked hard for your promotions."

He glances at Fiona, and back at me. "I think you're wasted here."

Fiona steps forward. "Colonel …" He waves her away.

"I'm offering you a chance to join the coalition. To join the new UK Army, when we're ready to stand by ourselves again." He watches me, still smiling. "We need your skills, Katrina. We need people with discipline. People who can get things done."

"Sir, I …" My voice fails. I don't know what to say.

"I'm not going to give you your old job back. I think it was a mistake, making you an assistant – isolating you from the chain of command. And without proper leadership, you have a habit of crossing lines we'd rather not cross."

I can feel the colour rising on my face. He's talking about Elizabeth, and Margaret. With a jolt, I realise he's talking about Saunders.

"I have your release papers. It's my decision, what happens to you when Fiona's finished with you." Fiona starts to protest, but Ryan ignores her. "I can send you back to prison. Hand you over to the coalition. Or I can give you a chance." He watches me, the ghost of a smile on his face. "I want to give you a chance."

I'm staring at him. I'm trying to understand what he's saying.

This is my answer. This is what happens next.

This is how I keep my freedom.

"You need a strong chain of command, and a lot of training before we can put you to work. We need to make sure you stay on the right side of the lines. But I think you can do that, with the right guidance." I nod, finally taking in what he's offering me. "I'm willing to invest in you. You'll be starting at the bottom – Private Smith. Can you handle that?"

Given the alternatives?

"Yes, Sir. Absolutely." I can't stop myself from smiling.

"Two weeks, then? I'm sure Fiona could use your help for the Victory Day celebrations." She nods. "But after that, you work for me."

He checks his watch. "Two weeks from today, have your bags packed. We'll pick you up at noon." He points at my knee. "And bring the PowerGel. You're going to need it."

"Yes, Sir." I'm grinning now. I can't help it. "Thank you, Sir."

Ryan shakes my hand, and Fiona's, and leaves us standing in the lobby, out of place between the velvet sofas.

"Well," says Fiona, eventually, her voice cold. "Go and take a shower, and meet me in the office. We have plenty of work to do."

JUNE

Victory

Bex

I pull the dress from the suit carrier, and drape it over the back of the sofa.

Gail chose it on our shopping trip, after I rejected the pink ball gown. And it's beautiful. Simple. Silver-grey, like a shadow. Fitted, knee-length, with sequins that catch the light.

I didn't want to come. I didn't want to be here, but I promised Charlie. So I'm back at the Royal Hotel, in my room next to Mum's, on the corridor with my friends. I didn't think I'd have the chance to wear the dress – not after I walked out on Fiona.

But here I am.

I take the lid off the shoe box, and pick up the silver-grey sandals with their low heels and glitter. There's a tiny shoulder bag on a sliver chain, and a necklace that sparkles in the bright lights.

I look at the outfit. This isn't me. Jeans and T-shirts, cargo trousers – even Fiona's smart suits – but not this. It feels too exotic. Too high-profile. Promising that I'm something I'm not.

And I realise that it's another uniform, like the RTS fatigues. Like my armour. Dress up and blend in. Wear what everyone else is wearing and hide behind the disguise.

I shrug off my jacket, and carefully take the dress out of its plastic wrapping.

*****

It's Victory Day. Charlie promised Fiona I'd be here, and my friends have been calling me ever since the funeral, making sure I haven't changed my mind.

Reminding me about the dress. Promising me a party before they all leave London.

We've spent the afternoon on the stage in Hyde Park. There were speeches and medals, and confirmation that Fiona will be our new Prime Minister after the election last week. The King hung a heavy gold star round my neck on a broad purple ribbon, and the vast crowd clapped and cheered. I closed my eyes as he presented medals to my friends, and handed a medal in a box to Saunders' parents. I blocked out the sound of the crowd, cheering for us.

It sounded too much like the crowd at Horse Guard's Parade. Too much like the people who shouted for Margie to die.

Margie made a speech, and the whole crowd fell silent. She talked about her imprisonment, and she talked about facing the firing squad. She asked us never to put anyone through that again. Dr Richards gave everyone a history lesson, leaning on a walking stick at the lectern, and reminded us to learn from our past. Charlie talked about friendship and working together. Dan thanked everyone he could think of. Amy cried, and talked about Joss. She told the crowd to build a better country together.

Jake and I refused to speak. I'm not the Face of the Resistance any more, and I said everything I needed to say on the day we saved Margie. Fiona doesn't get to use me again.

Mum watched from the VIP box with the other parents and families. I thought she might burst with pride, but I couldn't wait to get off the stage, and away from the crowd.

I couldn't wait to get back here, to my room, and close the door.

I want this to be over. I want to be invisible again.

*****

There's a knock on my door, and Dan calls my name.

I stand in front of the mirror, checking my outfit. Checking that I have enough clips and hairspray in my hair. I straighten my necklace and my dress, and walk to the door.

Everyone's waiting. Dan and Jake in their black bow ties and dinner jackets, and Maz in his kilt. Margie, in a long, fitted black dress. Charlie in a stunning shade of green, and Amy, rocking the pink sparkling ball gown I turned down. And Mum, in a midnight blue jacket and trousers, the silver bird necklace at her throat.

She breaks into a grin as she sees me, and I can't help smiling back.

Charlie steps forward and gives me a careful hug. "You look amazing, Bex."

"You, too."

"That dress ..." She steps back and looks me up and down. "You're going to upstage Fiona tonight." She shakes her head, and makes a face. "She won't like it."

And I'm laughing. "She paid for it! And I don't care what Fiona thinks."

Dan holds out one arm to Margie, and one to me, and I'm about to take it when Maz steps in.

"Bex of the Resistance. May I have the honour of escorting you to the official Victory Day ball?"

I'm blushing as I take his arm, Charlie grinning at me over his shoulder. I might be upstaging Fiona, but Maz is upstaging all of us in his kilt. And he's walking in with me.

I feel as if I'm floating as we take the lift to the lobby.

Changes

Ketty

Fiona sends me out in a taxi when she realises I don't have anything to wear for the party. She calls the department store and books me a personal shopper, then tells them to send her the bill. I have half an hour to pick out an outfit that works with the PowerGel.

The third outfit I try on is a pair of wide black trousers and a tight silver sequined halterneck top. The assistant hands me a pair of flat shoes, a sparkling hair clip, and a long necklace with an oversized black pendant, and I'm back in the taxi.

Twenty minutes. I still have time for a shower.

*****

There's a smile on my face as the taxi pushes through the crowds on Park Lane. The road is closed, but when I show the pass Fiona gave me, the soldier at the barrier waves us through.

I don't have long to enjoy this power. Tomorrow at noon, I join the army. Colonel Ryan's people will pick me up from the hotel, and I'll start my new life as Private Smith. A uniform, a gun, and no one but myself to take care of. Work hard, get noticed, climb the ranks.

This is a world I understand.

And this is what I want.

I need to take this chance. I need to take my life back. I need to learn to work inside the lines.

I need to leave the RTS and the Home Forces behind. I need to start again.

It seems impossible that two and a half months ago, I was behind bars, wearing a prison jumpsuit and begging the guards for painkillers. This afternoon, I waited backstage in Hyde Park, assistant to the most powerful woman in the country. Fiona addressed the crowd, and the King hung medals round the necks of my recruits. I wore the suit Fiona bought me, and held the new Prime Minister's briefcase while she stepped out on stage and formally agreed to form His Majesty's Government. Tonight, I'm dressing for a ball, and by tomorrow night I'll be back in uniform, and all this will be behind me. The Home Forces, prison, the choices I've made.

My bags are already packed. It can't come soon enough.

*****

"Katrina!" Fiona looks up from the mirror, and the stylist holds her hair in place with one hand while she turns to look at my outfit.

She nods. "That looks good. Are you ready?"

My hair hangs loose, with the clip on one side above my ear. The halterneck fits as if it was made for me, and there's no hint of the PowerGel under the wide trousers. I've put a new battery in the power pack, and there's a spare in my pocket. I'm ready.

"Whenever you need me."

"Could you run down and check that the ballroom is set up? And make sure the journalists don't get inside. Keep them in the lobby for me." She turns back to the mirror, and the stylist resumes sliding clips into her hair. "I'll meet you down there."

"There's no hurry, Fiona. I've got this."

She smiles. "I don't know what I'm going to do without you."

Run the country. Order someone else around. Take credit for Franks' confession.

I'm smiling as I leave the room.
Whatever you do, it's not my problem.

*****

I check the official photographer's ID, and let her into the party. Everyone else – the newspapers, the TV cameras – I line up in the lobby outside the ballroom. There are bouncers on the door, and I make sure they know to keep the reporters outside.

Fiona waits until most of the guests are inside before striding through the lobby and addressing the cameras. She's wearing a floor-length off-the-shoulder dress that makes her look more like a princess than a Prime Minister, and the photographers love it. She talks to all the reporters, and answers questions for the news channels and the papers. It takes twenty minutes, but she's smiling when she walks past the bouncers and into the ball.

VIP

Bex

There's a wall of cameras outside the ballroom. Photographers and TV reporters and journalists, all wanting to take our photos and ask us how we're feeling.

I can't do this. I can't pose for photos and pretend that I'm fine. I can't pretend that I'm not hurting. I wish Saunders was here, and Dad, and Will. I don't want to smile for the cameras, when I'm thinking about them. About everyone we've lost.

My footsteps slow, and I'm turning away when Maz puts a hand on my arm. I try to tug away from his grip, but he doesn't let go.

"No, you don't."

The cameras are in front of us now, and Maz is gripping my elbow. I can't walk away.

I roll my eyes. "Did Charlie put you up to this?"

He grins at me. "What do you think, Rugrat?"

I glance over my shoulder. Charlie is walking behind us with Mum, and she catches my eye and winks.

They've planned this together.

"I don't have a choice, do I?"

"No, you don't. Now smile, and let's get inside." He grins at me again. "Where the drinks are."

We line up in front of the reporters. Dresses and dinner jackets, kilts and sequins, arms round each other's waists. Maz is on one side of me, and Dan is on the other, and they give me the strength to stand and smile as the cameras flash and the photographers shout.

When the reporters start calling out questions, Maz holds up his hand.

"That's it, ladies and gentlemen. We have a party to go to." And he offers me his arm again.

"Thank you," I say, quietly, and he smiles. I take his elbow, and he walks me into the Victory Day ball.

*****

"That dress looks amazing!" Gail puts her hand on my shoulder and kisses me on the cheek. "Never mind the Face of the Resistance – you're the belle of the ball!" She looks around at the packed ballroom. "I bet everyone wants a photo with you."

She has to raise her voice, over the music and the conversations. It's a stunning party – the room is decorated like something out of a fairy tale, and there are almost as many waiters as guests, pouring drinks and carrying trays of food. The room is crowded with important people. New MPs, Fiona's staff, and everyone who supported the Opposition in Exile.

I nod. "It's getting boring. All these important old men posing for the cameras with their arms round my shoulders." I shudder, thinking about it. I'm the prize everyone wants on their arm tonight. The Face of the Resistance, all dressed up for their entertainment.

"So you're hiding in the corner?" Gail looks around.

"Hiding?" Dan sounds offended. "This is the VIP table! We're the VIPs – and this is our table!"

Gail smiles, and Margie moves Dan's glass out of reach while he's looking at us.

"You're enjoying the bubbly, then?" She whispers to me, grinning.

I give her a grin back. "Dan definitely is."

"Sit down! Sit with us, Gail!" Dan waves at the empty seats in front of him. Gail glances at me, and we sit down. Maz tops up our glasses from the bottle he's sweet-talked from the waiter.

Dan leans both elbows on the table. "So, Gail. Has the elusive Bex told you what she's planning to do with her life?" Gail shakes her head, and Dan rolls his eyes. "So we can't even force you to tell us. Have you told anyone, Bex?"

I shake my head, smiling. Mum knows, but I haven't told the others.

I'm not going back to school, and I don't know what they'll think. I don't know what they'll say.

But I have to tell them sometime.

"Go on, Bex. Tell us what you're planning."

I take a deep breath, and put both hands on the table. "OK. But you mustn't laugh."

"We won't laugh. I promise." Dan sounds serious, suddenly. Charlie nudges Maz, and the table is silent.

I can't meet anyone's eyes.

"I'm joining the Fire Service. The London Fire Brigade."

I look up. Dan looks stunned. Margie watches me, nodding.

Charlie takes my hand. "That's brilliant, Bex." She smiles. "Teamwork, protecting people, keeping people safe. I can't think of anything better."

I smile back. It's wonderful, knowing that Charlie understands. The others might take longer to see why this is what I want to do, but having Charlie in my corner is good enough for now.

"Wow." Dan sounds stunned. "Wow. OK." He runs a hand through his hair.

Margie nods. "So you're really not coming back to Rushmere with us."

"I'm not. You'll have to deal with being the famous kids all by yourselves."

She laughs. "I think we can handle that." She nudges Dan. "I think that's what he was born for."

"And your Mum's OK with this?" Dan's still trying to process what I've said.

"Mum's fine with it. I think she likes the idea of me living at home."

"This deserves a toast!" Maz raises his glass. "To Bex." He thinks for a moment, holding his glass high. "Bex of the Fire Brigade? Fireman Bex?"

"Fireman Bex!" And my friends are laughing, and raising their glasses.

"Good decision," says Gail, quietly, as she puts her glass down on the table. "Just remember to look after yourself, too." And she gives me a quick, tight hug. "Keep in touch, Fireman Bex."

I watch as she walks away, into the crowd. That was my first goodbye of the night, and I realise that there will be plenty more before the party's over.

Working

Ketty

I spend the next three hours standing where Fiona can see me. Bringing her drinks, and taking away empty glasses and plates. Finding the people she wants to speak to next, and letting them know that the Prime Minister would like to see them. It's boring, but it keeps me occupied.

Tomorrow can't come quickly enough. This isn't my kind of party – no dancing on the tables, or singing with the band. No one to draw lipstick war paint on my face.

No one to walk home with.

Conrad was the last person who tried to walk me home, but it's Jackson I think of. Staggering back to Camp Bishop from the bar in Leominster, laughing about the people we flirted with. Trying to look sober at the gate, so the guards would let us back inside. Trying not to wake the recruits as we stumbled to our rooms.

I loved you, Jackson. I understand that now.

Did you know?

Did you love me?

Fiona catches my eye, and I walk over to see what she needs.

Plans

Bex

"So what about you, Amy? What are you planning to do next?" Charlie puts her glass on the table, raising her voice over the music.

"School. With Jake." She can't hide a smile when she mentions her friend. "I'm going to finish school. Then I'm going to university and I'm going to study politics. I'm going to make sure this never happens again."

"Good for you," says Charlie, smiling.

"And what about you? What are you going to do after this?" Amy waves her hand at the ballroom.

Charlie looks at Maz, and grins. He grins back.

"Go on," he says. "You tell them".

"Maz and I," says Charlie, blushing. "We're going to open a restaurant." She shrugs. "Might as well do what we're good at!"

Amy holds out her hands, and Charlie takes them in hers. "That's so sweet, you two! Can we come and visit?"

"And will you serve proper sandwiches?" I can't help laughing as Dan leans towards them, drumming his finger on the table. "Proper sandwiches are very important."

"We know, Dan," says Maz, smiling. "You'll have to come and test them for us. Give us your seal of sandwich approval."

Dan nods, and sits back in his chair. "Deal."

*****

355

Dan's laughing. Maz is filling the glasses, and Amy is trying to persuade Jake to sit with us. The music is loud, and the room feels more and more crowded. Neesh and Caroline have both come to the table, and they've both wished us good luck for the future. They've both said goodbye.

And it's too much. I can't think, sitting here – I need to go somewhere quiet. I need some fresh air. I whisper to Charlie that I'll meet them on the roof, and I walk away from the table.

Mum's sitting with Dan's parents, so I walk past their table and tell Mum I'll see her for the fireworks. I have to elbow my way through the crowd, and the photographer follows me, asking for a final photo before I leave. I wave her away, and walk out into the lobby.

It's quiet out here. The reporters and the cameras have left, and it's just the receptionist and the velvet sofas. There's a lift standing open, so I step inside and press the button for the roof terrace.

And I'm finally on my own. No goodbyes. No photographers. No important old men. No Fiona.

I ride the lift to the roof, leaning against the wall and resting my head against the gold-framed mirror behind me.

Whatever I do, people still want something from me. Fiona. The party guests. The reporters. Just being here isn't enough – I have to get dressed up and answer questions and pose for photos.

I need some time on my own.

Lines

Ketty

The VIPs have gathered at a table in the far corner of the ballroom. My recruits, and their groupies, looking like film stars in their ball gowns and Black Tie, laughing as they sit with their backs to the room. It's as if all they care about is each other.

Every time Bex stands up, she can't cross the room without five or six people asking her to pose with them for photos. She might have quit as Fiona's Face of the Resistance, but that doesn't stop hers from being the most recognisable face at the party – and the most photographed. Fiona must be furious.

So I'm surprised when I notice her leaving the ballroom, shaking her head and waving the photographer away when she tries to take another picture.

Not enjoying yourself, Guest of Honour?

I pull my watch from my pocket. The fireworks will be starting in half an hour, and we're all expected on the roof terrace to watch the display. I think about Bex, and her evening walks at Camp Bishop. How she liked to be alone at the end of the day.

And I think about what happens tomorrow. Colonel Ryan's unease with the lines I've crossed. His expectation that I'll do better with a strong chain of command.

My determination to prove him right.

I need to draw a line under everything that's happened. I need to start again.

I tell Fiona that I'm stepping out, and I follow Bex up to the roof.

Rooftop

Bex

The lift doors open, and I'm in a glass lobby. There's a bouncer here, but he's one of Fiona's guards, so he smiles and opens the door for me as I step out onto the roof.

The view is astonishing. I walk to the parapet, looking down onto rooftops, and out over Hyde Park. The crowd fills the park, and there's a band on the stage. Everyone's dancing, and the streets are full of people. The light is fading from the sky, and the skyline of London is picked out in silhouette against the glowing streets and the spotlit buildings.

The ball is supposed to be our party, but it's really just a way for Fiona to use us one last time. A way to parade us in front of the people who helped her in the OIE, and the people who'll be helping her run the country.

Out there – that's the real party. That's where everyone else gets to celebrate what we've done.

I lean against the parapet, and think about the people who should be at our party. People who should know how this ends, and how our new world begins. Dad. Saunders. Will.

Dr Richards is here because Will threw himself in front of the bullets that were meant for her. He didn't live to see this – to see the revolution. To see Victory Day.

And it was the armour we stole that led the Home Forces to him. He took care of us at Makepeace Farm, and we sent him into a trap.

"I'm sorry, Will," I say, looking down at the party in the park. "You should be here. You should see this."

I'm here because Mum took my place. She convinced Ketty that I wasn't hiding in her room at the nursing home. She went to London. She wore the orange jumpsuit and she sat through the interrogations that should have been mine. Without her, I wouldn't be here. And if I hadn't put her in danger, she could have stayed with Dad.

And now Dad's gone.

"We're OK, Dad," I say to the rooftops. "We're OK. We made it."

My friends are here because Saunders saved us. He stopped Ketty from breaking in, that night at the bunker. He kept us safe, by putting himself in danger. If he hadn't …

There would have been other resistance cells. Other Faces of the Resistance. Other front-line dolls.

But we wouldn't be here to see this. We'd have been on the execution platform with Margie, or dead before we left the bunker. And there would have been no one to rescue us.

"Thank you, Joss." I whisper. "Thank you."

The door to the roof terrace opens and closes behind me, and I wait for some other drunk MP to stumble over and ask for a photo. But when I turn round, it's Ketty standing behind me, the soft lights under the parapet shining on her silver top.

Jackson

Ketty

Bex turns from the edge of the roof, her film-star dress catching the light, and I don't know what to say.

What do I need her to hear? An apology? An explanation?

What would let me close the door on the things I've done? The lines I've crossed?

What would Colonel Ryan expect?

I step forward, looking down on the crowds of people, dancing as the sky grows dark.

This is too hard. I feel completely exposed.

Grow up, Ketty. Get through this, and move on.

"I'm sorry, Bex," I say, looking out at the rooftops. "I'm sorry about Saunders."

She closes her eyes and takes several deep breaths, then she opens them and fixes me with a glare.

There's steel and anger behind her eyes. It's a look I've seen before, from her mother in the interrogation room. I take a step back.

"You're *sorry*?" She says, through clenched teeth.

"He was brave, Bex. He was so brave." I shake my head. "But he was in my way."

"I know he was brave, Ketty. He was my friend. I didn't need to *shoot* him to find out how brave he could be."

"If he'd opened the shutter when I asked …"

"And let you in? Let you put bullets in the rest of us while we were sleeping? How *brave* would that have been?" She takes a step towards me. "Do you even know what brave is?"

I think about Dad, shouting while I packed my bags. The look in his eyes as he held the kitchen knife in his

360

fist, stepping towards me. The sound of the door, closing behind me when I walked away.

You have no idea, Bex.

She shakes her head, watching me. "We were running from you, and your commanders, for nearly a year." Her voice is quiet, but she throws every word like a punch. "We slept under bridges, and in barns, and in a safe house with a line of locks on the door. We moved, and we kept moving. We left people behind, and we put people in danger, just by being there. We watched you torture the people we loved on TV. We watched, and we couldn't do anything to stop you.

"But we didn't give up. We stuck together. And I forgot to be brave, for a while. I know how that feels. I spent a long time blaming myself for everything that went wrong. But I moved on, and my friends helped me. I needed my friends, to help me be brave again." She looks over my shoulder and holds out her hands. "Where are *your* friends, Ketty? Where's *your* tribe? Do you even know how to have friends?"

I stand up as straight as I can.

This is for you, Jackson.

"I did. I had a friend. And it was your friend who killed him." She looks down, nodding. "When Dan shot Jackson outside the coach, he never woke up. They kept him breathing for months, but he never came back." I look out again, over the crowds and the stage. This is too hard, but I want her to hear what I have to say. I want her to understand. My voice is quiet, and I'm fighting back tears. "I loved him. And I think he loved me. I've only just understood that. I miss him, and I think about him all the time. I carry on without him every day, and it's hard, Bex. It's really hard."

She gives me a long, cold look. "Yes, it is, isn't it?"

Saunders

Bex

I stare at Ketty. At her face, lit up by the spotlights in the park. She's trying not to cry, talking about Jackson.

And she still can't see what she's done.

We took Jackson from her, and she took Joss from us. And it hurt, losing a friend. Knowing that he died to keep us safe.

"Do you know what you did?" I can't help shouting, trying to make her understand. Trying to make her feel what I'm feeling. She looks at me, her eyes shining with tears. "Do you know what we lost, when you killed our friend?"

She shrugs. "Another member of your gang?"

I roll my eyes. I can't believe she's not making the connection.

"My friends aren't disposable, Ketty. I can't just say goodbye and skip away and get a new friend. I cared about Joss Saunders. I cared about who he was, and what he wanted, and what we went through together." I shake my head. "He might have been just another recruit to you, but to me he was a person. He was brave, and he was talented," she raises an eyebrow. "And he loved Amy. He was protecting Amy."

She bows her head.

Understanding

Ketty

I can't meet her eyes. She's right – I didn't see Saunders as a person. I saw him as a prize. As someone to conquer. As an obstacle in my way.

Just another recruit.

And to her? Jackson must have been just another instructor. Just another person in her way.

"I'm a soldier, Bex," I say, quietly. "I had orders to follow, that night. At the bunker." I look up at her. "I'm sorry they ended that way."

She gives me another cold stare.

"You *were* a soldier, Ketty. What are you now? Fiona's puppet?" She points at my outfit. "What do you do? Pick up Fiona's post and answer her phone? Fetch her coffee and sandwiches?"

She's mocking me. She has no idea how I got here. No idea what happened to me in prison. And no idea what Fiona asked me to do.

But she's right, and the realisation is like a bullet.

I have been Fiona's puppet. I have been fetching her post and making her coffee.

I've been doing everything she asked – anything to keep me out of prison. And I haven't given it a second thought.

I think about Penny, in our cell. Calling her a glorified postman. Making her feel small, because what she did at the Home Forces didn't matter.

Private Penny, who fetched the post and smiled and saluted and had no idea what was going on upstairs.

And tomorrow, I'll be Private Smith.

Will I matter?

This is about survival, Ketty. Keep it together.

"I'm still a soldier, Bex." I lean against the parapet and look out over the park. "Basic training starts tomorrow. They've busted me down to Private, and I have to start over. But I'm still a soldier."

Bex nods, watching the crowds. "This feeling," she says, glancing at me. "Losing someone you love? Don't forget how it feels. You'll be a better soldier, if you can hold onto that feeling."

If you can understand what it means to cross the lines.

I nod, brushing tears from my eyes.

She's right.

If I want to impress Colonel Ryan – if I want to earn my freedom – she's right.

Fireworks

Bex

The door to the roof terrace slams open behind us, and Dan and Margie step out.

"Bex! Where have you been? It's fireworks time!" Dan sounds drunk, and there's a half-empty glass in his hand.

I look back at Ketty, but she's stepped away, into a dark corner of the roof. I turn and smile at my friends.

*****

The fireworks are stunning, and our view from the rooftop is the best in the city. They're launching the fireworks from locations all around London, so where we're standing, we're surrounded by light.

It feels amazing, knowing we're the guests of honour. Knowing that all this is for us – for me and my friends.

I stand with Dan. He has one arm round Margie's waist, but the other he throws round my shoulders.

"Do you remember, Dan?" Margie asks. "Your version of Victory Day had fireworks."

I laugh at the memory. "In the library, at Rushmere! You promised us fireworks."

Dan stands up straight, and looks out at the dazzling display. "So these are my fireworks." He nods, smiling, his eyes shining. "Not bad, Dan. Not bad."

Mum sits next to me, holding my hand. Amy's with her parents, and Jake stands with his Dad – his Mum's standing with Saunders' parents. Dr Richards stands with one of the MPs, debating something over the loud music from the park. Charlie has one arm round Maz, and his arm round her shoulders. She glances at me, and I give her a smile. She grins back at me.

I look around at everyone's faces, lit up by the fireworks. We're here, and we're alive. We're not running any more.

The fireworks are for us. And they're for Joss, and Will, and everyone who fought to defeat the Home Forces. For everyone who couldn't be here.

I squeeze Mum's hand. "These are for you, Dad."

Beginning

Katrina

I'm the first out of bed on the first day of training. The first through the showers and the first to get dressed. The other women in the barracks are only just stirring as I check my uniform and straighten the beret on my head.

I look at myself in the mirror on the back of my locker door. Camouflage fatigues. Polished boots. Hair neatly up and off my collar. Everything straight and regulation-smart.

And the name tag on my chest. Private Smith.

Katrina Smith, officially. I haven't asked them to change their records.

It's the name Mum and Dad gave me. The name I couldn't pronounce.

And it's the name I'm using for my second chance at building a life, and earning a place in the army. Leaving Corporal Ketty behind.

I look at my reflection.

I'm here. I'm alive. I've done things Colonel Ryan wouldn't approve of. I've messed up. I've crossed lines.

And I've done things that make me proud.

I've learnt what I can do. I know how strong I am. I know how hard I can push myself.

I think about bandaging my own gunshot wound, on the coach. Sending help to Jackson, and keeping the recruits calm.

I think about learning to walk again. Pushing myself to walk end to end of the corridor at the hospital in Wales, again and again until they let me leave.

I'm smiling at the memory of walking without my clothes through the dining room in prison, turning humiliation into victory.

I close my locker and walk along the corridor to breakfast. There's no one here, and the doors are still locked. I stand outside, first in the queue.

There are noises from the bunk rooms. People getting up, getting dressed, talking and laughing.

I look around at the empty corridor.

What are you doing here, Ketty? Starting again?

What do you want?

I want what I've always wanted. I want to be good at my job. I want to be the best.

I want promotions and responsibility and authority, and I want to deserve everything I get. I want to earn it.

No secrets. No manipulation. No backstabbing.

No Conrad. No Lee. No Bracken.

They're giving me another chance. They've given me a PowerGel, and they're going to train me to follow their rules.

And this time, it's simple. If I want my freedom, I need to earn Ryan's respect without crossing his lines.

There are no short cuts. I have to work my way up, and win my promotions. I need to be the best. The first, the smartest, the fastest.

Every day.

No mistakes. No excuses to put you back behind bars.

It won't be quick. It will take time, and hard work.

But I've done it before.

Discipline, determination, backbone.

I can learn to do it again.

I'm here, on day one, and I'm ready. I'm making a start.

And that's enough, for now.

SEPTEMBER

New

Rebecca

I'm up early, pulling on cargo trousers and a polo shirt for the first day of training. Mum's still asleep as I pack a rucksack with the things I'll need.

Everyone's moved on. Dan and Margie are back at Rushmere, and Dr Richards has a flat in the grounds of the school. Amy and Jake are at home. Charlie and Maz have chosen Brighton for their restaurant, and they're looking for a place to rent.

The Royal is a hotel again – not the headquarters of a political movement. And Fiona's moved into 10 Downing Street. It's still strange, seeing her on TV. Knowing that she saved my life, and that I worked for her, for a while.

I'll see everyone again. I can imagine us all in Charlie's kitchen, drinking tea and tasting her new recipes.

She's promised to invite us to dinner when the restaurant opens.

*****

After the party and the fireworks, we all ended up in Dan's room. We raided the mini bar, and sat around, swapping stories and feeling grown up and fabulous in our party outfits.

And no one wanted to leave.

Charlie and Maz crept out, around dawn, and the rest of us piled onto the enormous bed, and slept, curled round each other, in our ball dresses and dinner jackets. Dan and Margie stole the pillows, so I rested my head on

Dan's legs, and Amy curled up with her head on my waist.

Falling asleep, surrounded by my friends, I felt safe for the first time since we were conscripted. Since we began our long march to Camp Bishop. I felt protected.

I felt free.

This is my tribe, and I won't lose them.

There's a photo in a frame on the wall, next to Saunders' sketch. It's the photo from the ball, as we all stood in the lobby, facing the cameras.

My tribe, smiling. Safe. Dan and Maz holding me up, and making sure I didn't miss out.

It was an amazing night. Charlie was right – I'm glad I was there.

*****

I pick up my registration documents from my desk and put them in the top of my rucksack. *Rebecca Ellman*, the acceptance letter reads. *Trainee Firefighter*.

This is my chance to build a new life, and a new identity. To be someone other than the Face of the Resistance.

I don't need to be the figurehead, or the leader, or the inspiration. I can choose to be me. I can choose to help people, when they need it most. I can choose to stay out of the spotlight.

I think about waking my friends in the middle of the night, and getting them out of the bunker. I think about running through the farmyard, trying to save Margie and Dr Richards.

Margie was wrong, in the department store. *This* is what I was born for. Not the inspiration and the cameras and the attention.

I want to help. I want to stand with people when they need it.

I want to be brave.

Rebecca Ellman. I can live with that. Leave Fiona, and Ketty, and Bex of the Resistance behind, and move on.

I'm smiling as I pull the rucksack onto my shoulders.

There's a line of cards on my desk. Best wishes from my friends, and from Mum. Everyone sending me their support as I start my new life.

We're all carrying scars. We've all been hurt and used, and we've all lost people we loved.

But we found people, too. We found each other, and we found out what we're capable of.

We learned to be brave.

I open the front door quietly, and step out into the chilly morning air.

I need to be brave, today. Stepping out of my old life, and into something new.

But this is what I want, and I know that they're all behind me, cheering me on.

And that's enough, for today.

Note

Alcoholism is not a weakness – these are Ketty's words, not mine, and they come from her unique understanding of her childhood experiences. Addiction in any form is acknowledged to be an illness, not a choice. I do not advocate treating alcoholism as a weakness, any more than I intend to present Ketty as a perfect role model.

Reviews

First, thank you so much for reading *Victory Day*. I hope you enjoyed it, and I hope you'd want to recommend it to other people. Please, please do!

Here's why this is important.

I want to write more books, but I can only do that if there are people reading the Battle Ground series. How will readers find out about the Battle Ground books? I can buy all the adverts in the world, but the best way to reach new readers is through personal recommendations.

If you enjoyed this book, you can help me to write more, just by telling your friends and followers about it.

It's as simple as that.

Head over to Amazon. Give the book a star rating, and tell other readers why they might want to pick it up and read it. Tell them what you liked about the story and the characters. Tell them about other books you think are similar to *Victory Day*. Give them a reason to read this book instead of something else. Reviews don't need to be long – Amazon reviews can be as short as 20 words.

If you have an account on GoodReads or Library Thing, head over there and copy-and-paste your Amazon review. And if you have a blog, a YouTube channel, or an account on Instagram or Twitter or Facebook, drop your review on there as well. If you've read the rest of the series, reviews for the other books would be amazing – thank you! Tag me (@RachelChurcherWriting on Instagram, @Rachel_Churcher on Twitter, or Taller Books on Facebook), and I'll repost your reviews when I see them.

This really makes a huge difference.

Thank you. You're a wonderful person, and I really appreciate your support.

Don't miss the next book in the Battle Ground Series!

Balancing Act (Battle Ground #6) tells Corporal Conrad's story, revisiting the events of *Darkest Hour*, *Fighting Back*, and *Victory Day* from a new perspective ...

The Battle Ground Series

The Battle Ground series is set in a dystopian near-future UK, after Brexit and Scottish independence.

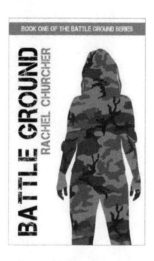

Book 1: Battle Ground

Sixteen-year-old Bex Ellman has been drafted into an army she doesn't support and a cause she doesn't believe in. Her plan is to keep her head down, and keep herself and her friends safe – until she witnesses an atrocity she can't ignore, and a government conspiracy that threatens lives all over the UK. With her loyalties challenged, Bex must decide who to fight for – and who to leave behind.

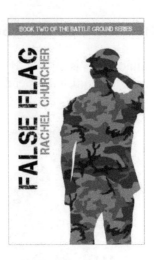

Book 2: False Flag

Ketty Smith is an instructor with the Recruit Training Service, turning sixteen-year-old conscripts into government fighters. She's determined to win the job of lead instructor at Camp Bishop, but the arrival of Bex and her friends brings challenges she's not ready to handle. Running from her own traumatic past, Ketty faces a choice: to make a stand, and expose a government conspiracy, or keep herself safe, and hope she's working for the winning side.

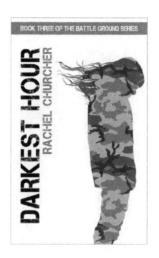

Book 3: Darkest Hour

Bex Ellman and Ketty Smith are fighting on opposite sides in a British civil war. Bex and her friends are in hiding, but when Ketty threatens her family, Bex learns that her safety is more fragile than she thought.

Book 4: Fighting Back

Bex Ellman and her friends are in hiding, sheltered by the resistance. With her family threatened and her friendships challenged, she's looking for a way to fight back. Ketty Smith is in London, supporting a government she no longer trusts. With her support network crumbling, Ketty must decide who she is fighting for – and what she is willing risk to uncover the truth.

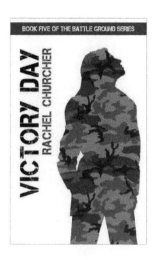

Book 5: Victory Day

Bex Ellman and Ketty Smith meet in London. As the war heats up around them, Bex and Ketty must learn to trust each other. With her friends and family in danger, Bex needs Ketty to help rescue them. For Ketty, working with Bex is a matter of survival. When Victory is declared, both will be held accountable for their decisions.

BOOK SIX OF THE BATTLE GROUND SERIES

BALANCING ACT

RACHEL CHURCHER

Book 6: Balancing Act

Corporal David Conrad has life figured out. His job gives him power, control, and access to Top Secret operations. His looks have tempted plenty of women into his bed, and he has no intention of committing to a relationship.

When Ketty Smith joins the Home Forces, Conrad sets his sights on the new girl – but pursuing Ketty will be more dangerous than he realises. Is Conrad about to meet his match? And will the temptations of his job distract him from his target?

Balancing Act revisits the events of *Darkest Hour*, *Fighting Back*, and *Victory Day*. **The story is suitable for older teens.**

Book 7: Finding Fire and Other Stories

What happened between Margie and Dan at Makepeace Farm? How did Jackson really feel about Ketty? What happens next to the survivors of the Battle Ground Series?

Step behind the scenes of the series with six new short stories and five new narrators – Margie, Jackson, Maz, Dan, and Charlie – plus bonus blogs and insights from the author.

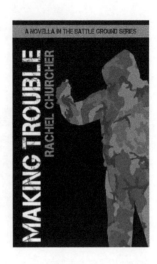

Novella: Making Trouble

Fifteen-year-old Topher Mackenzie has a complicated life. His Mum is in Australia, his Dad is struggling to look after him, and Auntie Charlie is the only person who understands. When his girlfriend is forced to leave the UK after a racist attack, Topher faces a choice: accept the government's lies, or find a way to fight back.

Download FREE from freebook.tallerbooks.com

Acknowledgements

The Battle Ground series represents more than a year of hard work – not just for me, but for the people who have supported me and helped to make it happen.

A huge thank you is due to my amazing proofreaders, who have given up their time to read every book and send me helpful and insightful feedback. Thank you to Alan Platt, Holly Platt Wells, Reba Sigler, Joe Silber, and Reynard Spiess.

Special thanks to Holly, for the inspiration for Ketty's outfit for the Victory Day Ball. You were right – it suits her!

Thank you to my *Victory Day* beta readers, Jasmine Bruce, Diana Churcher, James Keen, and Karen MacLaughlin, for encouragement and insightful comments.

Thank you to all the people who have given me advice on the road to publication: Tim Dedopulos, Salomé Jones, Rob Manser, John Pettigrew, Danielle Zigner, and Jericho Writers.

Thank you to everyone at NaNoWriMo, for giving me the opportunity and the tools to start writing, and to everyone at YALC for inspiration and advice.

Thank you to my amazing designer, Medina Karic, for deciphering my sketches and notes and turning them into beautiful book covers. If you ever need a designer, find her at www.fiverr.com/milandra.

Thank you to Alan Platt, for learning the hard way how to live with a writer, and for bringing your start-up expertise to the creation of Taller Books.

Thank you to Alex Bate, Janina Ander, and Helen Lynn, for encouraging me to write *Battle Ground* when I suddenly had time on my hands, and for introducing me to Prosecco Fridays. Cheers!

Thank you to Hannah Pollard and the Book Club Galz for sharing so many wonderful YA books with me – and for understanding that the book is *always* better than the film.

Special mention goes to the Peatbog Faeries, whose album *Faerie Stories* is the ultimate cure for writer's block. The soundtrack to *The Greatest Showman*, and Lady Antebellum's *Need You Now*, are my go-to albums for waking up and feeling energised to write, even on the hardest days.

This book is dedicated to my tribe. You know who you are.

About the Author

Rachel Churcher was born between the last manned moon landing, and the first orbital Space Shuttle mission. She remembers watching the launch of STS-1, and falling in love with space flight, at the age of five. She fell in love with science fiction shortly after that, and in her teens she discovered dystopian fiction. In an effort to find out what she wanted to do with her life, she collected degrees and other qualifications in Geography, Science Fiction Studies, Architectural Technology, Childminding, and Writing for Radio.

She has worked as an editor on national and in-house magazines; as an IT trainer; and as a freelance writer and artist. She has renovated several properties, and has plenty of horror stories to tell about dangerous electrics and nightmare plumbers. She enjoys reading, travelling, stargazing, and eating good food with good friends – but nothing makes her as happy as writing fiction.

Her first published short story appeared in an anthology in 2014, and the *Battle Ground* series is her first long-form work. Rachel lives in East Anglia, in a house with a large library and a conservatory full of house plants. She would love to live on Mars, but only if she's allowed to bring her books.

Follow RachelChurcherWriting on Instagram and GoodReads.

Lightning Source UK Ltd.
Milton Keynes UK
UKHW010640120922
408721UK00002B/448